There are many mews cottages in London and many pigeon-haunted cul-de-sacs like the Trident. There are dogs like Flicky, cats like Lucifer, and at least one handsome rag-and-bone mule called Michael, but the man in the mews and all the other characters in this story are entirely fictitious.   JOY PACKER

CONTENTS

I

MOTHER AND DAUGHTER

MRS OLIVIER STOOD IN THE OPEN DOORWAY AND stared up the steep narrow staircase that separated the two garages under the mews cottage.

'We call it Jacob's ladder,' said her daughter, Rachel.

'So you should,' cried Mrs Olivier joyfully. 'Light streams down from on high.'

'Rain too from time to time,' smiled Rachel. 'Those skylights have been known to leak.'

Mrs Olivier drew a long breath as she stepped over the threshold of the mews cottage, thereby crossing her own private Rubicon. She knew well that there was a chance – a risk carefully considered and calculated – that her return to London after an absence of over twenty years in South Africa might prove disastrous both to her and to her daughter. She had made up her mind to accept that risk and she had no intention of looking back. Her course was irrevocably set. She prided herself upon her force of character. 'I act as I think best and take the consequences.' When Rachel had been goaded into protesting that other people took them too, her mother agreed blandly. 'Consequences can never be contained. They spill over – like wars. It's enough to mean well.'

Rachel picked up Mrs Olivier's suitcase and followed the swinging red coat and shapely legs up the seventeen steps of Jacob's ladder.

'The trunk you sent by sea arrived yesterday,' she said to

the straight back mounting the stairs ahead of her. 'I un-
packed it for you. You've surely brought more summer
things than you need? This is London, not South Africa.'

'I'm an optimist. Anyway, London can be hot. The last
summer I was here – so long ago –' She broke off with an
exclamation of pleasure. 'Oh, darling! This cottage really is
heaven! Inside as well as out.'

Five doors led off the small landing and all stood open to
reveal the full extent of Mrs Olivier's tiny domain for the
next few months. The top step of Jacob's ladder was the
springboard to a bathroom papered with rosy cupids
floating on fleecy clouds. On one side of it was a studio and
on the other a large dining-kitchen, both lit by generous
skylights. The kitchen table, covered by a fanciful cloth,
was set for two.

'I thought we'd have grilled steak and salad and cheese
here instead of going out,' said Rachel. 'I've a bottle of claret
too.'

'Inspiration! You've thought of everything.'

The landing hooked round to a bedroom and sitting-
room facing one another and looking out upon the mews.
Geraniums and forget-me-nots nodded in the window-
boxes. Mrs Olivier gazed past the pink and blue frieze of
flowers to the cottages opposite, each exuding the personality
of its owner. Some were austere, others colourful. Elegant
wrought-iron grilles protected the windows of ground floor
living rooms that had once been stables. Dwarf trees stood
sentinel outside gaily painted front doors garlanded with
wistaria, clematis or jasmine. There was even a vine.

'A vine – here in London!' Mrs Olivier was overcome.
'A healthy one at that. See, the leaves are unfurling.'

'It bears no fruit,' said Rachel at her side, looking down
into the mews. 'Like the double-flowering peach there in
the churchyard garden. Beautiful but barren.'

The cul-de-sac of this third branch of Trident Mews was bounded by the high brick wall of a churchyard tucked away behind the turmoil of the main road. Magnificent sycamores, limes in young leaf and the froth of blossom swayed over the wall, scattering golden leaves in autumn and fragile petals in spring.

'There must be birds here,' said Mrs Olivier.

As if to prove it, a pair of hands reached from an open casement to crumble bread upon the cobbles below. Pigeons and sparrows alighted on the manna from heaven with a soft whirr of wings, and the bolder birds fluttered up to perch on the bountiful outspread hands. A sleepy black cat and a sleek miniature dachshund looked on with apparent indifference, and then suddenly the dachshund launched himself among the birds with a loud aggressive bark. As they scattered in confusion he addressed himself to the vine. He well knew that pigeon-greed would soon enable him to repeat his pouncing performance.

'Who's the little golden dog?' asked Mrs Olivier.

'Flicky. He belongs to the young Dixons who live opposite. They haven't been married very long.'

'And the gorgeous child?'

A small boy had swooped round the corner on his bicycle. He pulled up and dismounted with the dare-devil flourish of a Mexican bandit, seeming to fling invisible reins across an imaginary pole before swaggering into the next-door house.

'His name is Colin and he often comes to stay with his aunt, Jane Rafferty. She's Canadian. Her husband, Ginger Rafferty, used to be a test pilot. Now he's in some sort of business in the city — to do with aircraft, of course.'

Cars were homing after the day's work or play. Some were driven straight into their stables, others pressed close against walls as if tethered there. A few received a sketchy rub-down before their owners disappeared indoors. These were the racy beloved ones, canvas hoods down, long noses quivering as they came to rest with a final roar of the accelerator.

'That black cat down there, washing himself in the tub with the dwarf orange tree, surely that's lucky.'

Rachel smiled. 'Could be. But black cats have been known to ride broomsticks over the chimney-pots and this one belonged to a couple of pretty witches. There used to be night-time revels here in the mews, I can tell you! But one day the witches disappeared and Lucifer was left behind. How did you know he was a boy-cat?'

'Witch's instinct, perhaps. Who feeds him?'

'Anybody. If he's hungry or thirsty he miaows and some-body usually comes up with milk or fish or something. Jim says he's waiting for another witch, then he'll settle in with her.'

Mrs Olivier turned from the window with a laugh.

'Jim. That would be Jim Fleet — your steady?'

A faint flush stained Rachel's fair skin. 'I suppose you could call him that.' She went to a small cupboard on the landing. 'Look, this is where the booze lives. I got in whisky, gin and dry sherry, a few tonics and a syphon. It's past seven o'clock. Time for a sundowner.'

'Yes indeed, gin and tonic with ice for me, if any.'

'Of course. A slice of lemon too.'

Mrs Olivier leaned back in the arm-chair and closed her eyes. From the kitchen she heard the inviting clink of ice cubes being removed from their container under the tap. How strange. When last she had seen London she had been a young woman of twenty-two, not much older than Rachel was now. That had been another life, another London, and she had been another person. She heard her daughter's light step.

Rachel put down the glasses. 'I've no cigarettes. I counted on you to bring in your duty free ration.'

'In my suitcase. Right on top. Here's the key.'

'I'll get them.'

When Rachel returned with a tin of cigarettes she was frowning. 'Look, Ma, do you still need things to make you sleep?'

'Oh, those – the pink jobs? Yes, when I'm worried I take one or two, or if my mind gets over-active. Since your father died they have become rather a habit.'

'You've a good supply,' remarked Rachel dryly.

'I thought I might have trouble getting them here. You need a prescription.'

'It's your business.'

She lit her mother's cigarette and one for herself. Mrs Olivier looked round with appreciation.

'Everything in this room agrees with everything else.' She smiled. 'Yes, my dear, for once that goes for you and me too! But seriously, it's all in perfect taste. That narrow corner cupboard and the bureau between the windows are gems, and I love the gate-legged table with the Greek urn on it. As for the almond blossom, well that must be you, bless your heart.'

Rachel looked pleased. 'I'm glad you like Eve's atmosphere and my flowers. The place is welcoming and lived in, I think.'

'How did you get it at such short notice?'

'It was fate. Eve Kelly, the owner, is Jim Fleet's sister. She's a novelist, a real career-girl. But she surprised us all by suddenly marrying an American and taking off for New York. That's how I was able to jump in and snap up the cottage for you.'

Mrs Olivier turned this information over in her mind, and felt a glow of relief. She had flown from the Transvaal farm to England for the sole purpose of getting to know this young man, Jim Fleet, though she had no intention of admitting as much to Rachel. If this was the background of Jim's sister, Eve, then Eve must be a young woman of breeding and discrimination. It was a good omen. Like the black cat. Mrs Olivier pressed the stub of her cigarette into an ashtray and looked at her daughter searchingly.

'So the owner of this delightful place is your boy-friend's sister. Is she a friend of yours too?'

'Naturally.'

The gentle inquisition, thought Rachel resentfully, and instinctively prepared her defences.

'I never know quite what the term boy-friend implies,' said Mrs Olivier with a half smile. 'Suitor or lover?'

Rachel laughed shortly. 'Quaintly old-fashioned words. Suitor – lover? They have no meaning these days, except in Victorian fiction. What's the difference between a suitor and a lover, anyway? The suitor asks for the maiden's hand in marriage, and the lover just makes her his mistress. Would that be it?'

'Near enough, I expect. Can you define boy-friend equally exactly?'

'Good gracious, no! Boy-friends vary. Some are suitors and some are lovers. Some are both. Some are neither.'

'And Jim? What sort of boy-friend is he?'

How well she recalled these maternal interrogations, the sudden sharp probe of a hollow needle, drawing off some innocent admission to be crystallized later into a false and ugly form. She must guard against this violation of her secret self. She said stiffly:

'When you meet him you can form your own opinion. He's coming to fetch me later this evening.'

Mrs Olivier accepted the snub with an easy graciousness that surprised her daughter.

'That'll be nice. I'm looking forward to meeting him. Remember, when you flew home to be with me last year after your father died — how restless you were to get back—'

'To my job. They couldn't hold it open indefinitely.'

'Are you sure it was only the job calling? I wondered at the time if there wasn't some man — Jim perhaps.'

'I'd only met him two or three times then.'

'Two or three times! That, in certain circumstances, could be enough to drag you half way across the world. Are you sure Jim wasn't the magnet that pulled you back to England?'

Rachel gave her mother a long direct look from eyes light and clear as green water in sunlight. 'Am I sure of this? Am I sure of that? I'm never all that sure about anything. Especially motives. Are you?'

'My own motives — yes.'

'Are you really so sure — even of those? Can you explain why you've come back here after all these years? You wouldn't do it for Pa.' Remembered indignation roughened her soft deep voice. She went on. 'After we'd had those bonanza years on the farm Pa wanted to take us all to Europe. He longed to see it again and have Hans and me see it too. You stamped on it. And if I hadn't insisted on coming here after I left school — if my father and brother hadn't backed me up — you'd have stamped on that too. You never thought of us, only of yourself. Oh, I know it was tough — '

'You know nothing about it!' interrupted Mrs Olivier fiercely. 'How should you? You've been protected all your life.'

'You've told me your story vividly enough and often enough. I'm not lacking in imagination. You said you'd never revisit your beloved London after the horrors of the war — your home destroyed, your parents killed. That was horrible. I understand that very well. But you had good memories too. More recent ones. After all, you met my father here when he was in the South African army, you married him here, and I was born here. Couldn't you lay the other ghosts with things like that – living happy memories?'

Mrs Olivier clenched her right hand, a strong practical hand.

'The moment your father was due for repatriation we sailed for South Africa. I could hardly wait to get on board that ship – to get away.'

'Was that why you married him? To get away?'

'Rachel!'

'We were talking about motives a moment ago. I just wondered. You never seemed much like a real farmer's wife to me. You managed, but you didn't belong.'

'Perhaps I wasn't an ideal farmer's wife, but to me the farm was wonderfully satisfying. Between us, your father and I buried my bad city memories under the Transvaal veld. War, violence, death – horrors you can't conceive of – all were buried layers deep by the new life I learnt to love. Believe me, Rachel, my past was better dead. I had no wish to revive it.'

'So you always told me. Yet now, it seems, you feel differently. Why else should you be here?'

Rachel, having shifted from defence to attack, was watching her mother warily. What a powerful expressive face she had, with those high cheek bones and brown almond eyes, the smooth black hair brushed severely off a wide forehead and coiled in the nape of her neck. She looks, Rachel thought, like a Russian, like the wife of the first cosmonaut, Gagarin. Especially now, with the memory of suffering so clearly reflected. Rachel recalled the press photograph of the spaceman's wife, taken while she waited for news of her husband's historic achievement. It was a compelling unforgettable head, pride and love battling with anguish and suspense. Something of the same quality transformed Mrs Olivier's face at this moment. Under her daughter's scrutiny it softened and melted, the lines of strain obliterated by tenderness.

'Darling,' she said slowly. 'I thought you needed me.'

Her mother's answer was the one Rachel had most dreaded. It's Jim, she thought. She's here to get the answers about Jim. Why can't she let us alone? If you look at new-born rabbits the mother eats them. The thing between Jim and me is too young for inspection, and if she crashes in she'll destroy it. Every instinct in Rachel cried out against interference. She mastered a sense of panic but not the terror in her voice.

'What can I say, Ma? You put me on a spot. I'm making my own life my own way, and it's all right. I'll be twenty-one in a few months' time. I don't need a keeper.' Her nails bit into her palms and Mrs Olivier was shocked at the intensity of her daughter's emotion. 'I was hoping – you don't know how hard I was hoping – that your coming here had nothing to do with me. That it was for your own sake entirely.'

If Mrs Olivier was bitterly offended she hid the fact. Her impulsive bid for her daughter's confidence had appeared to Rachel simply as a threat to her independence. How easy it was to antagonise the young! How jealous they were of their freedom, how cagey about their love affairs, how re-luctant to consider advice, much less invite it. Mrs Olivier forced a smile, intended to be reassuring.

'Perhaps there's more self in it than I realised. Perhaps, after all, I was wrong about the motive. The very instant I stepped out of the taxi and saw the window-boxes and the little red door of this mews cottage I fell in love with Lon-don all over again. I'm happy here, darling. I shall lead my own life this summer and you can go on leading yours.'

The gesture with which she seemed to throw away their differences was a little over-acted. 'More than anything else at the moment I want a hot bath.'

'And, afterwards, a steak. Underdone.'

'I drool at the prospect!'

Rachel laughed. Her face cleared and she went to the kitchen with her heart a shade lighter. Perhaps, after all, everything would be all right.

Jim Fleet turned his little yellow sports car into the quiet well of Trident Mews. He swung sharp right into the third prong, where the lights of his sister's cottage glowed behind the curtained windows. As he cut the engine he nerved himself to meet his girl-friend's mother.

It was ten o'clock and he felt he had given them ample time to eat their first London dinner together and break the ice of a reunion to which Rachel had not looked forward. She had some sort of down on her mother.

He rang the bell and pushed lightly at the door. It opened and he leaped up Jacob's ladder, two steps at a time. Rachel was on the landing. She was wearing her neat office skirt and a blue pullover. He caught her quickly in his arms.

'You take my breath away – you always do!'

She laughed and made a warning gesture.

'Come and meet Ma – '

Mrs Olivier rose as the tall young man entered. She put out her hand and felt the firm grasp of his long fingers. She was quite remarkably aware of his hand, its cool strong authority. South Africans shook hands more frequently than English people and there was, in her opinion, a good deal to be said for a handshake. The first touch, however formal or impersonal, could prove to be the key to a stranger's character.

She studied Jim Fleet with frank interest. Weird-looking but arresting, she decided. That terrible yellow turtle-necked sweater murdered his sallow skin, but what of it? His brilliant dark eyes were sunk in sooty caverns, his chin, slightly cleft, was carefully and aggressively sculpted and his unusual head was topped by a shock of thick black hair. His smile was sudden and young. He said:

'I've had known you anywhere from that snapshot of Rachel's. All the same, you're a surprise.'

'How's that?'

'You're so completely unlike Ray. I'd expected something – some point of similarity – in personality if not in appearance.'

She laughed. 'Personality! You haven't had much time to judge, young man. Will you have something to drink? Whisky – '

'Beer, please.'

'I'll get it,' offered Rachel, who had catered for his tastes.

Mrs Olivier offered Jim her cigarette case. 'Smoke?'

'Not now, thanks.'

After her bath she had put on black slacks and a red velvet overblouse. Dramatic, judged Jim. She moved with athletic grace. She was taller than Rachel, altogether larger. More animal. He wondered what age she was. Somewhere in the early forties?

'Your sister's home is adorable,' Mrs Olivier was saying. 'I'm going to be happy here.'

'We all hope so,' he said. 'Eve gave me a list for you. I saw her and her husband off yesterday by the *Queen Mary*. She was sorry to miss you.'

He drew a folded sheet of notepaper from his pocket and handed it to Rachel, who had put a foaming tankard beside him.

'You'd better decipher this, Ray. Eve's writing is past hope.'

Rachel stood with her back to the electric fire. She unfolded the list.

'Useful people,' she read aloud. 'And their telephone numbers. Very thoughtful. It's perfectly legible, Jim.'

'Tell me more,' said Mrs Olivier.

Rachel chuckled. Her laugh, like her voice, was deep and soft. Only emotion ever pitched it high.

'Here we go. I like this. Doctor, Cyril James, knows everybody in the mews inside out. Booze, Leslie, open till eight p.m., prompt delivery. Papers, Smith. Laundry, White Elephant, calls Thursday. Gas Company — that would be stove and geyser. Serious plumbing, Mr Bradshaw. Odd jobs like leaks in taps, emergencies of all sorts, care-taking, explosions, Mr Ferrit. For general information apply Mrs Know-all — that would be Jane Rafferty next door, a help and a honey.'

'Mrs Know-all, help and honey, sounds fine,' said Mrs Olivier. 'But what about explosions? What is likely to explode? And who is Mr Ferrit?'

'Oh, anything could explode,' said Rachel. 'Fuses — the sort of thing one needs a man to cope with. Mr Ferrit is the man in the mews. He's lived here for years and he does all the odd job and handy-man stuff. When people go away they leave him a key and he keeps an eye on things. For instance, if there is a deluge he pops in to see that the place isn't swamped by a leaking skylight or anything else. If a fire started he'd be on the spot and so on.'

Mrs Olivier smiled as she took the list from her daughter.

'Life in the mews sounds full of hazards. I'll keep this list by the telephone.' She turned to Jim. 'Very thoughtful of your sister to provide it. Mr Ferrit appears to be the key man. I'll underline his number.'

'I think it would be a good idea if you'd show Ma how the TV works,' Rachel suggested to Jim. 'I'll tidy up the kitchen in the meantime, and then we'll be off. Ma's had a long day. It's rather a splendid TV,' she added.

'Shan't I help you wash up first?' he asked.

'No, I'll stack. Mrs Meadows'll be in at eight-thirty tomorrow. I'll only be a few minutes.'

'Mrs Meadows is Eve's treasure,' grinned Jim. 'Cherish her, Mrs Olivier, and she'll cherish you in return.'

He moved over to the 'splendid' television set. They heard Rachel singing to herself in the kitchen.

'I love it when she does that,' said Mrs Olivier. 'I want her to be that way always. Happy.'

She spoke with such passionate sincerity that he looked at her in astonishment.

'Why should you doubt it? Ray's a happy person by nature. She goes round laughing and tossing her head in the air. Not a care in the world.'

'That's how she must stay. Carefree.'

'Asking a bit much, isn't it? As a permanent condition, I mean. After all, life's made up of contrasts, ups and downs, light and shade and the rest of the clichés.'

She was at his side, kneeling by the instrument, and her perfume came to his nostrils, heavy and exotic.

'Reveal this thing's secrets!' she commanded, as if he had not spoken. 'I'm very stupid about mechanical devices.'

'Is that so? I shouldn't have thought you were stupid about anything, Mrs Olivier.'

'I don't like mechanical things.'

'Don't let the TV hear that. Like cars. You mustn't talk against your mechanical friends in their presence, or they turn on you. Now this knob, here – this gives you power.'

'Good,' she said. 'I'll remember that knob. I respect power.'

His left eyebrow climbed his forehead, but he did not comment.

'Look who's here,' called Rachel from the landing.

The black cat oozed sinuously into the room and began to rub himself against Mrs Olivier's calves. She stroked his plush coat.

'What a fine cat! How did he get in?'

'I heard him miaowing outside, so I let him in and gave him some scraps and some milk.'

Jim's eyes danced as he looked from Mrs Olivier and the cat to Rachel, who stood in the doorway.

'There's an affinity between these two,' he said. 'Lucifer is going to settle down at last. You'll see.'

'Lucifer?' said Mrs Olivier. 'Rather a sinister name, and he certainly has a ruthless face. I like him, though. Perhaps I'll adopt him. Perhaps not.'

'That's over to him,' grinned Jim. 'It's he who decides. If Lucifer adopts you, you might as well go quietly.'

'Take him out,' she laughed. 'I'm not selling my soul to the devil tonight.'

Jim picked up the protesting cat.

'Come on, old boy. We're all saying goodnight now. To-morrow is another day.'

They clattered down the stairs. The cat, hanging over Jim's arm, looked to Mrs Olivier like a dead snake dangling from a shepherd's crook.

So this young man with the strong interesting face would drive her daughter home to the small basement flat she shared with her South African friend, Liz Joubert. And then what? How much did they mean to each other? How well did they know each other? Was this a lasting relationship or a temporary love affair, or even a mere infatuation? Mrs

Olivier watched the little yellow car reverse and turn and roar out of the mews. My daughter is a stranger to me, she thought. So different from my son! Hans, two years younger than Rachel, had always been easy. His sister had been the difficult one – the unknown quantity.

2

THE MAN IN THE MEWS

UNDER THE FROSTY SPRING STARS JIM SLIPPED his arm about Rachel. She was driving his little open sports car because she drove well and he liked to be free to watch her profile and feel the supple warmth of her shoulder under his hand. Blunt nose, appealing line of chin and throat, pale hair blowing off a high clear forehead, even her ears intrigued him with their dainty convolutions. She was a poem, and she was his girl. She loved driving Yellow Peril.

'You must bring your mother to the ancestral home,' Jim said. 'The dear cow-girl's dying to meet her.'

'Your mother? Why should she want to meet my mother?'

'She's trying to persuade Dad to go with her to South Africa. She has a hankering after Africa and she wants to stay on a ranch.'

Laura Fleet, affectionately known to her stepson as 'the dear cow-girl', had, during the war, been a land-girl on Ravenswood, the Fleet estate in Sussex. She had remained on at Ravenswood after the war was ended and had finally married the owner, General Sir Jasper Fleet.

'That's too easy,' said Rachel. 'She'd always be welcome on Môreson. So would any of you, for that matter. And of course Ma would love to see Ravenswood.'

Suddenly she felt light-hearted. So did Jim. The stars spun filaments of silver in her streaming hair. He laid his cheek against hers.

'Next weekend then. I'll get off a bit early and collect you both about five o'clock. We'll be at Ravenswood for a late dinner. I'll let Laura know.'

'Lovely, oh lovely.'

She felt his gaze absorbing and memorising her features.

'You're not much like your mother,' he said.

'I'm not like my father either — except that he was fair, too.'

'Did she make any fuss about your not staying in the mews cottage with her?'

'I told her I couldn't let Liz down. After all, Liz and I have shared a flat for eighteen months, ever since I came here. Ma understood. She was rather nice about it.' She hesitated. In the sickly street-lighting the frown between her brows seemed no more than a brush mark on a paper mask.

'Go on, Ray.'

'Ever since Ma arrived I've had the feeling that she's holding herself in check — making a definite effort to stop herself taking me apart.'

'Why should she take you apart?'

Rachel swung the car off the Fulham Road into a quiet crescent where dignified Georgian houses curved pleasantly round a railed garden. The fragrance of lilac and syringa hung on the city air. A powerful motor-cycle was parked against the curb outside the end house where a light showed in the basement. Rachel drew up in the shadow of a plane tree some way behind the motor-cycle.

'Tom Standish must be with Liz,' she said. 'Shall we go in?'

'No. Let's leave Tom a clear field. We'll talk here a few minutes. Then I'll go. You're whacked.'

She lay back with her head in the hollow of his shoulder.

'Why should your mother take you apart?' he repeated.

'Habit. She always has done.'

'Only you? Or other people too?'

'Chiefly me. Never my brother, Hans.'

'Now why should that be?'

'It was as if she wanted to dig out something bad in me.'

'What sort of something bad?'

'When I grew up I realised it was sex. She wanted to kill it in me.'

He chuckled. 'She didn't do very well.' But Rachel said seriously:

'What got me down was the way she made everything natural seem ugly. Not evil, just plain ugly.'

'For instance?'

'When I was about thirteen we were putting down a new bore-hole on the farm. An Italian was in charge, his name was Roberto, he was very dark and good looking and I was crazy about him. I can remember his eyes right now – '

'Can you indeed?' He nuzzled her ear. 'To hell with Roberto!'

'He had horrible hands. He bit his nails. I had to make myself forget about his hands and concentrate on the rest of him. I used to hang about the borehole watching him operate that drill, pretending to be interested. Anything to be near him. Ma got mad.'

'Quite right.'

'She was . . . brutal. So cruel and contemptuous. She told me he was laughing at me for an infatuated kid – accused me of romanticising my barnyard instincts. I've never forgotten the way she said that – with real bitterness. She made me feel ashamed and self-conscious.'

'Darling, you exaggerate everything. You always do.' He touched her cheek with his long vibrant fingers.

'Why Ray, your face is burning!'

She lifted it suddenly to his, straining towards him, her

arms about his neck, her lips parted. She clung to him as if she greatly feared to lose him.

Down in the area, where the light showed, the basement door opened and closed. Whispered voices floated up the steps, a man and a girl saying goodbye. Jim and Rachel drew apart as a man's figure bounded up the area steps. Tom Standish did not pause or look about him. He sprang on to the big motorcycle and started her up with a roar. The next moment he was racing down the Fulham Road.

Jim whistled under his breath. 'What's up with Tom? You'd say the devil was after him!'

Rachel shivered. 'I must go to Liz. No, Jim!' She shook off his restraining hand. 'Something's happened between those two. I'm worried about Liz.'

He went with her to the top of the area steps.

'Shall I come in?'

She shook her head. 'No. Ring me at work tomorrow.'

She hurried down the steps and was suddenly swallowed by the backdoor that had once been the tradesmen's entrance to a grand mansion. He turned away, obscurely troubled. As he headed for his own bachelor flat two blocks further on he wondered what drama had upset Tom Standish. Liz was a great girl for scenes. No repressions there. Everything on a plate.

Rachel let herself into the basement flat that in more spacious days had been the housekeeper's private quarters. The sound of sobbing came to her ears – great gulping choking sobs like those of a child in dire need of comfort. She went into the living-room. Liz, clad in pyjamas and a dressing gown, lay on the divan weeping uncontrollably. Rachel sat down and put her hand on her friend's thin heaving shoulders.

'Whatever's up?'

'Tom. His destroyer's standing by to sail for the Far East.'

'But surely he has leave coming to him?'

'It's cancelled. He's on his way to Portsmouth now. To rejoin his ship.'

Liz sat up, her dark hair ruffled, her small pale face blotched with tears. She looked plain and pitiful.

'I'll never see him again, Ray. He's not the type to stick to a girl thousands of miles away. You have to be with Tom to hold him. You have to be there when he needs you. I've had it. You know I have.' She began to tremble.

'You'd better go to bed,' said Rachel quietly. 'I'll get you a hot bottle and some aspirin.'

'Ray – I told Tom I was scared – '

'What did he say?'

'He didn't believe me.'

'He didn't want to believe you.'

'He said what could he do anyway – even assuming it might be true? There isn't time to get married. There isn't time for anything. The responsibility's all mine.'

'We'll talk about it tomorrow. We'll make a plan. Now you must get some sleep or you won't be fit to go to the office in the morning.'

Liz dragged herself up. She stood white-faced, swaying on her feet.

'I love him,' she said thickly. 'That's the hell of it. I love him.'

Tom Standish shot over Putney Bridge and down Roehampton Lane. At this time of night it would be quicker to go through Kingston than take the by-pass. The river gleamed on his right, strangely tranquil compared with the turmoil inside him. A fine kettle of fish if Liz were justified in her fears! What the devil could he do about it? There'd never been any talk of marriage between them and he hadn't a bean in the world outside his pay. He'd blown everything he possessed in giving Liz a good time these last months.

And they'd had a good time. They'd lived it up. He was saturated, ready to call it a day, give his mind to his job and go on to the next adventure. China. He was twenty-two. Surely you couldn't be pushed into matrimony at twenty-two? No time for that anyway – not even for a shot-gun wedding. Or would her parents make her follow him?

He'd had too much to drink. The trees at the side of the road were crowding in on him. Water again – this time on his left – the silver stretch of the lake at Ripley. The roar of the engine didn't drown the thin singing in his ears. Always a sign of one over the odds – that mosquito whine in his head. Dazzling head-lights rushed towards him, mesmeric, blinding, rendering invisible the tail-light of the vehicle ahead of him. When he struck the solid square back of the van he was travelling at ninety miles an hour, oblivious of danger.

Even his crash-helmet couldn't save him as he flew over the handle-bars head on to instant death.

Mrs Olivier had taken one of the little pink torpedoes that usually guaranteed her four hours' sleep. But tonight her overstimulated brain and emotions were impervious to such mild sedation.

Jim Fleet and Rachel. Precisely what were they to one another? *Precisely* nothing, of course. The word precise had no meaning in the fluid concept of a developing relationship between a man and a girl. She – Rachel's mother – must wait and watch and decide what was best for her daughter.

The church bell chimed the hour of midnight. Mrs Olivier counted the twelve strokes and enjoyed their echoing resonance. She reflected that the nearby church was endowed with a full-throated bell, but did not pause to consider that it might possibly hold a message for her and suggest a boundless and much-needed source of spiritual guidance. In her

hours of need – and these had been many and desperate –
Mrs Olivier had never looked beyond her earthly father
and later her husband for help.

How quiet it was! The Trident, flanked by the tall build-
ings that formed a massive back-drop to the three rows of
mews cottages, was insulated from the normal traffic sounds
of London, but at intervals the uncanny peace was ripped by
the roar of a low-flying jet trailing its supersonic shriek in
the direction of London Airport. At first Mrs Olivier's
muscles had tensed as she waited for sounds that did not
come – whine of bombs, crash of glass, thunder of collapsing
masonary. Curious how the old reflexes continued to func-
tion after so long a gap. More than twenty years. But then
the realisation that the sky was rent by commerce and not by
conflict flowed over her in a tide of pure relief and her nerves
ceased to flinch. This was no longer a city battered, dis-
embowelled and licking grievous wounds, this was London
reborn, the phoenix risen from the flames of war. Mrs
Olivier too had sustained her own personal wounds of war,
scars still sensitive, areas unhealed and unsafe, but she was
glad that she had come home. For home it was. Already she
could see the years of the high-veld farm in retrospect, a
prolonged period of exile and regeneration, a life apart, an
experience with profound and healthy consequences
On his father's death the farm had passed to Hans though
the homestead was hers for as long as he wished to live in
it. Already she felt herself shaking off a part of that shell
which had been her home and her armour for so many years.
Hans was eighteen, at agricultural college. Soon he would
take the reins from his Uncle Christiaan who was running
the place with his own adjoining property.

Was I only a visitor all those years? wondered Mrs Olivier.
Rachel had implied as much and Rachel was subject to curious flashes of perception. Mrs Olivier breathed deeply of

London's air. Yes, here was where she really belonged. She said it aloud to lend the thought substance. 'Here is where I really belong.'

All hope of sleep had fled. She was very wide awake. She threw off the bed-covers and pulled on her quilted dressing-gown. She went to the window and listened to the immediate small sounds that threaded and emphasised the stillness of the night. A squeal of brakes on the ramp leading into the Trident, a taxi rattling over the cobbles on its way out of the mews and the stealthy purr of a late-comer's engine.

The young Dixons had put their little dog out, and now the girl opened the door to call him back into the house.

'Flee-kee? Flee-kee!'

The muted high-pitched notes, up-down up-down, were repeated in her quiet sing-song voice till the small golden animal consented to hear and obey.

There was the soft thud of the closing door, a pause and the metallic whisper of runners on a steel rail as the young wife drew the bedroom curtains and turned out the light.

All the little houses were in darkness now. Only a few lanterns illumined the length of the third prong of Trident Mews. They suited this backwater where once the rich and noble had kept their horses in the stables and their falcons in the attics. Out of the silence Mrs Olivier evoked faint echoes of bygone days, snorting and stamping, the clatter of hooves on cobbles, the rough voices of coachmen and the eerie cries of the birds.

The homeless black cat was slinking along the Dixon's wall. He sprang lightly on to the tub which housed the dwarf orange tree and settled under the umbrella of leaves in his brooding sphinx-like attitude. Now a new sound, soft and needle thin, fell on Mrs Olivier's ears – a tuneless tenuous whistling. A little wiry man had rounded the corner and was strolling down the mews. His springy step was silent for he wore rubber soles and his hands were thrust into the pockets of the stove-pipe trousers that accentuated the skinniness of his legs. Bowed jockey legs. Insect legs and an insect voice. His leather jerkin widened his shoulders grotesquely and a peaked cap was pulled down over his left eye. Mrs Olivier was interested. A bad sleeper perhaps, out for a late night airing? He didn't look a likely tenant of any of these expensively converted cottages, yet he had the confident air of one entirely at home in his neighbourhood. His promenade took him down to the church wall, where he paused to enjoy the leafy scents of the night. Then he sauntered back, observing the sleeping houses as he did so until he reached the tub in which the cat dozed. There, facing Mrs Olivier's red front door, he stood still, his head raised. Mrs Olivier half expected him to chant, 'One o'clock and all's well!'

But he appeared to have frozen. He had stopped whistling and she had an uneasy feeling that he was spying upon her. Of course it was impossible. In fact, it was the other way about. It was she, in the darkened room, who was the invisible watcher. She would like to have withdrawn and gone to bed, for the chill of the spring night had become more penetrating, but the immobility of the man in the mews gripped her too. He and she – both were turned to stone. Could he be contemplating a forced entry? Taking stock of her open window? Hardly. A potential thief would scarcely be likely to announce his presence by whistling. The intangible bond between them held her inexorably. How very odd, she thought. I'm nervous. More than that, I'm afraid! It was a long while since she had known the definite sensation of fear. Was there a chain on the front door? Had she fastened it? Her mind was numb with the encroaching cold and she could not remember. It was Lucifer who released her from the spell. He jumped down from the tub and began to rub

himself against the intruder's thin calf. The man bent to
stroke the animal and suddenly Mrs Olivier's nerves
slackened. The cat evidently knew him – the lucky black
cat, the familiar of witches.

The little man straightened up and went his way. Mrs
Olivier heard his tuneless whistle fade as he turned the
corner and disappeared into the night. It echoed vaguely
through her dreams and was with her still when she woke
at eight o'clock to see sunlight streaming through her window. It was subtly interlaced with the other morning sounds
of the mews – a hose and a bucket in use, a milk trolley
rattling over the cobbles, cars snorting and gasping as they
warmed up and roared off to the battle of the parking place,
a man's step, the click of heels, greetings and the slap and
slither of papers as the news-boy flung them on to doorsteps
with erratic accuracy. In wet weather he pushed his papers
through the mouths of letter-boxes, but when the sun shone
they flew right and left from the carrier on the handlebars.

Mrs Olivier got out of bed and surveyed the scene.
Directly beneath her window a man was washing a white
Jaguar. He wore faded denims and a cloth cap with a wide
peak. As he worked he whistled through the side of his
mouth. So it's you – the night prowler – back by day, bright
and early! A harmless looking beast now you're out of the
shadows. She felt exhilarated as she went to the bathroom,
on the threshold of a new life. She turned on the hot tap.
Instantly the weak pilot jet in the gas geyser sprang into
active life with a loud plop.

'Explosions – Mr Ferrit!'

She smiled to herself as she scattered perfumed crystals
into the water.

The skylights might have their disadvantages, but, as she
lay in her hot bath, she was aware chiefly of their charms.
She looked straight up into the unclouded blue of the morn-

ing sky. A jet tore across it like a toy, its thunder and its whine following in its wake, and there was the less impressive and more intimate scrabble of pigeons, cooing and preening on the long panes. What big pink feet they had! Mrs Olivier was so enthralled with her unusual angle on the common pigeon that she failed to hear a key turn in the front-door lock and a quick step on the stair. When she emerged from the bathroom Mrs Meadows met her at the kitchen door.

Mrs Olivier saw a slight grey-haired woman with lively blue eyes and a friendly smile, while Mrs Meadows observed a tall figure in a quilted gown, a mane of flowing dark hair and a pale face, untouched by make-up. If she wasn't so big she'd be like one of those Russian ballerinas, Mrs Meadows thought. It was her habit to translate life into terms of the theatre. Both her father and her husband were employed at theatres and her mother had, in her time, been wardrobe mistress to a corps de ballet. Mrs Meadows loved the stage and all that pertained thereto.

Mrs Olivier's pale morning face brightened as she smiled down at Eve Kelly's daily help.

'I've heard about you from my daughter, Rachel. I'm so glad you can help me out while I'm here.'

'You must rest and enjoy yourself while you're in London,' said Mrs Meadows firmly. 'Now why don't you go back to bed for a start and read your papers in peace – *Express* and *Telegraph* Miss Rachel ordered – I brought them upstairs. I'll get your breakfast, you can have it in bed on a tray.'

'A marvellous thought. Coffee, toast and marmalade.'

'And grapefruit. Miss Rachel brought in everything she thought you might need. She took the morning off to meet me here. "Look after my ma," she says. "Order milk and buy bread and see she doesn't run out of things. She likes half a grapefruit with her breakfast and instant coffee made with milk." '

'Bless you both!'

'Your daughter's a great friend of Miss Eve – Mrs Kelly I should say, but I keep forgetting.' Mrs Meadows' eyes twinkled. 'She's a great friend of Mr Jim's too.'

'So it seems,' said Mrs Olivier dryly. They both laughed.

As Mrs Meadows told her husband afterwards, 'We took to each other at once. She laughs easy. But there's something sad in her eyes, haunted, you might say.'

'*You* might,' he retorted. 'Not me.'

'How d'you know? You haven't seen her.'

'You're the fanciful one, old girl.'

So, on her first morning in the cottage, the basic pattern of Mrs Olivier's London summer was established. Breakfast in bed, an exhaustive study of the sensational and conservative view of events as presented by the *Express* and the *Telegraph* respectively, followed by a conference with Mrs Meadows on what household necessities were required and where best to make the purchases. After that she set off with her shopping bag and learnt to know her neighbourhood.

When Mrs Olivier went out into the Trident that first morning in London she felt both rested and intensely alive, pervaded by a spring-time sense of anticipation. She was about to explore an old well-loved terrain and invite new acquaintances.

The night prowler had finished polishing the Jaguar, which was back in its lair, and he was busy on a vintage Bentley two doors further down. The humbler cars in the mews were washed by their owners or not at all. The man's peaked cap was under the long open bonnet and a small cheroot dangled from the corner of his lip. She addressed his bent back.

'Good morning.'

Her greeting floated into the cold mechanical heart of power and speed. He straightened his back and turned to stare at her.

'Mornin'.'

She smiled at him, turning on her charm. 'I'm a stranger here. Can you tell me if I can get out that end of the mews?'

She knew the answer perfectly well – Rachel had given it to her the evening before – but that was none of his business.

'It's a cul-de-sac. No exit that way. Would you be the new tenant of Number Eleven?'

'I would. I'm Mrs Olivier and I arrived from South Africa yesterday afternoon.'

'I thought as much. I've been keeping an eye on the place for Mrs Kelly. These are lawless days, ma'am. It's not a good idea to leave a house unoccupied. I passed by your place last night – or early this morning, I should say – and I sees the window open and I thinks, the lady's turned up.'

'You must be Mr Ferrit?'

'That's right.'

She smiled. 'Mr Ferrit – explosions.'

He looked startled. 'Wha's 'at?'

'I'm quoting from the list Mrs Kelly left for me. In an emergency I call on you. I gather you have a key to the cottage.'

He preened. 'Tha's right. Quite a number of people like me to have their keys when they're away. Just in case. Man and boy I've lived in the mews. Isn't anything I don't know about it.'

Mrs Olivier was not finding it easy to sum him up. He stood with his feet apart, a square of oily cotton waste in his left hand and the stub of the little cheroot in his right. The peak of his cap, pushed far back on his forehead, did not shade his lined leathery face. The eyes were small and beady and glowed with a feverish life of their own, his mouth was narrow, no lips. His age? – Fifty – sixty?

'Which is your house?' she asked.

'It's in the first prong. The short one that leads through to the church. In my grandfather's day all this was owned by a duke. A great judge of horse-flesh 'e was – the duke, I mean. My grandfather was his coachman with a dozen men under 'im – footmen, outriders, grooms, stable-boys, the lot. Did themselves proud in those days! An' look at the present duke, reduced to turnin' 'is stately 'ome into a public show for the 'oypoloy with slot machines, juke-boxes, ice-cream an' coffee bars, the 'ole blinkin' bag o' tricks.'

'Times change. Would you want to go back to horses in the mews?'

He grinned, swaying back on his heels, a little wiry fellow with a jockey's bowed legs and strong hands.

'Not me!'

He flicked away the chewed stump of his cheroot and indicated the Bentley with a jerk of his head.

'All the 'orses that ever stamped in the Trident are boiled down under that one bonnet, ma'am. Tha's good enough for me.'

She was hatless and the pale spring sun was caught in her shining black hair. It picked out the fine crow's feet just beginning to form at the corners of her eyes and fell also on the classic planes of her face. Over forty she might be, but hers were ageless features stamped on the coin of time with firm precision. Her neck and her body were young and she moved with pride. Mr Ferrit found his gaze returning to her face again and again.

'You been 'ere before?' he asked.

She shook her head.

'Funny,' he frowned. 'Could o' sworn I'd seen you some-where before. I know your face.'

She smiled. 'Hardly likely – unless you've been in South Africa. I've lived on a farm in the Transvaal for the past twenty years.'

'Never been back to London in all that time?'

'Never.'

She looked at her watch. 'Half past ten! I must be on my way, Mr Ferrit.'

He grinned. 'Harrods is your way, I s'pose.'

'Good guess.'

'You know the short cut?'

'Tell me.'

'Don't turn left out of the Trident. Turn right at the first prong – that's past my place – and cross the churchyard, then follow the long stone path to the left of the church and it'll bring you right out into the Brompton Road.'

'Thanks. I'll do that.'

He watched her straight back and the sway of her red coat, and his face was puckered with an effort of recollection. He pulled off his cap and scratched his balding head. Whatever she might say, and wherever she might have been, he had seen her somewhere before. You didn't forget a dial like Mrs Olivier's. That for sure.

3

RAVENSWOOD

THE MAY SUN WAS HOT, BUT CLOUDS WERE BANKING over the sea.

'There's going to be a storm,' said Jim.

Rachel raised her head, distending delicate nostrils to sniff the air with delight.

'I can smell the rain coming – the soft freshness. The sea too. The grass, the earth, everything! Even you – warm sandalwood.'

He laughed and bit her ear as they sat on the grassy hillside above the Sussex Downs.

'Truly,' she said. 'Like the sandalwood chest my father inherited from some ancestor who'd lived in Java in the days of the Dutch East India Company.'

'When would that have been? Sixteenth century?'

'Middle of the seventeenth.'

'Just about the time my ancestors acquired Ravenswood.'

The sweeping gesture of his hand took in the green landscape spread before them. The swelling hills were crowned with dark arborial rings, ritual groves dreaming of ancient sacrifice. Green vales fell away from them in fertile folds, flanked by wheat fields, ruffled by the breeze and bounded by woods and hedgerows. It was a soft productive feminine landscape, billowing down to the shores of the English Channel, now streaked with silver where the westering sun gashed the clouds. White sails filled and leaned before the wind and overhead the white gulls planed in bright unseen currents. Jim was pervaded by calm contentment. Here at Ravenswood he was at his most complete, and he knew that Rachel too succumbed to its quiet magic. They could see the slate roof and twisted chimneys of the old Queen Anne manor house but its mellow flint and stone walls and beautiful shell porch were screened by trees.

'It's beautiful – all this,' she said. 'So different from my own country, so much more intimate.'

'Smaller, you mean? It looks wide enough to me.'

'It's wide,' she agreed. 'And not a house in sight. Yet when you are on the veld you have a feeling of . . . infinity. The horizons really are far and the sky is much higher. You can see the weather for hundreds of miles. You can say. "Look, it's raining over Johannesburg," and there's the rain actually slanting out of heaven on to a city fifty miles away.'

'It'll soon be slanting over Ravenswood,' he said. 'I give it less than half an hour.' But he did not move.

'And the land,' she went on. 'This isn't just an endless stretch of grassland with a span of oxen, a piccaninny and a windmill to mark the human touch. Or a mine dump, a dam and a clump of trees. It's a countryside of parks and villages and great estates, every square foot of it matters to somebody.'

He was watching her, stirred as he so often was by her sincerity. Her appreciation of Ravenswood sharpened his need of her. She had never been a stranger here. The place had known and welcomed her from the first.

'This land has been cherished,' she was saying. 'You have only to look at it to know that it has been loved and cared for. It has taken and it has given.'

'Which is, after all, the essence of love. To take, to give, to create.'

His words switched her thoughts to Liz. Womanlike, Rachel instinctively narrowed the wide conception down to the individual circumstances. Love's cycle. To take, to give, to create. She saw again the thin blotched face of Liz, swollen with weeping, sick with apprehension. 'China – it's so far, Ray! I'll lose him . . .' And, perhaps, even as Liz had spoken, the greater loss might already have been hers. Liz too was out of London this weekend, staying with her dead lover's family in Hampshire. How was it going for Liz?

'You're shivering,' Jim said.

'I'm not really cold. But the sun's gone in.'

He sprang up and pulled her to her feet.

'We must run for it. The squall's coming up fast.'

With one accord, still holding hands, they sprinted towards the copse on the lee-side of the hill. She had thrown off her momentary depression and tossed her friend's burden to the rising wind as she gave herself with laughter to the exhilaration of racing the rain. Panting, they reached the fringe of trees just as the storm clouds, split by forked lightning, broke in thunder to deliver their first heavy drops of rain.

'I hate lightning!' She hid her face against his chest, rejoicing in the protection of his arms.

Boughs creaked and groaned overhead as they leaned against the sturdy trunk of a tall elm, seeking the shelter of its dense summer foliage. The warmth of their bodies steamed through their clothes and they stood, breathless, listening to the storm around them, shaken by the force of another within their own breasts. Her heart pounded under Jim's palm. Neither the chunky wool sweater nor the frail rib cage of flesh and bone could stop it pouring her strong pulsing vitality into his hand. It spilled over and engulfed him – this life force that was Rachel. Her face was lifted to his and his lips tasted the stinging coldness of her cheek and the eager warmth of her mouth. The full force of the squall shook them and the high unearthly keening of the wind in the topmost branches of the elm vibrated down the length of the trunk through the receptive nerves of the man and the girl who had become part of the tree and of the storm.

They had never been more alone, more secret and secure than here in the copse on the green hillside isolated by the brief elemental fury of the passing storm. She was beyond thought or words. She and Jim were one with nature's sudden fury and with each other. She was ice and fire, yielding and possessing. Her skin, close knit by the wind's arctic needles and sprayed with intrusive flurries of hail, flamed too with the burning blood of awakened passion.

'Hurt me, I love you!'

She did not know if she cried the words aloud, if they were carried away in the fierce gust that burst upon them, or whether they remained locked inside her, agonised, ecstatic and unspoken.

General Sir Jasper Fleet enjoyed his game of bridge. He had trained his good-natured second wife to be a sound player and a useful partner. 'You stick to the conventions, my dear, and leave the deviations to me.' He had also taught his son some of the intricacies of the contentious game, but Jim regarded the conventions of bridge as he did all other conventions – merely as a reasonably safe guide to be followed by the mediocre herd. Since he did not place himself in this category, his play was jagged with deviations.

'No humility,' said Sir Jasper of his son. 'Jim prides himself on being an individualist.'

When Mrs Olivier admitted that she played bridge her host was genuinely pleased.

'That gives us a four. I'm sure Rachel won't object to lending us Jim.'

Lady Fleet intercepted the look that passed between Rachel

and Jim, and laughingly advised them to bow to the inevitable. 'After all, it's your own fault, Rachel. I've often offered to teach you.'

Sir Jasper patted his wife's blunt practical hand. 'My dear, your optimism does you credit, but I once tried to initiate Rachel into the rudiments of bridge and I assure you she is unteachable. Not because she's unintelligent,' he hastened to add for Mrs Olivier's benefit, 'but because she has an infinite capacity for closing her mind to any subject repugnant to her.'

Fortunately Sir Jasper had no objection to soft background music – in fact, he found it soothing – so Rachel put on a long-playing record and curled up in a big chair by the fire to listen to Dvorak's New World Symphony and watch the players.

Jim's father fascinated her. He looked, she thought, like a small bearded satyr, mocking, wiry and wickedly alive. In fact, General Sir Jasper Fleet held an impressive and varied record of achievement. A gallant fighting officer of the first World War, twice wounded, he had in the second played a more subtle part. As a key man in the Security Service, his fame in initiated circles was a legend. In the wider circles of the uninitiated it was even greater, for he was the author of the intrepid secret agent Gerald Bourne, whose exploits were printed, screened and syndicated throughout a world hungry for adventure and the inside dope on the mysterious international maze of espionage and counter-espionage where the lone wolf ranges dangerously, a super-criminal or super-investigator, whichever way you care to look at it. Gangster or policeman, slayer or saviour, Gerald Bourne was universally acceptable, for were not the motives of this bold hero consistently beyond reproach? Gerald Bourne was a man specially selected to carry out dangerous missions for his country's good. How he accomplished these tasks was described in the riveting novels of John Speed, the pen-name of Jasper Fleet.

Rachel was a devoted fan of Gerald Bourne, but she regarded his creator with reservations. She suspected that Jasper Fleet, like Gerald Bourne, possessed a hard steel core of active cruelty and it never surprised her that his first wife had left him. Her successor, the 'dear cow-girl' to his two children, was impervious to his querulous moods and the darts and arrows of his outrageous tongue. Ravenswood was Laura Fleet's real love and she had no intention of allowing its irascible master to talk her out of her joy in it.

'He likes to break his prisoners,' she had told Jim once with her wry attractive smile. 'It's something he does very well. But he can't hurt me – much – because I've neither the brains nor the sensitivity to feel an adequate degree of humiliation. I'm humble already. But he destroyed your mother.'

'If you had neither brains nor sensitivity you couldn't possibly have made that statement,' said Jim, who was very fond of his stepmother. 'You have a philosophy of life and your own immense integrity. Both are impregnable.'

'Philosophy of life? Not consciously.'

'Perhaps not. It's a very simple one. You leave people in peace. You never try to prise things out of them and they can't prise anything out of you.'

She laughed. 'Maybe there's not much to prise.'

'Only good, and that's hardly worth an extensive excavation. Not to my father anyway. His line of country examines the bizarre and the tortuous, the slightly shameful, the disloyalties and petty treasons – '

'That's been his job.'

'He was happy in his work. It echoes on in his Gerald Bourne novels – overtones of sadism. Subtle tortures. Warped psychological explorations.'

She'd laughed and rubbed her hand up the back of Jim's head as she'd done in his childhood.

'You're pretty analytical yourself, my boy.'

Jim had repeated Laura's remarks about his father to Rachel.

'She talks to me about him as if we were a pair of psychologists discussing a case. I sometimes think she's so frank with me because she wants to help me understand the nature of his venom. It's in his make-up and he can't help expelling it from time to time. It's fairly well contained in its secret poison sacs but the fangs are there. Under stress, or in the cause of duty or just for the hell of it, he bites and the victim is paralysed or destroyed. One has to find one's own private antidote. My mother couldn't take it. She never developed immunity. The final, obvious and only antidote for her was another man. So she walked out on us. Mental cruelty wasn't fashionable then – especially in England – so my father divorced her for desertion.'

'How old were you when your mother deserted him – deserted all of you?'

'I was six. Eve was eleven. It was worse for her. She was temperamental and artistic – '

'And you, I suppose, were a cabbage – *you*!'

'Not exactly. But the cow-girl was always full of comfort for me. She took me everywhere, hay-making, milking, to see the young pheasants and the baby partridges. She showed me nests and steeped me in country lore. I tagged along wherever she went. Ploughing, reaping, harvesting. When I had to go to prep school I lived for the holidays, and there she always was, big and beautiful, wholesome, my friend.'

'She's all that still.'

'Yes, only now I don't take her for granted. I can see that she drew out a sting – that she wouldn't let me bear malice towards my mother or judge my father. She accepts people as they are. Eve saw less of her. Eve was at boarding school when our mother took off. I was luckier. Laura was good enough for me.'

'Did you see her often – your own mother – after she left?'

'Never. She had no access to us.'

'That was cruel.'

'I'm not so sure. She married again and had another family. When your life goes sour on you perhaps it's best to start again and cut away the past. Completely.'

'Is it possible?'

'*Your* mother thought so. Or so she led you to believe.'

But he had said it sceptically. As Rachel watched the game dreamily, that half-forgotten conversation with Jim ran it-self over in her mind. Could the past ever really be cut away? Surely only a major operation could do that, and even then the long roots might go too deep and far to be eradicated. Could Sir Jasper forget the lovely girl he had lost as much through his own intolerance as her frailty? Could Jim's mother forget her own children? And what about Rachel's own mother? Could she really claim to have put away those memories she had locked in a sort of Blue-Beard's chamber, for ever *tabu*? If so, she had been caught up in it again. Death had left her free, but London – or perhaps Rachel – had drawn her back into the danger zone. Liz. How could Liz put away her short tempestuous past with Tom Standish who had been killed on the Portsmouth road? Would she even try? Poor Liz, who was still too shocked to face the future. And what about me? Rachel wondered. This even-ing in the copse on the hill. Nothing can ever be quite the same again for Jim and me. It may be better. It may not. She dared not look across at him for fear of meeting his eyes. Her bones melted. There was no need to look at Jim. His strong irregular features were burned into her memory; the way his eyes changed when he wanted her, the touch of his long-fingered hands that could be so gentle or so possessive. Her lids dropped and she floated on tingling sensations of near faintness.

'My daughter's asleep,' said Mrs Olivier, making the cards. 'Your deal, General.'

Rachel sat up quickly and caught the flash of laughter in Jim's glance.

'I was enjoying the music,' she said.

'The New World's not exactly soporific,' said the General, sorting his hand with satisfaction. He was in a winning vein tonight.

Rachel's eyes, looking outward now, wandered from his satyr's face with the thick thatch of wiry steel-grey hair and the aggressive little beard to the calm absorbed countenance of his partner. Laura Fleet was much younger than her husband but she had given him no children, and this was an abiding sadness and mystery to her, for she was a fine stalwart woman who looked like the mother of all living. Now she was past the age of child-bearing and her thwarted maternal instinct poured itself out on every baby creature on the estate. Her resignation was without rancour. No one who had as much as she could be considered barren. She has a look of innocence, thought Rachel. She's older than Ma but she seems much younger. It's her fairness and the moon face. They don't age. Laura and Ma are both outdoor women, but Laura's skin is fresh and healthy because of it and Ma's is burned dry and pale like winter bracken. Laura's outlook is innocent too. Young. She sees all the aspects of nature as part of one divine law, whereas to Ma it's a constant reminder of the 'baser side of human behaviour'. It's the self she wants to ignore.

How differently they played their cards. Sir Jasper always twisted his as he placed them on the table. 'He wrecks them,' Laura often complained. But she never tried to check him.

For her part she dropped her cards quietly from her hand on to the velvet cloth. Jim was quick and neat, while Mrs Olivier played with decision.

'Game and rubber,' said Laura.

She gathered up the cards and put them away in their box, leaving the adding up to the other players.

'We never start a new rubber after ten o'clock,' she said. 'We've country habits. Who's for church tomorrow?'

She turned to Mrs Olivier with her open smile. 'It's not compulsory. Jasper and I always go. The young ones generally come along but they don't have to. And if you prefer to lie in or laze about the garden, please be honest.'

Mrs Olivier threw an inquiring glance at Rachel, who said aloud: 'Lady Fleet means it, Ma. Do as you like. I shall go to church.'

Mrs Olivier had risen. She took a florin and a sixpence from her purse. 'Half a crown I owe you, Sir Jasper.'

He passed the coins across the table to his wife.

'For the collection box, my dear. A nightcap, Mrs Olivier?'

'Nothing for me, thanks. What time do you leave for church in the morning?'

'Ten fifteen,' he said. 'No need to commit yourself. If you aren't ready downstairs by then we leave you to your own devices.'

'It's a sweet little church,' said Laura. 'Twelfth century.'

'How interesting,' said Mrs Olivier politely.

Rachel feared that her mother would not be 'ready downstairs' at ten fifteen next morning. It was her father who had laid the foundations of her spiritual values. It was he who had taught Rachel the Ten Commandments, those simple Old Testament laws of a pastoral people. The bible had been his Great Book and every evening it had been his habit to read some passage of it aloud to any members of his family who cared to listen. Rachel had always enjoyed that peaceful half hour and the sound of her father's rumbling voice enriching the ancient tales and proverbs with its warm depth. Her mother usually stayed to listen, her dark head bent over her mending, the picture of a dutiful God-fearing wife and mother. Yet Rachel, ever sensitive to the moods of others, had been aware of the withdrawal of her mother's spirit, of the strange sad way in which it ebbed from her shadowed expressionless face, a retreating tide leaving a desolate empty shore. Not even driftwood to light a fire. Nothing.

'Sometimes I think she doesn't really believe in God,' Hans had said once to his sister, his eyes wide and apprehensive at the magnitude of his suspicion.

She had answered, intuitive and suddenly afraid.

'It's more than that. She believes in Him, but she hates Him.'

The fearful thought completed itself in her mind. 'She's turned against Him – the way she turns against me.'

4

JIM AND RACHEL

MRS OLIVIER WAS VERY NEAT AND CORRECT IN HER
tailored linen suit with her grey and scarlet kerchief round
her neck.

'I can put it over my head,' she said to Laura Fleet, who
laughed.

'Not necessary. The church is twelfth century but the
congregation is strictly twentieth.'

Rachel looked at her mother with surprise. Mrs Olivier
was evidently doing her best to conform.

The little stone Norman church stood among the trees of
Raven Park, the great house which had once belonged to the
Fleet family and which was now a school for retarded children. Half a dozen of the little backward boys sang in the
choir. Their well-scrubbed faces might be dull, they might
shuffle their feet and pick their noses, but when Miss Pike,
the music mistress, played the opening bars of psalms or
hymns the children were transformed. It was a long time
since Mrs Olivier had heard the singular effortless purity of
boys' voices raised in songs of praise, uncomprehending,
emotionless as birds, pouring forth the high golden notes for
the sheer joy of it.

The white and purple lilac in the silver altar vases had been
arranged by Laura Fleet, the Lessons were read with forceful
effect by Sir Jasper, and Mrs Olivier was astonished to hear
Jim's baritone, true as a bell, raised lustily at her side as he

flung back his head of black unmanageable hair and let fly. He was a bony young man, all corners, and his hands on the hymn book held her fascinated. Virile Rodin hands, the past and future written into them. Would she be willing to put her daughter's life into those hands? She looked past Jim to Rachel.

They were in the family pew directly in front of the lectern, and the light, filtered by stained glass, poured on to Rachel's hair, pale as ripe barley. Her profile was devout, eyes downcast, a glowing shell-like cameo.

'Let her be happy!' Mrs Olivier pleaded silently, and added her recriminations. 'Don't give her the raw deal You gave me. Give her a fair chance. Don't let the sins of others be visited upon this child.'

Polished brass and bronze plaques gleamed on the ancient walls. They bore the names of Fleets killed in action in old imperial wars and modern world wars. A peal of bells had been donated in memory of James Fleet, a midshipman in the Royal Navy lost at sea in Nelson's day.

By the time they emerged into the green and silver of the showery morning Mrs Olivier had reached a major decision. She had determined that, come what might, Rachel must be allowed to get her man. But she sensed resistance from a formidable quarter. She knew very well that she, Rachel's mother, had been invited to Ravenswood on approval, so to speak. If she measured up to the standards set by General Sir Jasper Fleet her daughter would be welcomed. Otherwise not. Mrs Olivier was intelligent enough to know that there were serious gaps in her own past unaccounted for by a sojourn of twenty years in a far country. She had no fears about Môreson. If the Fleets visited the Transvaal farm they would be pleasantly surprised. It was a farm of which anyone might justifiably be proud with its many morgen of grain and cattle lands supporting tenant farmers and supplying the new mining towns on the Reef with meat as well as wheat. It was here, in her native England, that Mrs Olivier knew herself to be vulnerable. She had not played bridge with General Fleet without observing his tactics. He was astute at introducing well-timed strategic bluffs. He played his cards with an eye to the psychology of his opponents and he learned as much from the tone or hesitation of the caller as he did from the call itself. He was, as he admitted, disconcertingly devious. She had the disturbing impression that, for all his excellent manners and considerable charm, he was not accepting her at her face value. He was assessing her worth from many angles and after his own tortuous fashion. He's dangerous, she thought, I must go carefully. The long-forgotten habit of watching her step and minding her tongue reasserted itself and at once it was unconsciously reflected in her eyes.

By five o'clock the sun was shining and the family met in the garden-room for a late tea.

Jim and Rachel were the first there. She gazed out at the green lawn spread under the broad umbrella of a giant horse-chestnut.

'How I love this room!'

'Rather like a greenhouse,' he said. 'It was an open sun-terrace once and my grandfather had it glassed in.'

The roof was glass too and light bamboo blinds could be drawn across any of the panes at will. French doors led on to the lawn bounded by a high wall of weathered brick and flint. Fruit trees in espalier were crucified against this wall in a living glory of leaf and late blossom, and a lavish herbaceous border bloomed in its shelter. Beyond it the lilac trees tossed prolific sprays of white, mauve, and a deep rich wine. A peahen strutted delicately across the grass, placing her feet with fastidious care, and her mate descended suddenly from the wall with a cross between a jump and a flight. He landed heavily with a raucous 'paap' like an old-fashioned motor horn.

Laura Fleet had joined Jim and Rachel as the male spread the jewelled fan of his tail in all its courting splendour.

'No need to give him chocolate cake to make him show off – not at this season.'

She turned to the tea-tray. 'We won't wait for Jasper and Mrs Olivier. They've gone to see the golden pheasants.'

'The golden pheasants are even more glam than the peacocks,' said Rachel. 'One just goes on and on looking, not able to believe in all those miraculous colours.'

Jim watched his stepmother pour the tea. 'My father has fairy-tale tastes – exotic birds and a beautiful cowgirl.'

'Put a chunk of cake in it!' said Laura. 'And give Rachel this cup of tea. Here come the others.'

Mrs Olivier and the General had strolled through the moon-gate in the wall and paused to watch the love pavane of the peacock for the benefit of his mate, who coyly ignored it. As they came into the garden-room Sir Jasper said:

'Mrs Olivier admires the magnificence of our peacocks but not their early morning serenades.'

'Did they wake you?' asked Laura.

Mrs Olivier smiled. 'At dawn. I've never heard such mournful screeching.'

She sank into an easy chair and Jim put a cup of clear tea beside her. She shook her head at the proffered sandwich. 'Nothing to eat, thank you.'

'I'm so used to their noise in the mating season I've stopped noticing it,' said Laura, 'But it is rather horrific – that drawn-out "ow-oh-ow-oh-ow" followed by fearful cries of "he-alp! he-alp!" '

Jim said: 'It gets them that way, like cats. You'd never say it was love, you'd think it was murder.'

'Each man kills the thing he loves . . . ' said the General. 'Quote – Oscar Wilde.'

Mrs Olivier had taken a cigarette from her case and as he lit it for her Jim saw that her face had gone pale and stony and her hand was shaking.

'Tired?' he asked. 'Dad's apt to walk our guests off their feet if they let him.'

'A bit,' she confessed. 'I'm in poor training.'

'Tomorrow we'll give her a mount,' suggested Sir Jasper kindly. 'Let her ride.'

'I've no riding things,' she said. 'In any case, we go back tonight.'

Laura refilled Mrs Olivier's tea-cup.

'I'll lend you a shirt and slacks. And why go back so soon? Stay till Tuesday and you can go up to town with me. I have to be in London by lunch-time. It'll be company for me on the drive.'

'Why don't you do that, Ma? I'll leave a message for Mrs Meadows.'

Rachel's tone was eager and Mrs Olivier chuckled softly. The life had returned to her pale face.

'You'd certainly be more comfortable in that little car without me. Thank you very much, Lady Fleet. I'd love to stay on.'

'Do make it Laura.'

'I'd like to. My name is Ann.'

'Ann. A good old English name,' remarked the General.

'I am English,' said Mrs Olivier.

'It must be fun meeting your old friends again after twenty years,' said Laura. 'Or is it a bit of a shock?'

A queer little silence fell, and Rachel, who had been watching the peacocks, turned to look at her mother. Such an ordinary question, yet she knew it was one her mother would find difficult to answer. She felt the blood rise to her cheeks and a faint prickling round her forehead where the fair hair sprang back, soft and strong.

'It's not easy to pick up the threads,' Mrs Olivier said. 'There's a Rip van Winkle feeling about coming home after such a long time. People have drifted away, the points of contact have become . . . remote.'

'Rachel says you're a Cockney by birth,' Sir Jasper plugged his pipe and struck a match.

'Near enough. My parents lived in Bloomsbury. My father was a doctor.'

'Was?'

'They – my father and mother – were killed in the blitz. A buzz bomb. I was in the WAAFs then – in London too.'

'How sad – how dreadful for you!' cried Laura, dismayed at the revival of tragic memories. Sir Jasper drew on his pipe.

'Mrs Olivier – Ann – lived dangerously, my dear. All those who remained in London on the job took chances in those bad old days. I salute them.'

'The war to end wars.' Jim's eyes were hot in their smoky sockets. 'All those sacrifices, yet our generation grows up under the shadow of the bomb!'

'And makes that an excuse for futility,' snapped his father.

'Some do. Not many. We feel the need to live before we die. That's how it gets most of us.'

'Live – the little word that can mean anything from yowling at a Pop-singer to begetting a bastard under a hay-rick.'

'Not a very wide range according to you. A to B.'

Rachel saw the colour leave Jim's face. The General pursued his theme.

'If you'd said "achieve something", I might have been more impressed. "Live" is too vague a term for my precise mind.'

Laura cut in.

'To come to earth, Jim, what time are you and Rachel proposing to leave this evening?'

'After supper. No hurry. The later the better, in a way. Less on the roads.'

But the General was not to be deflected. 'So you can step on it. Speed. That's a vital part of living, I suppose.'

'Our time may be short.'

'Or extinguished altogether by the great god Speed.'

Jim had recovered his good humour. 'Father,' he said, 'you're being contrary. I'm going to take Rachel round the garden and show her birds' nests.'

They sauntered out into the soft evening, through the moon-gate into the kitchen-garden and on up the hill.

'The old man riles me,' said Jim.

'He does it on purpose. He likes to get a rise out of you.'

'Achieve something. What the hell can one achieve in the city?'

'You could make a fortune and you could feed it into Ravenswood.'

'Ah,' he said, 'now you're talking.'

The season of summer holidays and night travel had not really begun and Yellow Peril made good time through the Sussex lanes. On long drives Jim took the wheel.

Jim drove fast but well. She was never out of control. When they hit the main Portsmouth road he let her go. As they left the lake at Ripley behind them Rachel shuddered and her hand pressed harder against the warmth of his leg.

'Extinguished – your father said – by the great god Speed . . .' She closed her eyes to shut out the picture of a buckled motor-cycle and a broken human body. Tom Standish.

Jim said: 'Poor Tom.'

'Poor Liz.'

'What'll she do?'

'I don't know. She's with his people now till Tuesday. Her boss is away and she's got a few days off.'

'Will she tell them – his people?'

'That's her intention.'

'Would they have married?' he asked.

'I doubt it. Tom isn't . . . wasn't . . . the marrying kind.'

'I am,' he said. 'If you were caught that way I'd marry you.'

'It would need that, would it?'

'No. It wouldn't need that.'

After a while she said: 'How extraordinary. Would that mean – could it be – a proposal of marriage?'

'It could,' he said. 'It is.'

'Jim. Please stop the car.'

'No.'

She laughed softly and leaned against him. His hands did not leave the wheel, nor his eyes the road. The shadowy retreats of Barnes Common fell behind them and they were crossing Putney Bridge and roaring through the long empty wastes of the King's Road. Jim cut up left into the Fulham Road and the crescent where she lived.

Under the plane tree he stopped the car and sprang out, opening the door for Rachel and slinging her small suitcase out of the back seat.

'You can lock yours in the boot,' she suggested.

'It'll be safer in your flat.'

She turned abruptly and ran down the area steps ahead of him. Her fingers trembled as she fitted the key into the lock.

In the tiny hall he put down the cases and took her in his arms. 'Tuesday,' he whispered. 'Liz gets back on Tuesday, you said?' Her throat was dry. She could only nod her head.

'I love you,' he said. 'Ray, my darling, I love you.'

5

NEXT DOOR NEIGHBOURS

LAURA FLEET DROPPED MRS OLIVIER AT THE MEWS cottage at noon on Tuesday. Jane Rafferty was just emerging from the next door house and stopped to talk to them.

'How's Eve? Liking New York?'

'Loving it,' said Laura.

'I wonder if they'll come back?'

'More than doubtful.'

'Disaster! Eve was my favourite neighbour,' Jane turned to Mrs Olivier. 'When are you coming in for a drink with us?'

'Whenever you say.'

'What about this evening?'

'That would be very nice.'

'Around six then. Any old time that suits you. I must fly. I'm hideously late.'

Laura said: 'Which way are you going?'

'Sloane Square.'

'That's hardly out of my way. Hop in.'

On the narrow table on the landing upstairs Mrs Olivier found a scrap of paper. She unfolded it. 'Hope you had a lovely weekend. Lilian Meadows.'

She was touched and warmed by her daily help's message. It was as if fingers of friendship brushed the lonely core of her heart. It was curious – this homecoming that was not a homecoming. She had a sudden overpowering desire to know what had happened to certain people intimately associated with that other life – the life before Gerhard

Olivier had swept her out of Europe into the golden heart of the African continent. Her friend, Cheryl, for instance. Cheryl had been a WAAF too, her room-mate, as close to Ann then as Liz was to Rachel now, sharing secrets and confidences. It had been painful to part with Cheryl.

'We must keep in touch,' Cheryl had said. But Ann Olivier had looked at her with haggard desperate eyes. 'No! We must never meet again. Everything that has happened must be buried. Finished for ever.'

'Surely you can trust me, Ann?'

'I daren't.'

She would never forget the hurt in Cheryl's eyes. What had become of Cheryl? Why wonder? What did it matter to her now? Mrs Olivier dumped her suitcase on the bed and began to unpack it. Her features set into a cold hard mould. Rachel would have recognised the look and flinched. You could never touch her mother when her face turned to stone. To try was to hurt yourself.

Laura Fleet turned into Sloane Street at the Pont Street intersection.

'What do you think of your new neighbour?' she asked Jane Rafferty.

'I don't know a thing about her,' said Jane, 'except that she doesn't appear to have many friends. Like most of us, her door's always open but Lucifer, the cat, is about the only visitor, or so Mr Ferrit tells me, and he – as you know – is the eyes of the mews.'

'She's been lost in Africa for a couple of decades. Difficult to pick up the threads after such a gap.'

'Does she try?'

'There was a tragedy. Parents killed in the blitz.'

'So Rachel told me. But even so, I can't quite see why it should eliminate all the rest – the other ties. Rather a pathological attitude, isn't it?'

Laura agreed with such evident relief that Jane shot her a sharp glance.

'What does Jasper say?'

Laura hesitated. 'Jasper's holding his horses. Where do you want dropping? This side of Sloane Square or the other? I'm going to the Embankment.'

'Put me down here. This'll do well. Why not look in for a drink this evening, Laura? Stay to a meal and avoid the outgoing rush.'

'I might come in for a noggin. But I won't stay and eat.'

'I'll fix some sandwiches for you. Shall I ring Jasper?'

'Yes, do. Tell him I won't be home to dinner. See you later, then.'

When Jim and Rachel drew up alongside the mews cottage in Yellow Peril that evening they found Mr Ferrit busy mending a leaking tap in the Raffertys' garage next door. Jane's white Jaguar gleamed in the gloom like a modern speed goddess, sleek, ferocious, swift – Artemis of the autostradas. The black cat brooded on the bonnet.

'I'm surprised you allow that,' said Jim.

Mr Ferrit shrugged his shoulders in the leather jerkin. 'Lucifer does as 'e likes. Mrs Rafferty had the Jag out this afternoon and the bonnet's nice an' warm. Chilly this evening, more like winter than summer.'

Rachel had her own key to the cottage and was fitting it in the lock when he called suddenly.

'I was forgettin'. There's a message for you from Mrs Rafferty. Both your mothers is over at her place. She says for you to go in there for a drink.'

'Thanks,' said Jim. 'We'll do that thing.'

Mr Ferrit resumed his work, whistling out of the corner

of his mouth. The travesty of a popular tune followed them up Jacob's ladder. So did Lucifer, the cat.

'Wants his sundowner,' said Jim.

Rachel set a saucer of milk on the kitchen floor.

'What about you?'

'I'll sting the Raffertys. When are we going to break the news to our respective relatives?'

She perched precariously on the landing rail, waiting for Lucifer to finish his milk. Jim took a quick step towards her.

'Don't do that! You could go over backwards down Jacob's ladder. That rail's wobbly.'

She laughed as his arms went round her waist. He stood between her knees, supple and lean, and she slid down against his body. Would they ever get used to one another? Would she ever see him, touch him, hear his voice – or even his name spoken – without quickening from top to toe? When that happened they'd be old. Old – he and she! The prospect was more foreign than death. Death was a hazard. It sprang at youth out of the night or a clear sky. Old age crept up on dreary middle age. Old age was not for lovers.

'What are you thinking?' he asked, his mouth against her hair.

'That I can't imagine ever not wanting you.'

'Ah ... Ray ... '

But she broke away from him and went into the sitting room. The cat was there before them, washing its thigh with a periscope leg in the air and an arched neck. Jim pulled Rachel down beside him on the couch.

'We must make plans – proper plans. When are we going to be married?'

'In September, when I'm twenty-one. Before Ma goes back to South Africa.'

'Eve might want us to stay on here for a bit – as care-takers.'

'Cats might fly.'

Jim grinned at Lucifer. 'Some do. On broomsticks. Anything can happen.'

I'm lucky, she thought. It's usually the girls who want to settle down. The men prefer to let things slide. He's really keen on the altar and the marriage bed. But then he has Ravenswood. Without that he mightn't care so much. He wants to establish the succession. She smiled to herself. Like kings and queens. A new picture formed in her mind. Sir Jasper gone – a painless thought, though she'd miss further exploits of Secret Agent Gerald Bourne – and Jim the master of Ravenswood. There'd be children and an eldest son to grow up loving that fertile Sussex scene as his father loved it. She closed her eyes, dimly aware of the immortality bestowed by continuity of family and inheritance, and of the timeless blessings and obligations that fall upon those who love the land they own.

'You're quiet and far away,' he said.

'No further than Ravenswood. Will your father make difficulties?'

'I wouldn't put it past him. He's always impressing on me that it's a mistake to marry young.'

'Young? Twenty-four isn't very young.'

'From his point of view it is. You see, he was that age when he married my mother.'

'Do we – you and I – have to suffer because they made a mess of their marriage?'

'They take it out on us. All parents do. Children are twisted by the experiences of their parents.'

'Do you really think that?'

'Don't you?'

'It hadn't occurred to me. It was good between my father

and mother. Oh, they had the odd disagreement of course, but they got along well. I was the misfit.'

'Why should you have been? I can't think why. You're fiery, but with a gentle mouth.'

'Why? I've wondered too.' She got to her feet. 'We ought to go.'

'Shall we leave Lucifer here?' asked Jim. 'He's purring like a well-timed motor.'

'Why not? He's moved in with Ma to all intents and purposes. I'll be ready in a minute.'

Jim waited for her by the window, his hand idly caressing Lucifer's throat. How the animal did vibrate! In the mews below they saw Mr Ferrit go whistling on his way. The young Dixons came out of their house and crossed the cobbles into the Raffertys', leaving the dachshund, Flicky, to sulk outside. The cornucopia hands from further down the mews were dispensing crumbs and seed for the greedy pigeons and sparrows. Ginger Rafferty ran his powerful car into the garage. Rachel called to Jim. He turned from the window, and Lucifer's eyes narrowed to basilisk slits.

The red house-door slammed as Jim and Rachel left him to his own feline devices. A chill erratic wind funnelled down the mews, blowing the summer scent of geraniums over faint ground vapours of gasoline. The witches' cat brooded over the scene. He did not feel the cold, he was snug in his black velvet coat warmed by the distant glow of eternal Satanic fires.

The Raffertys' house was a strange shade of green, like summer on the point of death, picked out with a hot Caribbean tan. Purple clematis covered the tiny porch. Jim and Rachel entered without knocking and Mary Dixon called out:

'Don't let Flicky in!'

But Flicky had slipped past them and was being made

welcome by his hostess. No one had the heart to throw him out.

The Raffertys had turned the garage into a living room, its glass wall facing on to the mews was protected by a fanciful but strong wrought-iron grille. The huge window was touched now by the last rays of the sun which penetrated to these ground-floor rooms only once a day and briefly, as if for a goodnight kiss.

It was a room worth a kiss, pale salmon pink with touches of Madonna blue. An Adam fireplace, a Chinese ginger jar masquerading as a lamp and an artistic arrangement of dead flowers on a table near a dusky couch. A little bar had been bricked into the wall like a wicked nun and was resuscitated regularly at sunset.

Rachel said it was like going into a crypt, and a breath of incense supported the idea, but Jim contended that the room symbolised the reverse of Jane – 'the dark side of the moon' – the unlit mysterious aspect of that breezy outdoor young woman.

Ginger was mixing a lethal Martini. Ginger Rafferty, ex-R.A.F. officer and test pilot, director of companies engaged in the manufacture of various aeronautical entrails, was now earth-bound, an inveterate car-coper, trafficking only in the best and fastest the age of speed could offer him. He was the car connoisseur of the mews, an expert, revered by lesser men like Jim Fleet and Charlie Dixon. These two hung upon his words now, and Rachel, seeing the expression on Jim's face, knew that he had been sucked into a glittering masculine realm whence he would later emerge preoccupied and inaccessible with shining extravagant dreams in his eyes and supersonic songs in his ears. Young Mary Dixon threw a glance of experienced resignation at Ginger and his two disciples.

'That's the way it goes if you're fool enough to live in a

mews. It's their spiritual home as well, a place where they can talk their jargon and tinker at engines when they ought to be doing other things. Charlie won't even come in to a meal once he's got a bonnet open and a tool-box out – and he's a hungry hound.'

'Do you understand the jargon?' asked Rachel. Mary laughed.

'In self-defence, yes. I'm mechanic's mate. I do as I'm told and hold the spanner. One of these days I may rebel. In that case my ever-loving will be found coshed by a blunt instrument.'

Jane was doing her Mrs Know-all act for Mrs Olivier. She was familiar with every inch of her neighbourhood.

'I must have been here before in some other incarnation,' she said. 'Like Mr Ferrit. He's another one who knows every cobble and paving stone in and around the Trident.'

'Mr Ferrit – car-washer, caretaker, self-appointed night-watchman,' smiled Mrs Olivier.

'Watch him polish a car, whistling through the side of his mouth. He might be curry-combing a horse.'

'Is there a Mrs Ferrit?'

'No, he lives with his sister, who's a bit on the simple side.'

Ginger Rafferty appeared, cocktail shaker in hand.

'Mr Ferrit doesn't live his own life, Mrs Olivier. He hasn't got one. So he lives ours. Martini?'

'I still have a whisky,' she said.

Jane laughed. 'Old Emily goes to the pictures to lead her vicarious life. There, in the dark, she's the heroine. Mr Ferrit finds all the drama he wants here in the mews. We are the play.'

Ginger lingered a moment. 'I hope you aren't lonely here. There are times when London can seem as empty as the Sahara.'

'Never to me! It's my ant-heap.'

Ginger topped up Laura Fleet's glass. 'Here's a girl who thinks nothing of the ant-heap,' he said to Mrs Olivier.

'All cities stifle me,' Laura said. 'I like the wide open spaces. As a matter of fact, Ann has talked Jasper into taking me to South Africa for a short holiday. He's just turned in the typescript of a new Gerald Bourne and he needs a complete change.'

'Wonderful idea,' said Ginger. 'Next thing we know we'll have Gerald Bourne wallowing in witchcraft and ritual murder with a bit of diamond smuggling on the side.'

Laura looked at him thoughtfully. 'You're right. I must plug that angle. Africa might be a very good stimulus for Jasper's jaded imagination. He gets more depressed after every Bourne exploit and goes through agonies deciding that he's dried up.'

Rachel and Jim had gravitated towards her. Rachel said:

'We can't do without Gerald Bourne! The fantastic is the normal in South Africa. I'm sure it will inspire General Fleet. And the Transvaal at this time of the year is glorious.'

'But it's your winter. Who'd miss our glorious English summer for somebody else's winter?' Ginger Rafferty's grin was sardonic.

'A Transvaal winter is heaven,' chipped in Mrs Olivier. 'Bright and dry, sparkling air, hot sunny days and ice-cold nights. It's the perfect season for seeing our great wild life sanctuaries – the lion in all his glory, herds of elephant, white rhinos –'

'I could use a tour like that,' sighed Mary Dixon. 'Swop Flicky for a cheetah.'

Laura said, 'I can't wait. I must persuade Jasper to leave next week. Not a moment later. We'll go by sea, return by air. Ann's dreamed up a complete itinerary for us already.'

The marble clock on the mantlepiece chimed the hour and

Laura looked round in dismay. 'Surely it can't be eight o'clock! I ought to have been halfway home by now.'

Jim put his arm round her shoulder. 'I'll see you into your car. Jane's organised sandwiches and a thermos for you.'

When they were alone, Laura at the wheel and Jim standing at the open window of her car, his black hair wildly blown by the gusty wind, she seemed in no hurry to get away.

'Jim, are you serious about Rachel?' she asked quietly.

'Yes,' he said. 'Can you smooth the path with Pa? We want to get married in September. We thought we'd announce the engagement very soon.'

'Wait till we get back from South Africa.'

'Are you really going? I thought you were just shooting a line.'

'If you're serious about this South African girl – yes, then we're really going. And soon.'

She saw his recoil. 'Checking up on the Oliviers?' There was a bite in his voice.

'Don't be so touchy, Jim. I've always wanted to go to South Africa – you know that – only now it will be so much more interesting. Meeting people in their homes, staying on the Olivier's farm. If you're involved we can afford to be involved too. Otherwise not. See?'

He was disarmed but unconvinced.

'You like Ray, don't you Laura?'

'She's a darling. I'm your ally. Your father likes her too, but he may be more difficult. He'll probably want you to wait a couple of years. You know how he feels about young marriages.'

'A couple of years! Our generation can't afford to toss away two years.'

His eyes burned in their deep sockets. He had at times the look of a medieval saint, she thought, of one who will never recant. How intense they were – these sons of the last war whose own sons might well be sired in the deadly glow of Götterdämmerung.

'I hope to make your father see it that way. By the time we get back he should be your ally too. Have patience, Jim.'

'It'll make no difference either way. We've made up our minds.'

'Jim,' she pleaded. 'Don't despise your father's approval and willing consent. Approval is like a fine day. You can bask in it.'

She blew him a kiss as she pressed the self-starter and put the car into gear.

He watched her drive away, her broad friendly ungloved hand fluttering out of the window. But for her, he thought, my father and I would long ago have been mortal enemies.

6

RAG-AND-BONE MAN

WHEN JIM TOOK RACHEL BACK TO THE BASEMENT
flat soon after nine o'clock they found the mercurial Liz
back from the country in high good humour. She greeted
them with enthusiasm.

'I've just made coffee. How was your weekend at Ravenswood?'

'Wonderful,' said Rachel. 'And how did things pan out
for you?'

'Need you ask?' grinned Jim. 'She's on the crest.'

'I'll tell you. Sit down. Black or white coffee?'

'Half and half for me and black for Jim. And sugar for
both of us.'

Liz had drawn the curtains against the deepening summer
twilight that filtered uneasily into the area; the little flat was
cosy and homely. Rachel curled up on the divan and Jim
sat next to her. She dared not catch his eye. Last night and
Sunday night this warren in Fulham had been all theirs.
Then, too, the gay absurd curtains with their pattern of vio-
lins and lobsters had shut out the world. Last night, in this
room, they had eaten a meal cooked by Rachel and drunk
a toast to the future in mulled red wine.

'Being here on our own . . . it's like being married,'
she'd said.

He'd laughed, with his olive scooped-out face sparkling
with life and mischief.

'Is it? I've no experience – of marriage.'

'You'll learn.'

She was still a trifle light-headed as she sipped her hot coffee. But she made an effort.

'What were they like – Tom's folk?' she asked Liz.

'Fabulous,' said Liz. 'Well, not exactly. What I mean is – astonishing. Tom was an only child, you know. His mother is about the same age as yours, his father's not much older. When they realised what Tom had meant to me – '

She broke off, tears welling and brimming over. She dabbed at her eyes.

'Sorry, this happens. I never know what's going to set me off.'

'Were they kind to you?' Rachel asked.

Liz nodded helplessly.

'Did you tell them everything?'

'Everything.'

'Did they take it well?'

'Fantastically. I couldn't have believed it possible. I told Tom's mother when we were alone and she began to cry. But she was happy. She wants this child. She said that now she doesn't feel as if she'd lost Tom altogether.'

'Will she adopt it?' Jim asked.

'That's the idea. It seems they have money in Switzerland and we're going to stay there in a chalet near Gstaad – it's one they often take for winter sports. We'll go there in September and remain till after the baby is born . . . '

Rachel looked at her friend reflectively.

'And then?'

'Well, and then he's to be hers – theirs.'

'What about you?'

'They'll send me back to South Africa.'

'Where's the catch?' asked Jim.

'The catch. Before the child is born I have to sign a legal

document relinquishing all claim. I'm to part with him at birth. I'm never to try to see him again.'

'That might be tough on you,' said Rachel. 'You might begin to love this child. Perhaps you do already.'

Jim had risen. He took Rachel's empty cup and put it on the tray. He stood with his back to the electric radiator, his face set. He spoke roughly.

'Don't queer this excellent solution for Liz. Liz loved Tom. The child is incidental. An accident. Let it go where it will be wanted.'

Rachel stuck to her guns. 'I don't see how Liz can promise to relinquish all claims on her own baby at this stage. It's part of her, she may feel quite differently about it when he – or she – is born. She ought to be free to decide later.'

'They're adamant about the conditions,' said Liz. 'It seems Tom's mother always wanted several children, but after Tom something went wrong and she couldn't have any more. She's only forty-two now. It's not really very old. They'll probably adopt another as a companion to . . . mine . . . but the fact that this one is Tom's means a great deal to them both.'

'Of course, I see that,' said Rachel. 'I see how she feels. It's you I'm thinking of.'

'Then think on practical lines,' snapped Jim. 'How can a young woman earning her own living bring up an illegitimate child?'

'Why not?' said Liz suddenly. 'People do. For choice.'

'It's not fair to mother or child. And if Liz wants to marry later on it's a lot to ask the man to swallow.'

'Not these days,' Liz said obstinately.

'Not in theory, perhaps. In fact, yes. In any case mother-love is an overrated commodity. Even mothers who appear to love their children and are genuinely adored in return –are quite prepared to ditch their families if they get in the way.

I should know! Give this kid a chance to go to people who won't ditch him. Give yourself a chance to start again, Liz, and thank your stars for a lucky break all round.'

'I don't know that I want to go home to South Africa,' said Liz sulkily. 'That's a condition too. Get me out of the way. In fact, I don't count to them, I'm just the incubator.'

'It's all you deserve to be,' he said. 'Need your people know about this?'

Liz laughed shortly.

'My father would have a stroke. He's Victorian. And mother wouldn't be too pleased.'

'You don't have to tell them. No necessity to hurt them, surely.'

'I suppose not,' she said. 'I could go on working for quite a while. When I can't I'll just disappear to Switzerland. Nobody need be any the wiser.'

'Then keep it that way,' advised Jim. 'We know – Ray and I – but nobody else does. Grow up, Liz.'

She made a gesture to lift the tray, but he took it from her with his quiet smile.

'I'll put this out in the kitchen for you.'

As he carried the tray from the living-room Liz looked at Rachel with raised eyebrows. Rachel said:

'Jim's mother deserted him and Eve when they were little. She went off with her lover. Jim knows how it feels to be ditched as a child.'

'Poor Jim ... I didn't know. I suppose he's right. I suppose it's important to get a fair start in life – like I had. You too, Ray. My family may be straitlaced but they cared about us kids. They still do. We were never in doubt about that.'

Rachel took Liz's small soft hands in hers.

'Do you like these people – Tom's parents? Do you trust them?'

Liz faced her squarely. 'Yes, I do. They're trying to do

their best for me – and they truly want Tom's child. He'll be well off with them.'

'Oh, Liz, you talk as if you knew him – this baby. He's a person to you already. He's a son.'

'All the more reason to do the best you can for him.' Jim had come back into the room. 'Your son is part of the future, and it's not going to be an easy future. Every child born into it needs the best chance he can get.'

Liz stared at him. 'Who cares about the future?'

'Ray does. I do. Nothing – however catastrophic – can finally destroy life. In some form it'll go on. We aren't the last of the human breed – even if it sometimes suits us to pretend we think we are. So if you've any sense of responsibility towards yourself and your . . . son . . . you'll do the best you can for him without any thought for yourself.'

Rachel had never seen Jim so stern. This was his other side. Austere relentless. When he looked like that with his head back and up and his eyes smouldering, she knew that he was not to be shifted. A cold trickle of fear ran down her spine. I could be afraid of him, she thought. He could hurt me as no one else in this world could do. He has the power. He has it in him to be unforgiving. His standards are high. Can I live up to them? He doesn't live for the day like most of us. He accepts the dangers of the day, he has no illusions about that, but he doesn't reckon night must fall and no more dawns break ever.

When she had said goodbye to Jim on the doorstep there was rain on the wind. She stood shivering, watching him take the area steps two at a time. She went back into the flat and crouched at the radiator, warming her hands. Liz emptied the ash-trays and set the table for breakfast.

'What does Jim mean to you?' she asked.

Rachel didn't raise her head.

'Everything,' she said. 'Without him there'd be nothing.'

'One lives again,' said Liz.

'You have reason to.'

'Are you going to marry Jim?'

'In September.'

'We'll have to give up the flat about then. Or will you and Jim take it on?'

Rachel rose. She looked at Liz, her eyes bright with affectionate amusement.

'Basically,' she said. 'You're quite the most practical girl I know.'

Mrs Olivier sat at the little bureau and prepared to tackle her South African mail.

She had enjoyed her few days in the country and now that she had decided upon a definite course of action with regard to her daughter's future, her mind was more at rest. All her nagging secret misgivings were firmly repressed. She was set on her course and there would be no looking back. The visit to Ravenswood had convinced her that she had been right to come to England. Jim Fleet was a highly suitable husband for Rachel and Mrs Olivier intended to impress his family that Rachel was equally suitable for him. Then she would step out of the picture and take the modern point of view. Sufficient unto the day is the joy and the evil thereof.

. The wind of the night before had died down, but Ginger Rafferty, striding out of the Trident, used his umbrella as a walking stick, and Mrs Meadows had appeared this morning in her Marksy Sparksy macintosh looking like a pleasant parcel done up in polythene. Mrs Olivier could hear her singing at her work in the kitchen. She had a sweet bird-like voice elaborated by unexpected trills.

'Darling Hans,' wrote Mrs Olivier to her son, 'Rachel's boy-friend's parents are leaving shortly for a trip to South

Africa. I want them to stay a weekend at Môreson. Get
Cousin Jacoba to come over from Springs to act as your
hostess. And invite Oom Christiaan over for dinner. Tell
Jacoba to put her best foot forward. She'll enjoy doing that
to impress Oom Chris, if for no better reason.'

She put down her pen and a cynical smile touched her lips.
Jacoba would be delighted to play hostess for Hans at Môreson. The widow from Springs had set her cap at Christiaan
Olivier for the past two years, ever since the death of his
wife. Well, good luck to her! It was high time Christiaan
married again. For the first time since leaving South Africa
Mrs Olivier experienced a sharp pang of nostalgia. The
Transvaal air would be nectar now. Such bright winter air,
so much of it and so few people breathing it.

Her thoughts were interrupted by a sonorous Gregorian
chant from the mews, the rumble of wheels and the leisurely
clop-clop of hooves. She got up and looked out of the
window.

'Mrs Meadows,' she called. 'Come and see!'

Mrs Meadows came from the kitchen and leaned over
Mrs Olivier's shoulder at the window.

'It's Alf, the rag-an'-bone man,' she chuckled. 'And that's
old Emily Ferrit hobbling along beside him. His street cry
brings her straight out of her lair like a mating call!'

'What's he saying?'

'Any old lumber.'

'You'd never guess it, In-yo-lumb-ber. But it's rather
melodious.'

'Oh, that reminds me. Mrs Kelly told me to give him
some stuff she has stored in the back of Mrs Rafferty's
garage. I'll go and ask Mrs Rafferty for the key.'

Mrs Meadows flew downstairs and out into the mews –
really, she was rather a bird-like creature – and Mrs Olivier
followed more sedately.

Jane Rafferty opened the garage door. 'It's that junk over in the corner,' she said. 'I better run the Jaggy out, then Alf can get at it. I think he finds the mews rather rewarding.'

'It's iron they like,' said Mrs Meadows, as Jane drove her white Jaguar into the fitful sunshine. 'Bits of old bikes and machinery and iron bedsteads – that sort of stuff. Not so much bones these days. It used to be bones for the farms. What do you call the stuff that makes things grow?'

'Fertilizer.'

'That's it – fertilizer. And rags, of course. They can always do with rags.'

The chant had receded as Alf's progress took him to the end of the mews where he turned and began to retrace his steps. He was a tall bent old man in a long shabby coat with an ancient bowler on his head. He walked beside his flat cart with a big chest on it and a grey box and a sack, all of which he hoped to fill in the course of the day. His gnarled hand held the reins as he led a fine mule. At his elbow trotted Miss Ferrit, a wispy, toothless travesty of a female. But the mule! Now there was a fine beast. Large and glossy, his chestnut coat carefully clipped into a pattern.

'Gives him a sort of plimsoll line,' remarked Jane Rafferty with admiration. 'And I should say he was down to it. A well-fed brute.'

'Cargo nicely stowed,' laughed Mrs Olivier.

The mule wore blinkers and this suggested a sensitive and high-spirited nature. Mrs Olivier patted his strong neck while Alf loaded the twisted iron of an ancient tricycle, a battered iron fender, and a stained mouldy mattress.

'You have a splendid animal here,' Mrs Olivier said to Alf. 'I'm quite a judge of mules.'

'Michael,' said the rag-and-bone man with tenderness, producing a carrot from a deep misshapen pocket and presenting it to the mule on the flat of his hand. 'Ah, he's foine! And knows it, don't yer?'

He was about to move on when Miss Ferrit, who had been staring intently at Mrs Olivier, suddenly gave tongue.

'Yer know something'! One o' these days it's 'uman bones Alf'll be gittin' from one of these grarges. I'm waitin'. That's why I joins Alf when 'e comes singin' into the Trident.'

'Put a sock in it, Auntie,' said Alf mildly. 'I'm no body snatcher.'

Miss Ferrit laughed a little wildly and pointed a skinny quivering finger at Mrs Olivier.

'You there – you're one of Ernie's people. I know you!'

Jane took Mrs Olivier's arm. 'Pay no attention. The old girl's round the bend. Quite harmless, but gets fancies from time to time.'

'Who's Ernie?' asked Mrs Olivier calmly.

'Me brother Ernie – everybody knows Ernie Ferrit – he collects people like you – '

Mrs Olivier smiled. It was an odd tight archaic smile, with the eyes hard in a glacial face.

'I'm honoured to be in Mr Ferrit's collection.'

Jane's laugh was embarrassed.

'Sounds like Madam Tussaud's.'

She felt the arm under her hand stiffen.

'Come on, Auntie,' said Alf. He touched his bowler and moved on. The old woman, still muttering, trotted at his side.

Mrs Olivier stood rigid as the little cart rumbled round the corner. The echo of the rag-and-bone man's cry came faintly back to them with the stolid clopping of Michael's hooves.

Mrs Meadows had gone back to her work, leaving the front door ajar. Jane Rafferty looked at Mrs Olivier

anxiously. The sun shone on her chalky face in a cruel light.
It looked coarse and heavy.

'That poor simple wretch has upset you,' Jane said. 'Come
in with me and I'll make you some tea.'

Mrs Olivier allowed herself to be led into the crepuscular
gloom of the beautiful room. She sank into a chair and
closed her eyes.

'You ought to put your car back in the garage,' she
muttered.

'That can wait.' Jane called to her daily: 'Mrs Jackson, tea
please. Two cups.'

'I don't understand,' said Mrs Olivier. 'What did she
mean by . . . Ernie's people?'

'She's daft. I've no idea what she meant by Ernie's people.
That's new on me. Her . . . derangement . . . is apparently
fairly well known. There's a name for it. I can't remember
what it is. The form it takes is that she imagines the most
fantastic things. She thinks she's been on journeys and done
all sorts of things that bear no relation whatever to fact.
She may have seen something on T.V. to set her off, or
pictures in a magazine, or some news item, but there it is.
She has these imaginary adventures and if she meets you
she'll tell you about them with such conviction you're
tempted to believe her.'

Mrs Olivier lit a cigarette. She was regaining command of
herself.

'Rather a trial for brother Ferrit, surely?'

'Frankly, he's marvellous to her. That's why we all make
allowances for him. If he's tiresome – and he can be awfully
nosey and interfering and rather mischief-making – we
remember that he has old Emily Ferrit for ever round his
neck.'

'I've never seen her before.'

'She very seldom goes out of the house these days. Ferrit

does all the shopping and I fancy he does most of the cooking and cleaning too. She's his millstone. I suppose most people have a millstone of some sort – but it's not always quite so visible and voluble. . .'

Mrs Olivier smiled at Jane without much mirth.

'The invisible millstones might be worse. They could be round your heart as well as your neck.'

'Yes,' said Jane Rafferty slowly. 'None of us really knows much about each other, do we?'

7

TRANSVAAL WINTER

THE FLEETS SAILED FOR SOUTH AFRICA ARMED WITH invitations and letters of introduction. Laura was as excited as a schoolgirl and her happy anticipation was infectious. Sir Jasper looked forward most of all to the few days scheduled for them in Johannesburg where they were to stay with Captain T. S. Carstairs and his wife. Tommy Carstairs was Public Relations officer to one of the powerful mining groups. It was part of his business to help project a favourable image of South Africa abroad.

'He's always been prepared to attempt the impossible,' chuckled Sir Jasper to Laura, who had never met this hearty and persuasive man of the sea. 'That's how I first came to know Tommy Carstairs. In the war. He was a youngster in command of Coastal Motor Boats. He accomplished some tricky missions for us.'

'What took him to South Africa?'

'The course of duty. He was appointed to the Cape Station, fell in love with the country, and with a Johannesburg girl, and the rest followed as night the day.'

The mail-boat docked in Cape Town on a sunny winter morning. The Cape in June can be wet, wild and bitterly cold, or it may dream of vanished summer in an autumnal afterglow of haunting beauty. Skeletons of oaks are X-rayed on the white gables of the past; leafless vineyards rest after the vintage; new wine ferments noisily in the great teak casks that are housed in cellars as elaborate and dignified as the homesteads they adjoin. Tourists, trippers and holiday crowds depart, diplomats and members of the Government return to official residences in Pretoria, and the inhabitants of the Cape sit back in their comfortable homes and sigh with pleasurable relief. The Cape is theirs once more. The dark folk are less complacent. Winter woollies cost money, bare feet get cold, *pondokkies* are flooded when the storms come and God's sunshine will, for a spell, cease to warm their bones and light their homes.

The Cape smiled upon the Fleets and they were sorry when the time came for them to catch the Blue Train to Johannesburg. This luxury express conveyed them through the majesty of snow-capped mountains on to the pastel plateau of the Karoo, where Laura, ever responsive to nature, found her whole being saturated with the pervasive melancholy engendered by that vast scene. Distant blue ranges and *koppies* rose from shimmering lakes of mirage, and at sunset the wide empty land was drowned in waves of splendid colour, crude yet tender and so unforgettably luminous that they invaded the very soul of the beholder. At 6,000 feet above sea level the highveld spread its pale kaross of maize and hay, and man-made mountains and pyramids proclaimed the teeming underground life of the Witwatersrand, where the black ants worked in the bowels of the gold-bearing earth.

Captain and Mrs Carstairs lived in a modern mansion on the outskirts of the city. Their home was shaded by fine trees, and boasted an excellent hard tennis court and a lido-blue swimming pool. Their nineteen-year-old daughter, Jennifer, lived at home, and the Carstairs' garage housed three cars and a station-wagon to three people.

'Can it go on like this?' Sir Jasper waved a well-manicured hand at the evidence of luxury on all sides of him.

They were sitting in the loggia watching the lavender African dusk seep into the tawny carpet of the veld.

'Yes, in a modified form,' said Tommy Carstairs.

His wife's laugh was brittle and unamused.

'Tony's a wishful thinker. This way of life is on its way out fast – but fast. All that's left is the flick of its tail this side of the door!'

'Pamela is a pessimist,' said her husband.

'A realist,' she retorted. 'In any case, one man's pessimism is often another man's optimism. Especially in South Africa.'

Looksmart, the black butler in his white suit and red sash, set a tray of drinks on a marble table and returned silently to that exclusive zone of dark intrigue known as the 'boy's quarters'.

Tommy Carstairs indicated the departing figure with a jerk of his head.

'People forget that the alternative to us is them. Blacks don't like working for other blacks and even *uhuru* can't turn everybody into a bossman overnight. A good many of them realise that.'

'What's the answer?'

'A compromise. It'll come.'

'It'll come all right – one way or the other,' said Pamela grimly. 'The only real answer is live for the day.'

Laura sighed. 'It's the same everywhere. In Europe too we live for the day. Here it's the blacks, there it's the bomb. Is it really the twilight of the gods?'

'Of some gods, yes,' said Carstairs.

Sir Jasper stroked his neat imperial beard with a sensuous finger and thumb. His half-concealed mouth had a satirical twist.

'You have a potent god right here on the spot – universally worshipped.'

'Gold? Yes. And the high priests still wear white skins.'

Looksmart had turned on a light in the dining-room. It shone through the window on to the loggia table where Tommy Carstairs was shaking a cocktail.

'It would be interesting to have a telescope into the future – the distant future – when the Reef is all worked out and the great god, Gold, with it.'

Laura Fleet said: 'Then the ancient pagan gods will come into their own once more. There'll still be the land, the sun and the moon, seeds and crops, beasts and fertility.'

There speaks my cow-girl, thought Sir Jasper, and found a soothing magic in her words.

'Laura's first love is the land,' he said. 'She's a better farmer than I am.'

Tommy Carstairs put a cocktail beside her. 'You'll enjoy your weekend at Môreson. It's a fine farm, about ten thousand morgen and highly cultivated. Wheat, mealies, beans, potatoes, cattle. All very modern and productive. When Gerhard died young Hans inherited. He's rather a special friend of our Jenny.'

'Of course Christiaan Olivier really runs it for him at present, but Hans'll soon take the reins for himself. The Oliviers are born farmers.'

Pamela pronounced the name in the South African way 'Oollyfear'. 'Jenny's going to drive you out there on Friday afternoon and she'll bring you back on Monday. That'll give you a day's break before you set off for the Game Reserve.'

'It's sweet of Jenny to give us her time,' said Laura.

There was a sharp edge on that splintered laugh of Pamela's. 'The young do as they like these days. Your programme is right up Jenny's street. She loves a weekend at Môreson. In her own way she'll find it just as interesting as you will.'

The crow's feet crinkled round Sir Jasper's mocking

eyes. 'The Oliviers would seem to be a very interesting family.'

Jenny Carstairs had only recently acquired her driving licence but she had driven since her fifteenth birthday, and, like most of her generation, the 'feel of a car' came naturally to her. She chattered away as she drove the Fleets out to Môreson about fifty miles from Johannesburg. Mainly about Rachel.

'We were at school together and Ray used to come to our place on Sundays, and other times too. She was older than me – Hans is my age – but she was always marvellous to me.'

'You must miss her,' said Laura from the back seat.

'Yes, I do. But we all felt that she must get away. Her mother suffocates her.'

'That's quite a statement,' Sir Jasper glanced at the girl at the wheel. Jenny's nervous definite features might sharpen into the witch-like mould of her mother's face as she grew older unless she eased up and stopped trying to live every hour of the day and night.

'We can't be caged by our parents,' Jenny said. 'It's intolerable! Mrs Olivier tried to cage Ray – treated her as if she wasn't trustworthy and resented her boy-friends. Ray wasn't like a lot of girls – ready for anything – her mother should have known that and trusted her.'

'Perhaps she didn't trust the boy-friends,' suggested Sir Jasper.

Jenny snorted. 'Boys take their cues from girls.'

'I wonder Mrs Olivier allowed her daughter to escape from the cage and fly all the way to England,' Laura put in.

Jenny chuckled. 'I can tell you it sparked off the most imperial row! Everybody was in it and for once Mrs Olivier found herself with her back to the wall. Rachel's father and

Hans took her side and so did Oom Christiaan and even old Cousin Jacoba. Everybody had their say. I think the fact that Liz Joubert was in London and wanted Ray to join her clinched it. People felt that if Ray shared digs with Liz she'd be all right. Liz – they reckoned – was a thoroughly nice girl.'

'Do you?'

'She's not as dull as all that!'

Sir Jasper smiled. 'So, in the end, young Rachel set sail in a glow of approval?'

Jenny stole a glance at Sir Jasper. The father of Ray's boy-friend was a sly old fox, but he certainly had something. You couldn't dream up Gerald Bourne, Secret Agent, without being pretty terrific yourself.

'Except for her mother,' she said. 'Her mother didn't approve. She sulked. Do you know, she let Ray go off without one single introduction. We wrote to our friends in England to ask them to be kind to Ray while Mrs Olivier – who is English, mark you – didn't even give the poor girl a letter to so much as a maiden aunt!'

Jenny broke off every now and again to point out some landmark – a Bantu village with elaborate geometrical designs decorating the square huts; a herd of buck grazing with the cattle; an occasional dorp with its little tin-roofed single-storeyed houses, its trees, windmills and stream, dry at this season; a wireless or a satellite tracking station.

'It's wonderful tank country,' remarked Sir Jasper, gazing out over the flat expanse of the veld. Jenny laughed impudently.

'Gerald Bourne wouldn't have said that. He'd have thought it magnificent landing ground for a whole fleet of space-ships.'

'You must collaborate with Jasper,' said Laura. 'He's in one of his blocks.'

Jenny laughed. 'I'm full of ideas. Look, this is where we turn off. That's Môreson land up there on the ridge.'

They followed a parched watercourse for a few miles. It was fringed with tall reeds and bulrushes alive with little scarlet finches. At a wire fence and gate they rumbled over the first of the Môreson cattle grids.

'Now we're on Hans's land,' said Jenny. 'Oom Christiaan Olivier's borders with it.'

Men, women and children were lifting potatoes in the fields, the men in a travesty of European clothing, the women in blankets with piccaninnies lolling in slings against their backs or on their hips. In the mealie-lands the combine harvesters were at work, mechanically reaping and stacking the ripe grain. Up on the ridge a team of sixteen oxen ploughed the furrows at the pace of a bygone age.

Laura took in the wide golden scene with delight. The wind-ruffled wheat changed colour with every breath under a twittering cloud of plaguey little birds out to rob the ripening ears in spite of scarecrows, glittering tin pennants and humming wires struck by near-naked children. Down in the hollow a shining dam mirrored softly moving clouds tinged with evening pink and gold, the long stringy tresses of weeping willows bare of leaf but clothed with the exquisite nests of weaver-birds, the bovine faces of cattle and the twitching ears of a herd of blesbok. Wild duck and a wedge of geese circled over the water.

'There's the house,' said Jenny. 'Up on the rise.'

She turned the car into a long avenue of blue-gums culminating in a cypress grove, the slender dark spires accentuating the lonely peace of the only human habitation within sight.

Môreson homestead was a large single-storeyed stone house, sturdily built, roofed with red corrugated iron and surrounded on three sides by a wide stoep.

As Jenny drew up a tall deeply tanned young man in corduroys and a bush-shirt ran down the steps to meet them, followed by a massive grey-haired matron.

Hans Olivier bore a striking physical resemblance to his mother. He had her gipsy colouring, her well-proportioned limbs and animal grace. His eyes, as he greeted Jenny, warmed with pleasure. With the Fleets he was more formal.

'I'm so glad to welcome you, Lady Fleet and General Fleet. This is Mrs Wessels, our Cousin Jacoba. She mothers me when Ma's away.'

Cousin Jacoba beamed with kindliness and hospitality. She signalled the waiting house-boy to take in the guests' bags, while Hans turned to Jenny.

'I'll put the car away for you.'

'I'll come with you,' she said.

Cousin Jacoba led Sir Jasper and Laura up the red-tiled steps on to the wide stoep which was furnished with gaily-cushioned garden seats.

'We spend a lot of our time on this stoep,' she said. 'The veld is only monotonous to those who don't love it. To us it is ever changing, our favourite scene.'

'Our home has a garden-room too,' said Laura.

'Ann wrote and told me about it. She described your beautiful walled garden and the peacocks. Ravenswood sounds lovely. Would you like to come to your rooms now, or would you care for some refreshment first?'

'I think we'd like to wash and tidy up,' said Laura.

The house was built round a large living-room and dining-room connected by sliding doors. It had a homely atmosphere, Laura thought, and the heavy antique Dutch furniture lent it substantial dignity. Everything looked polished and cared for. Cousin Jacoba was obviously an excellent housewife. She fitted into her surroundings naturally. Laura tried to see Ann Olivier in this setting and found it curiously difficult. On horseback, galloping over the veld, yes. Yet somehow, some way, she felt that when Ann Olivier had come here she must have been taken right out of her context to begin life anew.

'We've put Jenny in Rachel's room, and we thought you'd be most comfortable here.'

Cousin Jacoba led them into a large bright double bed-room.

'Ann and Gerhard had this suite; it gives on to a sleeping-porch. The bed is made up there if either of you like to use it. Ann often slept out in the sleeping-porch. She was subject to nightmares and sometimes she couldn't bear being in a room – walled in, as she put it.'

'It's a beautiful suite,' said Laura. 'And Jasper may well want to sleep on the porch.'

'There's a dressing-room and your own bathroom too,' said Cousin Jacoba. 'Don't hurry if you want a rest, Lady Fleet. Mr Christiaan Olivier – Gerhard's brother – is coming over to dinner. He'll be here about seven o'clock.'

When Cousin Jacoba had left them Laura went on to the partially enclosed porch. The keen evening air poured in and she inhaled its grassy purity.

'Isn't it lovely – all this?' she called to her husband. 'Even a swimming pool down there under the trees. Darkest Africa doesn't do itself badly!'

He came and stood beside her.

'Not darkest Africa. That may come. But not yet.'

He looked at the divan bed covered with a fine kaross of jackal pelts.

'A pleasant place to sleep, I'd say. I'll try it tonight.' He paused thoughtfully. 'But tell me this. Why should our friend, Ann Olivier, suffer from claustrophobic night-mares?'

Laura laughed softly. 'Could it be a bad conscience?

That's what they say, isn't it? You'll never get a far-fetched or original answer out of me. You should know that by now.'

He patted his wife's shoulder affectionately.

'The clichés, the platitudes, the old wives' tales. I respect them all, my dear – along with the eternal verities.'

8

DINNER AT MÔRESON

CHRISTIAAN OLIVIER DROVE OVER TO MÔRESON IN his hard-used Chevrolet. A small buck was caught in the beam of his headlights and he stopped to let the animal escape. The night air was icy and the wheat under a young moon was, in Christiaan's eyes, a miracle of sheer living beauty. Tomorrow he'd have the harvester in these lands.

A letter was folded in his pocket. He knew most of it by heart.

'How right you were to urge me to come back here! after many heart-searchings I am at last of your opinion about Rachel. She must *not* be told – ever. The young man is right for her. I could wish that his people were less traditional in their attitude to life and property. I find it rather unrealistic in the England of today. The heritage of an estate means as much to them as it does to our old South African families. However, I've become more fatalistic every day. Love has brought out new qualities in my daughter. Or perhaps it is just that she has matured since being on her own and is less apt to fly into those unreasonable rages that used to upset me.

I have written to Hans that I want him to get Jacoba to act as hostess to the Fleets. She'll be willing – if only to be near you! Why don't you marry her? A wife is as necessary to a farmer as a windmill, and Jacoba is full of domestic virtues. Or are you looking for a young woman who will give you a second family?'

A broad grin spread over his weathered features. He was in his mid-forties, a sturdy bull-necked man, the father of two sons at University at the Cape. His 'young bloods', he called them, and they were enough family for any one man, he reckoned. But women were inveterate match-makers. Even Annetjie. It wasn't enough for her to engineer a marriage for her daughter. She must also do as much for himself and Jacoba. A left and a right. Where Jacoba was concerned, Christiaan had developed a high degree of sales resistance. The old girl was half a hundred, if she was a day, though he was compelled to admit she'd worn well.

But that evening he had to admire the way in which Jacoba entertained Ann's guests. She combined informality and humorous charm with gentle dignity. He liked seeing her at the head of Ann's table. She presides, he thought, that's the only word for it. But when the stuffed Môreson goose was set before her in all its fragrant golden brown perfection she deferred to him.

'You are the carver, Christiaan.'

They drank Rosé Constantia wine of the Cape with their meal, and, as his mood mellowed, Christiaan found himself drawn towards this English General and his wife – a fine big woman who showed a proper appreciation of the feast Jacoba had prepared for them. In fact, when he bowed his close-cropped blond head and said a heart-felt grace 'For what we have received we are truly thankful,' he felt that he was speaking for all at the table and telling the Almighty no less than the gratifying truth. He had found Laura Fleet a pleasant dinner companion, surprisingly knowledgeable about the problems of farmers the world over. As they left the table he said as much to the General, who smiled. 'During the war my wife was a land-girl. She really is a very experienced farmer – and loves it.'

'That's more than can be said for my sister-in-law. Ann

loves her horses and dogs, and she made a good thing of being a farmer's wife, but it wasn't really natural to her.'

'What can you expect of a Londoner, born and bred?'

'I don't know much about Londoners, but I know Ann.
She'll always surprise you. Now she's taken the plunge and
gone back to England I'm inclined to wonder if we'll see
her here again.'

They were standing with their backs to a crackling coal
fire. Jenny and Hans offered them coffee and cream while
Jacoba and Laura sat chatting comfortably on the sofa.

'Mightn't that depend on Rachel?' asked Sir Jasper. 'If
the daughter makes her home in England the mother may be
tempted to do the same.'

'Have you reason to believe Rachel will make her home in
England?' parried Christiaan. There was a deliberate thrust
to the quick question and for a moment it caught Sir Jasper
off guard. Suddenly he sensed that the spare open-faced man
who stood on this hearth-rug as if he was the master of his
nephew's house, was a force to be reckoned with. He was
Ann Olivier's brother-in-law and her ally. Rachel's future
was a matter of considerable concern to her uncle.

'She seems happy in England,' he said cautiously. 'But she
probably misses her family . . . and Môreson.'

Hans had joined them. 'If you're talking of Ray, she's like
my mother. She thinks Môreson is fine, but it's not really
in her blood. She'll only miss it from time to time. And the
same goes for us. She's dreadfully homesick sometimes –
especially if she thinks about it – but she can get along without us.'

He spoke in the quick way of many young South Africans
– impulsively, in rushes.

'She's always liked getting away from the farm. Oh, she
liked home too – but the getting away was more important
to her.' There was resentment in his voice. Hurt, too.

Christiaan put a huge hand on the young man's shoulder.

'Lucky you were born the boy, Hans.' He turned to their guests. 'Hans takes after his Pa. Môreson and its people are the centre of his life. He knows both – the farm and the Native – with his head and his heart.'

Jenny had turned on the radio and tuned in to a dance programme. The music – soft but insistent – lured Hans.

'She's going to teach me the lastest dance steps,' he grinned. 'Mind if we try them out on the stoep?'

'Of course not.'

The two older couples watched the young people go out through the open 'stable door'. They heard them laughing together as they rolled back a rug. But Hans did not take his partner in his arms.

'Man, do you call that dancing?' Christiaan asked the world at large. 'It's a Kaffir war dance! Nothing but stamping and squirming, and the man does one thing and the girl does another, and nobody gets to grips.'

Laura and Cousin Jacoba Wessels were absorbed and set apart in the inpregnable circle of two women engrossed in discussing a third. 'You see, my dear, Ann never really understood the girl. But at twenty-one Rachel will come into her money – only the income, mark you – but still it'll be enough to give her total independence.' Jacoba leaned towards Laura, who was most sympathetic. 'Lady Fleet, *my* daughter tells me everything. "Mommy," she says. "There's nothing I can't say to you." It was never like that with Ann and Rachel.'

'Confiding is mutual,' said Laura, who had been exploiting this truism for the past hour. 'Perhaps you gave your daughter your confidence in return for hers.'

Cousin Jacoba nodded gravely. 'I could always talk to Joanna, even as a little child. But Ann was never anything but close as a clam about her life before she met Gerhard.

Even now, I doubt if Rachel knows much about her mother's girlhood – the people in it. We all have people in our past, my dear. Relatives, childhood friends, and so forth. But not Ann.'

Suddenly conscious of greater density in her vicinity and of vibrations to which she responded, Cousin Jacoba looked up to see Christiaan's powerful bulk looming over the sofa.

'Scandal,' he chuckled. 'Don't deny it! When a woman talks scandal she has a special face – like a jackal tearing at a kill. Even you, my dear Jacoba, have such a face from time to time.' He was beaming at her as if even her jackal-face could charm him. But under the teasing lay the reproof.

The wine, the truth behind the words and the heat of the room caused a prickly flush to mantle Jacoba's throat and face. She had forgotten momentarily that these Fleets had a son who was Rachel's particular friend. Perhaps more.

'I must bid you goodnight,' said Christiaan in his court-liest manner. He bent over Laura's hand. 'You understand how it is in the reaping season. So I know you will excuse me. Tomorrow Hans will bring you over to my place, and then you will have to make allowances. It is only little sister to Môreson.'

The next few days went too fast for Laura. After Môreson they visited the Kruger National Park where the wild beasts roamed free in their well-watered woodlands while the humans were restricted to the safety of cars and camps. There, one evening, they watched a jackal take his turn at the lioness's kill, and Laura smiled to recall Oom Christiaan's remark to that amiable gossip, his Cousin Jacoba.

That night, alone with her husband in their *rondavel* under the stars, with the human sounds of the camp still about them, the scent of camp-fires and the great secret silence of nature in the thornveld beyond, she spoke of the subject uppermost in their minds.

'Well, Jasper, what do you make of it all?'

He did not pretend to misunderstand her. It was their habit to take short cuts with each other.

'I've come to the conclusion that Rachel has had a good environment and a sound upbringing.'

'I'm glad. I liked the Môreson set-up. Rachel's brother, Hans, is a truly fine lad and I've heard only good of her father. All the same, I'm still in doubt – '

'About Mrs Olivier?'

'Yes. It doesn't take Professor Higgins to tell us that she comes out of a very reasonable drawer – but still – '

'There are gaps.' He drew on his little pipe before continuing. 'There are only two things about Ann Olivier I'm a hundred per cent sure of – '

'What are those?'

'That she loves her daughter,' he said. 'And that she is a woman of singular determination.'

He paused. The camp had grown quiet. It slept early and woke at dawn. Beyond the thorn-fence they heard a leopard cough, and, far away, the strange yodelling call of a hunting lion, followed by a chorus of echoes. The ensuing silence was the more complete for the brief rift.

Sir Jasper said: 'We've seen for ourselves today how the lioness stalks and kills to feed her mate and her family. It is she who provides for her young and protects them. They are her responsibility. I think, Laura, my dear, that Ann Olivier is, in her own way, quite a lioness. Among lesser beasts she has a sort of majesty.'

The darkness of the night was festive here and there with the dance of fire-flies, or a sudden spray of sparks as a camp-boy raked a wood-fire before damping it down. There was starlight on the river. Laura saw the glow of her husband's pipe. She knew how he'd be looking now. Pleased with himself because he'd arrived at some definite and, in his own opinion, sensible conclusion.

'You respect her, don't you?'

'Yes, of course. One must respect a lioness.'

'Don't bluff yourself! Your respect has nothing to do with the animal kingdom. It's strictly human and rather professional. You've measured the worth of Rachel's mother by your own curious cruel yardstick . . .' Even when she paused he did not interrupt her. Strange widsom flowed through his cow-girl when the world about her was tranquil, nature's Eden, far from the turmoil of city streets.

'Ever since you've been in South Africa,' she went on, 'you've been trying to find out something concrete about the pre-Transvaal past of this woman who intrigues you. And all you've discovered – as I have too – is that others would like to learn more about her – from us! She's a riddle here, too.'

For a while she sat staring down at her blunt capable hands, lying quiescent and pale against the dark drill of her slacks.

'Well?' he said gently, 'you were going to suggest . . . the reason for my respect.'

'You have to hand it to her, Jasper. With all your skill and subtlety, with all your experience, you're no wiser about Ann Olivier than you were a month ago. Even after meeting her son and staying in her South African home her secrets are intact. From you . . . and from the people she has lived with all her married life."

'And so, Laura?'

'And so you pin a medal over her heart, my dear. Because under prolonged and persistent – if intermittent – interrogation she has held her tongue. *That* you respect. Even affection couldn't loosen it. She remains an enigma.'

He got up and came to her side. He touched her rich

brown hair, streaked with grey, springy glossy hair like a young girl's. With Laura he could never be devious. The door to the tortuous labyrinthine tunnels of his mind was locked by her strange perceptive innocence and she led him now, as always, into meadows bright with buttercups. He quoted the poet of a war she had been too young to know.

'There's wisdom in women, of more than they have known; and thoughts go blowing through them, are wiser than their own . . . '

Laura put up her large gentle hand and touched his beard. It was surprisingly soft. She was often astonished at its softness.

'I could fall for you,' she said.

And Mrs Olivier was forgotten.

9

ENGAGEMENT

MRS OLIVIER LOOKED INTO HER DAUGHTER'S GOLD-flecked water-green eyes and saw there a radiance that moved her heart.

'So it's all right?'

Rachel nodded. 'Jim met them at London airport yesterday. He rang me from Ravenswood this morning. We can announce the engagement whenever we like, and the General approves. I'm so happy . . .'

The shining eyes brimmed. Ann Olivier put out her arms. Rachel fell on her knees beside her mother's chair and buried her face against the deep soft breast. She was a child once more with strong tender hands stroking her hair. Safe and loved.

Let her be happy! pleaded Rachel's mother, as the Sunday morning chimes floated through the open windows of the mews cottage. Let her be safe – and those who come after her.

'Are you glad for me?' asked Rachel, at last.

'Yes. I'm glad you've chosen Jim and that he loves you.'

Rachel sprang up.

'With a September wedding we haven't any time to lose. It's the middle of July already!'

'What with the sales and the silly season, you're right. We must get cracking at once. Have you made any plans? Where will you live?'

'Right here, at first,' said Rachel with delight. 'Jim wrote to tell Eve some time ago and she says we're to have this cottage when you go – for at least six months! Free! After that she can't promise anything. She might sell it, or they may come back to London for a bit. She doesn't know.'

'In any case, it's a wonderful offer,' said Mrs Olivier warmly. 'It means you won't need to worry about furniture, linen, glass and all the rest of it for the present. You can see what the wedding presents bring forth and go from there quite quietly later on. We can concentrate on your trousseau. There'll be the invitations – '

'We don't want a fashionable wedding and a lot of fuss.'

'Darling, your prospective father-in-law is a celebrity.'

'It's not *his* wedding.'

But neither Rachel nor Mrs Olivier gauged the full extent of the interest aroused by the engagement. The latest and most popular of all the Gerald Bourne films was filling a West End cinema to capacity at every showing, and the new Gerald Bourne novel headed the lists of autumn publications. The social columnists, avid for gossip to break up the end of the summer dearth, pounced upon the news. One gossip column was headed 'SPY AUTHOR'S SON TO WED SOUTH AFRICAN HEIRESS'.

Rachel's eyes blazed as she brought the paper to the cottage in the Trident.

'Heiress indeed! And we'll be hard put to it to afford a pram! I could murder this wretched Onlooker, whoever he may be.' But Onlooker remained unscathed and unrepentant. When the news-hounds telephoned the cottage Mrs Olivier was high-handed with them.

'They give me no peace,' she complained to Jane Rafferty afterwards. 'It's infuriating. I refuse to be drawn.'

'You can't really blame them,' Jane said, reasonably. 'It's their business. And Eve was rather co-operative when they flocked round her for the same reason.'

Onlooker, thick-skinned and cynical, sent his photographer to take pictures of the cottage that had spelt Romance for both brother and sister. Mrs Meadows was disappointed when Mrs Olivier refused to pose. Mrs Meadows liked seeing people she knew in the papers. Rachel, antagonised by the heiress headline, also objected to being featured.

In the Trident the engagement caused a pleasant stir. The Raffertys rejoiced, and so did the young Dixons. Mary Dixon patronised Rachel happily. She had been married a year – no longer a bride, but a wife of experience. Mr Ferrit, of course, was interested. Nothing of importance could happen in the Trident without his active participation. He came round one morning especially to congratulate Mrs Olivier. He was wearing a new pepper-and-salt suit of sporting cut – the sales, thought Mrs Olivier – and a new wide-peaked cap. The scarlet door was ajar and he doffed his cap as he came up Jacob's ladder. Mrs Olivier observed that his thinning grey hair had been trimmed. This was evidently a formal call.

'I was just going out,' she said. 'But do come in for a few minutes.'

He hesitated on the landing. 'I wanted to offer my felicitations,' he said, very formally.

Her broad smile flashed. 'Thank you, Mr Ferrit. You'll take a glass of sherry with me? Or a beer.'

'I don't mind if I do, ma'am. Shall we say beer?' He stood in the sitting-room, bow legs apart, while she fetched ale off the ice and two glass tankards.

The day was oppressive and thundery. The flowers in the window-boxes had wilted, even the Dixons' lovely show of pansies and petunias opposite. The handsome vine had shed its leaves and the dwarf orange trees were sere and dispirited.

Lucifer rose lazily from the window-sill and jumped down to rub himself against Mr Ferrit's leg.

'He likes you,' said Mrs Olivier.

'We're old chums.'

Mr Ferrit raised his foaming tankard.

'To Mr Jim and Miss Rachel.'

They drank the toast. Mrs Olivier lit a cigarette and sat down. She indicated a chair and the open cigarette box. 'Help yourself.'

He sat down and took one of his little cheroots from his pocket.

'Do you mind if I smoke this?'

'Of course not.'

'This cottage,' he said, looking round him with a glint of pleasure in his beady eyes. 'It's got something.'

'It has,' she agreed. 'It has charm and distinction.'

'It 'as more'n that, ma'am. It breeds romance, if you ask me. Whoever comes in 'ere single goes out wed.'

He enumerated a list of previous tenants and gave a succinct history of their somewhat exotic love-lives, culminating in Eve Fleet's marriage to an American, and now her brother's engagement to a South African.

'And them young ones opposite,' he said. 'They did most of their courtin' at Mrs Rafferty's place next door. Of course it can't always work out so well. There was the young ladies Lucifer lived with . . . well . . . least said soonest mended there! That 'ouse – the one at the end – 'as a bad history. I won't go into that now. This is a pleasant occasion, Mrs Olivier.'

'You whet my curiosity,' she said.

He shook his head.

'Not today. I could tell you a thing or two about the Trident. But not all in one go.'

'Save it for another session, shall we?'

She rose with a touch of hauteur.

'You must excuse me, Mr Ferrit. I have an appointment with my dressmaker.'

'Of course, Mrs Olivier. I shouldn't 'ave kept you. These is busy days for you and Miss Rachel.'

He took the tankards into the kitchen and washed them under the tap, leaving them upside down on the draining board.

On the landing he picked up his cap and stood twisting it in his narrow predatory fingers.

'There was somethin' else, Mrs Olivier – somethin' I ought to mention.'

'Oh, yes?'

Her expression became attentive. She had been wondering where this call was really leading. But when he spoke she was taken aback.

'It's my sister, ma'am. Alf – the rag-an'-bone man – was telling me she upset you the last time 'e was 'ere in the Trident. I only 'eard yesterday when 'e came again and I 'appened to be around.'

'That was some time ago. I'd put it out of my head.' But she was frowning and he saw with interest that she had indeed been upset. 'Your sister said a strange thing, Mr Ferrit. She pointed at me . . . in quite a threatening manner . . . and said "I know you – you're one of Ernie's people." Now what would she mean by that?'

He shifted his weight uneasily from one skinny leg to the other and tapped his forehead significantly.

'She 'as funny fancies, Mrs Olivier. You mustn't pay attention to what simple old Emily says. Folk in the Trident understands Emmy Ferrit.'

His eyes flickered over her face as he talked and she thought suddenly of a snake she had once seen, its forked tongue quivering over a hypnotised mouse, making the flat head more than ever sinister.

'I 'ope you'll accept my apologies for what 'appened,' Mr Ferrit was saying.

She shrugged her shoulders impatiently.

'Forget it, and I'll do the same.'

'Thank you, ma'am.'

He sounded greatly relieved, and, as he ran down the steep stairs, nimble as a sailor skimming down a ship's hatch, he was already whistling softly through the corner of his narrow trap-like mouth. At the foot of Jacob's ladder he swung round and looked up at her.

'Shall I close the door?'

'No, leave it. I'm going out in a minute.'

She saw his silhouette against the hot dazzle of noonday; then he was gone.

Forget it, she'd said, and I'll do the same. But somehow the incident in the mews that windy day a month ago had haunted her ever since. The old witch-like hag wagging a finger at her; the flat cart; the big mule and the bent old rag-and-bone man in his long shabby coat and bowler hat. She could see Mrs Meadows and Jane Rafferty now, in the background – surprised and enthralled – the sun glinting on Jane's white Jaguar and on the green dustbin outside her house. She could hear again those last extraordinary words shrilled by Miss Ferrit in a high hysterical cackle – the climax of a crazy incantation. 'I know you! Ernie collects people like you!' There had been other things too at which she had hinted. Terrible things – poor dotty creature.

Mrs Olivier shuddered as she went into the kitchen and put down a saucer of fish for Lucifer. He was waiting for the gesture. While her hand was still on the saucer he was rubbing against it, purring and drooling. The smooth warmth of his coat and the tickle of his whiskers pleased her, but she pretended to scold.

'Don't nudge like that! You'll knock the saucer out of my hand.'

As she put it down she stroked him two or three times, her long fingers straddling his back which arched to her touch.

'You're lucky,' she said. 'Don't dare forget it! You're my lucky black cat – my mascot against all evil.'

Mrs Olivier slammed the scarlet front door behind her and stepped outside. The mews was deserted and drowsy in the enervating midday heat. Heat was curious in London, she thought. The air became vitiated, as if the millions of people breathing it had sucked the oxygen out of it. She paused to look up at the tired window-boxes. Lucifer had taken up his position in one of them. It was shaded by the overhanging brick brow of the window. He was washing. She smiled to herself. What ritualistic creatures cats were! Mannered and highly civilized, arrogant or servile as suited their purpose. His breath now would smell of fish and fur. She could almost feel the rasp of his tongue on her skin. She was very sensitive today. Simple things were over-significant.

The man with the camera stepped out of the angle of the garage opposite. He caught Mrs Olivier perfectly as she turned, hatless and relaxed, to face the full sunlight.

'No!'

She flung up an arm to cover her face, and heard the shutter click again. She saw red.

'Who tipped you off? *Who*?'

'You live here, don't you?'

'Get out!' she cried. 'Get away from me!'

Onlooker's news photographer was a seedy intrepid individual who had hunted the London jungle for many years in search of his prey. 'Wait till you see the whites of their teeth,' was his maxim. Smile or snarl, you picked 'em off. At least you got a reaction – something livelier than the wooden pose of the willing victim. There was, however, a certain spice of danger in getting uninvited, unguarded pictures of an unwilling quarry. As Mrs Olivier came at him the photographer took a risk to get his third shot. He knew a camera-smasher when he saw one, and this dark angry woman with her teeth bared was dangerous. He wasted no further time. Before she could reach him he had doubled out of the Trident with Flicky, the dachshund, barking lustily at his heels. Flicky had no objection to intruders, but fugitives he pursued as a matter of principle.

Mrs Olivier's bag had fallen on to the cobbles. She did not attempt to pick it up. She stood trembling violently, her face buried in her hands.

A bicycle bell tringed merrily as Jane Rafferty's small nephew banked round the corner with even more than his usual dash and élan. He no longer saw himself as a Wild West cowboy riding his trusty steed over the waving prairies of the Trident. That was childish stuff. He was a human rocket now, screaming through space at a million miles a minute. At the Raffertys' door he baled out, hungry after his fantastic flight. Then he saw Mrs Olivier leaning against the wall, shaking like an old car when the engine is too strong for the chassis. Colin touched her raised arm.

'I say, Mrs Olivier, are you all right?'

She took down her hands and the boy saw that she was ugly and old and wounded. Gradually her eyes focused his anxious face and the way his hair jumped up on the crown of his round fair head. His bike lay on its side outside Jane's garage. Of course, he was here for a long weekend – Friday to Monday. He had picked up her bag and he held it awkwardly, too chivalrous to give it to her till she was in some condition to receive it.

By a mighty effort of will Ann Olivier forced herself to smile. It was a dreadful grimace.

'I'm quite all right now, Colin. Thank you.'

'What happened?' he asked, wide-eyed. 'Did you hurt yourself?'

'A man shot at me,' she said, the smile still pinned on and twisting.

'Shot! Lucky he missed! Which way did he go? Was he on foot? Should I chase him on my bike?'

'He meant no harm,' she said slowly. 'He shot with a camera. I'm peculiar about cameras.'

Colin relaxed. 'There are tribes who think a camera is the evil eye. If you put it on them – to take a photo, I mean – they kill you. My Uncle Ginger told me that.'

'I know how they feel.'

She pulled herself together. She took her bag from the little boy and he saw that her face was no longer ugly, but sad under the smile with which she tried to thank him.

He watched her walk away, her heels clicking firmly on the cobbles, her back straight, and her head, with its coil of black hair, very high. As she turned the corner he skipped into the house to tell his aunt of his adventures.

Jane Rafferty listened entranced, and, like any born raconteur with a good audience, Colin added his own embellishments and made the most of his tale.

'So Mrs Olivier said the man's camera probably had an evil eye in it. That's why she was so scared.'

'If it was Onlooker's camera,' said his aunt, 'Mrs Olivier may well have been right. Sunday's paper could be interesting.'

IO

CRUEL CAMERA

ON THE FOLLOWING SUNDAY ONLOOKER'S COLUMN was headed by a sequence of three striking photographs. In the first a tall well-dressed matron is seen standing outside the narrow front door of a mews cottage; in the second her arm is raised to defend her face from impending injury; in the third, with head thrust forward and teeth bared, she is evidently about to charge a deadly foe. 'MEET CAMERA-SHY OCCUPANT OF ROMANCE COTTAGE' ran the impudent caption. Having failed to get an interview with the recalcitrant tenant, Onlooker had spread himself about the 'love-spell' of Number Eleven, and had quoted Mr Ernest Ferrit as saying 'They goes in single and comes out wed.'

The Trident reacted to the story with rage and fascination. The peace and privacy of their mews had been outraged, but Mrs Olivier had become more than ever intriguing. Colin, who was soon known to have 'rescued' her after the ordeal, found himself something of a hero, while Mr Ferrit, who had been misguided enough to shoot his mouth to the press, received black looks from all sides. Colin, returning from the Sunday school which his aunt compelled him to attend while she lolled in bed with his uncle, observed Mr Ferrit washing the vintage Bentley outside Number Six. Drawn by the slosh of water and the glitter of the long bonnet, he wandered along to watch.

Mr Ferrit's cheroot was in his mouth and he washed and polished in glowering silence.

'See the paper this morning?' asked Colin, casually.

'Which one?'

Colin told him.

'Yep,' said Mr Ferrit. 'Disgustin' business – them pictures of Mrs Olivier.'

"She looked like she was going to bite the photographer,' commented Colin. 'Pity she didn't.'

'Probably poisoned 'er if she 'ad.'

Colin grinned.

'My aunt said you let the side down, talking to the reporter.'

Mr Ferrit straightened up and assumed an expression of injured innocence.

'Listen, sonny, I'm not one to talk. I leaves gossip to women. But on Friday I chanced to meet a man in the Queen's 'ead round the corner. We gets into conversation and 'e stands me an old and mild. No 'arm in that. Next thing I know the bastard's puttin' words into me mouth – in print!'

Mrs Meadows didn't come to work on weekends. It was Mr Meadows who drew her attention to Onlooker's pictures.

'Shows a nice bit of temper,' he remarked. 'I like a woman with spunk, but you'd better keep on the right side of your Mrs Olivier, my girl!'

Mrs Meadows was loyal.

'She's allergic to photographers. She told me so. Even Miss Rachel hasn't a proper picture of her Mum. Only an enlarged snapshot. Mrs Olivier is very reserved, keeps herself to herself.'

In the basement flat in the Crescent Rachel was sleeping late. Liz brought the paper to her room with a cup of breakfast coffee.

'Wakey-wakey! It's past eleven.'

Rachel raised heavy lids. She stretched, cat-like and sensuous, half smiling, the last dance, the last embrace still warm in her somnolent blood.

Liz plopped on to her bed, looking sulky. She didn't feel good in the mornings. She pushed the paper under Rachel's nose.

'This'll take the Cheshire-cat grin off your face. Honestly, Ray, your Ma's playing her cards wrong. The more she fights publicity the more she'll get it.'

'I don't know what you're nattering about. Take that scandal-sheet from under my nose!'

Rachel sat up, running her hand through her rumpled hair. Her pyjama top was unbuttoned and one firm round breast was bare, the nipple pale and virginal. Liz averted her eyes crossly. She had begun to hate her own changing body and the young perfection of Rachel's pointed painful contrasts. When Liz allowed herself to think about the active exigent unseen life inside her she felt much the same horror that she'd known as a child when she'd heard a moth flying round her room in the dark, beating itself here and there, battering its gold-dusted wings, trapped and not wanted.

Rachel drank her coffee with lazy enjoyment.

'Wonderful coffee, Liz.'

She put down the cup and looked at the paper, yawning, languorous, indifferent. Liz watched her with malice. In her opinion everything was going just a little bit too right for her friend. Ray had no problems. She was all on the side of the angels, while Liz was off the hooks and swinging in space with the safety-net of social security wearing thinner by the hour. If she didn't have an imperial blow-up with Mrs Standish before this infant was born it would be a miracle.

'Onlooker always gets his man,' she said. 'Or his woman.'

Rachel gasped. The healthy colour ebbed from her face as Liz had known it would. Ray was so fair-skinned that emotions seemed to move visibly under the thin delicately veined surface.

'I'm going to throw up,' she said chokily.

'Oh no, you're not,' said Liz. 'We've had enough morning sickness in this flat without any more.'

Rachel fell back on the pillow, her eyes closed, the lids smooth azure. I bet she can see through them, Liz thought. Ray was certainly made of fine material, light bird-bones covered with pure silk, and laced with sensitive nerves and arteries that throbbed visibly if you as much as looked at them. Could such quality endure, or was it better to be a calico woman in the long run?

'As a matter of fact,' said Liz, 'this first picture is nice. I'd have known it anywhere, but this third one! I could never have told it was your mother.'

'I could,' said Rachel. 'I've seen that look.'

'When she's mad with you?'

The clear green eyes snapped open.

'It was only once. Once I saw her look like that. And then it wasn't really directed at me. There was a man . . . ' Rachel's voice tailed off, but Liz was interested.

'Go on.'

'His name was Roberto. He was an Italian and he was boring for water at Môreson – down where the lower windmill is now, and the big willow. You know the place.'

'Where the blesbok used to come and drink with the sheep?'

Rachel nodded. 'I was crazy about that man. I used to hang round him.'

'How old were you?'

'Early teens – maybe not even that. Twelve, perhaps. One evening, when he was going off the job, I tagged along. It was hot – lord, how hot it was – with lightning along the horizon. By the dam he said "Cut along home, kid. I'm going in for a swim." And I said "I'll swim too." He took off his clothes without another word and waded into the water and I did the same. Ma was out riding. She caught us.'

'In the water or out of it?' Liz was a glutton for detail.

'We were in, but our clothes were on the bank. I remember being scared stiff when I saw Ma leading her horse to the water's edge. She'd loosened his girth and the bridle to let him drink, and then she spotted my cotton pants and dress lying on the grass with Roberto's vest and dungarees.'

'What happened?'

'I stayed in the water, my teeth chattering with fright. I must say Roberto was superb. He walked calmly out – just as if Ma wasn't there at all – absolutely stark. He dried himself with his vest and pulled on his dungarees. His black hair was in tight little curls all over his head and he looked pretty terrific.'

She paused thoughtfully, new interpretations of a half-forgotten episode insinuating themselves into her consciousness. Liz said:

'Your mother can't have been very old then. Maybe thirty-one or two. Must have given her quite a turn – or even a kick.'

'She was young enough to understand very well what was making me tick when it came to wanting Roberto,' agreed Rachel. 'And she let him have it! She looked like this when she ticked him off – eyes blazing, lip drawn back, savage, like an animal.' She touched the paper with distaste.

'She had something to be mad about,' conceded Liz. 'Finding her little girl being led astray.'

'It may have seemed that way, but in fact there was nothing to it. I'd made all the running.'

'Did Roberto explain that?'

Rachel laughed with genuine amusement, and instantly knew the healing balm of humour. Some of the shock and revulsion she had felt upon seeing the revealing photographs of her mother was dissipated in mirth.

'Oh, Liz, I can see him now! A gorgeous beast, if ever there was one, looking down at my mother, not in the least put out by the situation, or by her ravings. He let her say her say – and it was quite a mouthful – and when she drew breath he put his hands on his hips and stood there admiring her. "When you are angry, Signora, you are beautiful," he said, "like a wild beast – magnifico! Don't worry about the cub. I like my women grown." And he strode off, up the rise, leaving her gasping and speechless beside her horse.'

'And when you came out of the water?'

'I came out like a pup with its tail between its legs, and she flew at me. But, now I come to think of it, she was probably quite shaken on her own account. After that I was sent to boarding-school.'

'She must have had something in those days,' said Liz. 'Damn, there goes the phone. Jim, I suppose.'

'I'll answer it.'

Rachel sprang out of bed and ran to the telephone in the living-room. Jim had been on the line to Ravenswood.

'That ghastly Onlooker stuff!' said Rachel. 'I didn't think your father read that paper!'

'He doesn't. Mrs Shane, our help, showed it to Laura.'

'Heavens! How did they take it?'

'Believe it or not, Dad thought it rather funny. He really is unpredictable. He said your mother looked very spirited with her fangs bared. Spirited – what a word! Laura's furious, of course, and so am I. If I could get my hands on that photographer I'd wring his neck. As for Mr Ferrit – wait till I can tear a strip off his ugly hide.'

Rachel giggled. 'You'd better cool off, or there'll be another drama in the mews.'

'We must go and see your mother. She's probably fed to the teeth. I'll fetch you in half an hour.'

Rachel and Jim expected a scene. They were prepared to make soothing sounds of consolation, or to laugh the whole thing off. In fact, they had begun to see it as something of a joke themselves. Nothing really to fuss about.

The scarlet door was, as usual, ajar and they bounded up stairs and into the sitting-room. Mrs Olivier was sitting at the bureau with an aerogram before her. It was blank. She turned as they came in, and Rachel's heart sank. It was her stony face. Her skin looked matt and dead and her eyes were cold. She had guessed their purpose in coming and she forestalled it immediately.

She went straight to the point.

'The whole thing is degrading. I allowed myself to lose my temper. That's the lesson, Rachel. If you lose control anything can happen. The wild beast takes over.'

Jim sat on the arm of a chair, one long leg swinging.

'You're taking this thing too seriously, Mrs Olivier.'

She turned slightly and raised her eyebrows. 'I don't think so. Every now and again something crops up to make us know ourselves a little better. We do well to learn from the experience.'

Rachel said: 'Please, Ma, don't take this to heart. It's a trifle. It's nothing.'

She was leaning against the window-sill; as Mrs Olivier moved her head to face her daughter she looked full into the light. Rachel saw the ice begin to thaw.

'We all remember different things about the same incidents,' Mrs Olivier said. 'I wonder if you remember a certain occasion when you were a child? You could be terribly stubborn, you could put on a most infuriating face,

very pale and absolutely closed. We had one of our set-to's
– just before I sent you to boarding-school. You'd made a
fool of yourself over a man called Roberto.'

'I'm here,' Jim reminded her.

'I hadn't forgotten,' she said over her shoulder, and continued to address herself to Rachel. 'We were in my bedroom
with the long mirror, I'd been scolding you, and you'd
given me no change, only that obstinate unyielding mask.
Suddenly I took you by the shoulders and swung you round
to face the mirror, and I said, "Look at yourself! Look!
Sulky, mulish, stupid – " and then, over your shoulder, I
saw my own face in the glass. I didn't like what I saw.'

'I remember that. I remember how you looked,' said
Rachel, and made no further comment.

Mrs Olivier said: 'I learnt a lesson that day, and I've learnt
another today. It doesn't do to fly off the handle. At best one
makes a fool of oneself. At worst . . . '

She broke off and Jim came to her side. He put an arm
affectionately about her shoulders and she drew comfort and
strength from the gesture.

'Let's call the matter closed,' he said.

She threw back her head and he felt her muscles brace
under his hand.

'Yes, Jim. From now on the subject is tabu!'

II

ENCOUNTER WITH THE PAST

MRS OLIVIER HAD DISCOVERED THE PECULIAR peace of the church playground at the back of the Trident. Really, it was less a children's playground than a tiny secluded park – a place of green grass, with solid wooden benches under enormous elms, limes and planes. It was in the heart of a veritable maze of mewses and the little flat-roofed houses that overlooked this glade of leaf-filtered light were painted blue, mauve, pink and primrose and sported bright canvas canopies over ornamental wrought-iron balconies that lent them an insouciant foreign aspect. They were, she thought, like a flock of Mediterranean migrants settling among their dingy London neighbours for the space of a summer season. The churchyard had become her retreat, and on the Monday afternoon following Onlooker's revelations she went there to find balm for her bruised spirit. For once her strong body ached in sympathy, as if that too had taken a beating and endured humiliation.

She sat on a bench under the branches of a plane tree already shedding its first flat golden leaves on the thinning grass beneath it. The name and date of the donor of the bench was carved in the hard wood. A good memorial to a human being, she thought. 'Remember Ann Olivier' and the date of her death. She'd like that. Better a bench than a tombstone.

A child threw a ball for a terrier, and a white poodle, being exercised by the Italian maid from one of the pretty mews houses, joined in the chase. An old shabby man excavated a stale loaf with deft fingers and scattered crumbs for the pigeons that flocked round him, perching on his arms and shoulders. A young woman lay on her back in a patch of sunlight, arms and legs bare, face to the pale evening sky, her string shopping bag limp on the grass at her side. Two women sat talking on a bench under a tall elm; the one rocked a pram whose occupant stared about him with the lofty disdain of an individual who expresses only what he feels. The bell in its turreted tower of mellow brick tolled five o'clock. Mrs Olivier closed her eyes the better to enjoy the refreshment of this green-gold dappled backwater in the life of a great city, whose murmur rose and fell like the tides of the sea. The terrier barked and the child cried, 'Chase it, boy, chase it!' The wings of the pigeons whirred as the dog pursued the ball into their midst. Mrs Olivier heard them rise and fly away and come down again. She could distinguish the evening calls of song-birds and the chirping of sparrows, small immediate sounds that fell into her consciousness with the cool comfort of rain on parched earth. Reflections floated quietly in and out of her mind without urgency. She wished that she knew the secrets of meditation. How good it would be to extract the very essence of her being from its problems and immerse it in the waters of Lethe – that stream of blessed amnesia.

But, when she opened her eyes once more, Mrs Olivier looked straight at a window on to the past she so earnestly wished to forget.

A pleasant-faced woman of about her own age was standing a few feet from her. She wore a blue linen suit and a pill-box hat which perched on her auburn hair without concealing its rich waves. She was small and plump with neat ankles and feet. Ann Olivier brushed a hand across her eyes incredulously. She whispered, 'Oh no, no . . . it can't be...'

It was too cruel – to be cornered like this with no hope of escape! After all this time. The little woman advanced with a warm friendly smile.

'Ann, how wonderful! You again, at last – after twenty years. I've been watching you while you dozed. You've hardly changed.'

'Cheryl . . .'

There was no answering smile on Mrs Olivier's face as she spoke the name softly, with apprehension. Her expression had lost its new-found serenity. It had become hostile and she had stiffened into an attitude of defence. But Cheryl refused to be put off. She sat down beside Mrs Olivier on the wooden bench.

'You aren't very glad to see me, are you, Ann?'

'Frankly, no.'

'I was afraid it would be like that. But the moment I saw those photographs in the paper yesterday I made up my mind to hunt you out. They were rather characteristic – all three of them. And your daughter – she must be lovely?'

'Rachel is lovely. She is happy. How did you track me down?'

'It was too easy. Onlooker gave the address away and I went there this afternoon but you were out. A little man was mending a leaking tap in the garage next door. He said I might find you here – that you often came to the churchyard.'

'The little man's name is Ferrit. Ferrit by name and ferret by nature. He's the man in the mews. Everything is known to Mr Ferrit.'

'You sound bitter, Ann, yet things haven't gone so badly for you, from what I can gather.'

'They've gone well, Cheryl. And I'm determined they shall continue to go well – especially for Rachel.'

'We were great friends once,' said Cheryl. 'you and I. You can talk to me.'

'We were friends . . . in another life. When we parted it was goodbye. Final.'

'Can one ever say that? Can anybody partition life . . . put bulkheads between the past and the present? Is anything ever – final?'

'God only knows. But one can do one's best to make it so.'

'But need you, Ann? Surely you can trust *me*?'

Ann looked into the sincere blue eyes of the closest friend of her youth. Cheryl, who had been so bitterly hurt by Ann's decision to make an end of everything connected with the past, was incapable of bearing a grudge. Warm, generous, loving, she still insisted upon offering the un-wanted gift of an outworn friendship.

'Did you marry your good-looking dentist – Johnny Braithwaite?' Mrs Olivier asked.

Cheryl's face shone with sheer contentment.

'I did, bless him. We have three children, two boys and a girl, and a house on Putney Hill.'

Mrs Olivier's smile was twisted.

'And when you saw those pictures yesterday, you said, "Good heavens, it's Ann!" And Johnny Braithwaite remem-bered . . . it was all rehashed between the two of you . . . everything.' She leaned forward fiercely and grasped Cheryl's dimpled ungloved hand. 'Admit it! You did talk about it – of course you did! And maybe your children joined in.'

Cheryl Braithwaite looked back at Ann Olivier, her gaze direct and fearless.

'I did point the pictures out to Johnny and we did discuss the situation. We said nothing whatever to the children. I made you a promise once and I've kept it – '

'Not from your husband!'

'Of course not. He knew, in any case. Who didn't, at that time?' She went on, more gently. 'I know how you must feel, my dear. I didn't hunt you out to make a nuisance of myself or remind you of things you'd rather forget. Quite frankly, I thought you might be . . . very lonely . . . that you might need one person, one true friend, who knew everything. Johnny thought so, too. He said "To begin with she'll want to know about her parents. That must have been the worst thing for her."'

Mrs Olivier put a hand to her throat. She seemed to choke.

'They are dead – to me.'

'They are dead.' Cheryl's voice was stern. 'You didn't think much about other people at that time, did you? You didn't stop to consider what it meant to your father and mother to have their only daughter write them off, to have her vanish without trace. Deliberately.'

'It had to be that way! There could be no half measures.'

'They sort of adopted me when you had gone. I saw them often. Your mother died two years ago. A heart attack. Your father went soon after. He'd been having dizzy spells. He fell under a train – in the Underground. It was during the rush-hour – a hot day. I couldn't even write and tell you. You left no address and you had forbidden me to try to find you, no matter what the circumstances.'

Reproach and condemnation had hardened Cheryl's tone. Ann Olivier said nothing. Her eyes were tightly closed, but Cheryl's information had opened the flood-gates of memory. The dear inconvenient ramshackle home, the gaunt over-worked doctor-father who was never too tired to make some little joke, the austere mother who faced war and the blitz without flinching but whose heart had been broken on the wheel of her daughter's headstrong temperament.

They had been so proud of Ann in her uniform of a WAAF officer, but she had given them only grief. Dykes of emotion began to crumble. Tears forced their way through lids closed against them and rolled unheeded down her cheeks. She did not attempt to wipe them away. She let them flow. Cheryl watched with horror and pity. Poor Ann, she has forgotten how to cry! I don't believe she's cried in years. Cheryl found those silent unchecked tears infinitely distressing.

The old man who had been feeding the pigeons had gone his way, the woman with the pram wheeled it down the stone footpath leading to the Brompton Road. Her friend walked with her and the baby sat up, straight and stately, observing the world into which an error of judgment had cast him. He smiled suddenly at his mother, who beamed back and spoke to him in the incomprehensible language reserved for infants, imbeciles and lap-dogs. They had a conspiracy and when her little duckie-wuckie smiled at her with such windy wonder she forgave him all his father's carelessness. The Italian maid put her mistress's white poodle on a lead, crossed the cobbles and closed a lavender front door behind him and her. The boy with the terrier frisked home to tea, his tireless dog springing up beside him, still asking for the ball.

The gardens were deserted.

'Here's a hankie,' said Cheryl. 'I'm sorry to have hurt you, Ann, but we – Johnny and I – thought you ought to know. We loved your old folk.'

'So did I.' Ann was clearly overcome. 'It was good of you both to take so much trouble.' She dabbed at her face and returned the handkerchief to its owner.

'What about you?' Cheryl asked. 'Your husband . . . ?'

'Gerhard died a year ago. Our son inherited the farm – a beautiful farm, Cheryl, and the boy's a fine lad. The house is mine for as long as I want it. Rachel . . . well, you read about her. She's going to marry Jim Fleet in September.'

An unspoken question sparked in Cheryl's eyes and Mrs Olivier answered it obliquely.

'If you can't wipe the slate clean you must smash it. I've done that. Try to understand! I don't want to hurt you, but you mustn't attempt to see me again. Really, dear Cheryl, you must forget today.'

The little woman rose with dignity. She looked down at her erstwhile friend compassionately. Ann's head was bowed her swollen lids veiled her eyes.

'I'll respect your decision,' said Cheryl quietly. 'But don't forget that if ever you need a friend I am there. J. Braithwaite. Putney Hill. It's in the directory. So long, Ann.'

'Goodbye.''

Mrs Olivier did not look up as Cheryl left her. She heard her friend's step on the pebble path and the squeak of the little iron gate. It would be good to call Cheryl back, talk freely, discuss knotty problems and seek advice. But Cheryl had a family – a husband to whom she was devoted. A secret shared is a secret no more. She sat on, steeped in the deep inner aloneness to which she had long ago condemned herself.

The sun had set behind the brick ramparts and the chill of evening crept through the darkening leaves. Ghosts walked in the shadowy glade. To the woman on the bench under the plane tree the quiet garden had assumed its other aspect. It was no longer a playground, but a graveyard now, where children romped and played over the dust of the departed.

Mrs Olivier closed the churchyard gate behind her and strolled along the first prong of the Trident.

This was the short unattractive arm with only half a dozen box-like houses on one side facing towards the fire-escapes of the huge concrete block which towered over the quiet well of the mews. In one of these houses – she was not sure which – Mr Ferrit lived with his daft sister, Emily. But Mrs Olivier was not thinking about the Ferrits. She had gone into the garden in search of peace and she had come out with an unhealed wound open and bleeding. It's like the stigmata, she thought, the agony of the cross resuscitated again and again – scars of nails and thorns and dagger-thrust, breaking open to bleed anew and repeat the two-thousand-year-old suffering of Calvary.

At sight of Cheryl a whole period of her life had risen from the grave to torture her afresh.

She moved like a sleep-walker on her way back to the sanctuary of Number Eleven. It was old Emily Ferrit who broke through the vision of the past and linked it with the present.

Miss Ferrit was trotting home from a blissful afternoon spent at the big cinema in Kensington High Street. She'd sat the picture through twice and had, for a few hours, been the beloved of a king. As she pattered over the cobbles in her shabby shoes she was decked in diamonds and ermine, a princess of shining beauty strolling with her royal lover through formal moonlit gardens. Tonight the moon would be waxing – a summer moon poking his glowing face through the window, beckoning her! Miss Ferrit, still dazed and moving erratically in the direction of home, bumped into Mrs Olivier.

The shock of the contact shattered the spells – each so different – that had held both women in their particular aura of withdrawal. Mrs Olivier recovered herself first.

'I'm sorry,' she said. 'I wasn't looking where I was going.'

Miss Ferrit was staring at her with half-crazed eyes.

'It's you,' she said. 'It's you again. *I know you.*'

Mrs Olivier shivered. The old woman gave her the creeps.

'Of course, I've lived in the Trident since May.'

'It's not that,' said Miss Ferrit. 'I know you because you're one of Ernie's people – one of the sort 'e collects.'

Mrs Olivier forced a smile. 'Oh yes, Miss Ferrit. You've told me that before. I wondered at the time exactly what you meant.'

'Ernie wouldn't let me say. Nobody knows about his people. Only me. Sometimes 'e lets me talk to them.'

She moved on, muttering to herself. Mrs Olivier watched her go, hunched and scrawny, off-balance mentally and physically, animated by her own fixed intentions. Purposeful.

Miss Ferrit hobbled over to the rickety chest-of-drawers in which she kept her few belongings and scrabbled in one of the two top drawers. It contained her own mending and her brother's socks in need of darning. With a grunt of triumph she drew out a news cutting. It was Onlooker's column of the day before.

'I cut 'er out for you. We can paste 'er into your book.'

Mr Ferrit was interested. His sister had the same photographic type of memory as his own, and, although her pre-occupation with his hobby irritated him she had upon occasions been useful. He was well aware too that the poor frustrated creature was driven by her uncontrollable hunger for vicarious experience.

They had cleared away the remains of their evening meal but the greasy tang of kippers still pervaded the small house. Dusty paper flowers in a metallic vase adorned the table. It was still broad daylight and cars snorted in and out of the

Trident. Somebody was giving a cocktail party in the second prong and the noisy buzz of voices, like a disturbed hive, floated out of the open windows on the quiet air.

'Never thought I'd see one of yours in the flesh,' said Miss Ferrit with happy wonder. 'Makes it all come real, somehow.'

'It is real. All of it is real.'

He spoke with grim satisfaction, the words and the thought behind them inducing a peculiar ringing in his ears and tingling in his blood, the onset of a familiar indescribably exciting sensation. His body was a hollow vessel filling consciously but almost imperceptibly with diabolical power. His sister grinned slyly. When his eyes glazed a little like that she knew that he would no longer try to resist his people.

'Get them out,' she whispered hoarsely. 'Let's play with them. Hide and seek. Let's find *her*.'

He went to his room and unlocked the drawer in which his people lived. A jet flashed across the skylight with its deep-throated roar and thin tearing whine. Mr Ferrit's hands with the grimy nails were not quite steady as he lifted the heavy scrap-book and carried it into the living-room. He set it on the table at which they had recently eaten their supper.

'I wish you'd git out,' he said roughly to his sister. One day, if she hung around long enough, she'd come to harm!

'I'm goin' to find 'er,' Emily persisted, oblivious of his secret fear and the insidious temptation to which she intermittently subjected him.

He sat with his head in his hands as she thumbed through the huge album. She leaned over the table peering down at the pages she riffled. Faces looked back at her from faded news clippings – grim, debonair, handsome, bestial, male, female.

She turned back the clock, ten, twenty, twenty-five years. Mr Ferrit's hobby covered nearly a quarter of a century.

'You'd best leave it alone, Em.'

He spoke harshly, struggling not to yield to the hot intoxication that invaded his whole body till sanity strained at her moorings. He reeled. He seemed to stand on the edge of a giddy height, only safe because the moment of abandon must be postponed until he was certain which of his people possessed him. Emily, too, was safe for the present, but one day he feared that she would stay in the room too long. Then she, too, would be one of his people. What had once been a passive interest to both of them had gradually, over the years, become an active obsession to Mr Ferrit, one against which he struggled well aware of his sister's peril – and his own.

Suddenly he could endure her interference no longer. Lithe as Lucifer, the cat, he sprang at her and snatched her inquisitive searching hands from the yellowed pages pasted over with items of news from other years. She uttered a strangled cry.

'Let go! You frighten me, Ernie.'

'Shut up, you bloody old scarecrow! I told you to leave it alone!'

'You're hurting my wrists,' she whined. 'Leave go of me, Ernie.'

She stared up at him, pleading and half afraid.

'When you gits this way you looks like one of them yourself! No wonder you scare the daylights out of me, Ernie!'

She saw his eyes widen suddenly as he looked over her shoulder at the open book. His grip on her wrists relaxed. He let her go and she fell against the table, whimpering.

He took no notice of her. She had ceased to exist for him. His gaze was riveted on the face that looked up at him across a period of twenty years. Even the smudge of newsprint failed to blur its dark gipsy quality. You had to look again. And yet again. It was a young face but it was marked with fate and tragedy. He turned the page and there it was again, but this time the tall pliant figure showed too, feminine and seductive. An arm was thrown defensively across the face, hiding the features. There was only the curve of the long neck and the dark head turned away from the flash-light. There were other pictures, too. A man, athletic and masterful, was with her. They were sitting on a beach, laughing and confident, evidently part of a picnic party. You could not look at it without being sure that they were lovers. And here she was again, with a baby in her arms, the usual mother-child studio portrait, the madonna expression softening the outlines of strength with conventional tenderness. Soppy stuff.

The heat had been shocked out of Mr Ferrit's blood. He drew a chair forward and sat down soberly to study the columns of that long-ago Sunday paper. Onlooker's paper. He found them absorbing. When Emily breathed down his neck he told her, not unkindly, to clear out and make him a cup of coffee. Strong. Mr Ferrit's mood of elation had passed. He was empty now and passionless, coldly calculating. Well, well! Who'd have thought it?

When Emily brought him his coffee he pushed the hard kitchen chair back and rocked to and fro on it for a few minutes. Like a dog sensing approval, she fawned on him.

'It's 'er, aint it? Remembered 'er face the second I seen it. You don't forget a face like that.'

'It's 'er all right,' he said. 'Yes, Em old girl, you done well. We've got somethin' 'ere. But what? That's what I've got to think about.'

12

DREAMY AUGUST

RACHEL GAVE UP HER JOB AT THE END OF JULY, AND August was, for her, a busy happy month. The wedding date was fixed for late September, and the young couple had stuck to their decision to have a quiet wedding in the little church at Raven Park, and the reception at Ravenswood.

Hans Olivier hoped to fly from South Africa for his sister's marriage and Jenny Carstairs, whose parents were taking a holiday in England and bringing her with them, was to be Rachel's bridesmaid. The only fly in the ointment was the unfortunate necessity to exclude Liz from the occasion.

'Mrs Standish says we ought to go to the chalet in Switzerland at the beginning of September,' she said to Rachel. 'What do you think?'

'If you want to keep the matter secret, then she's right. The fashions are all in your favour at the moment, but even so another month will tell a tale.'

'I s'pose so,' Liz pouted. 'I've written to my folk to tell them that I'm taking a job in Gstaad as companion to Mrs Standish and to learn French and German. They swallowed it whole.'

'It's the truth – even if it's not the whole truth.'

'What'll you do, Ray? Will you join your mother in the mews when I leave?'

Rachel looked round the little flat she and Liz had shared

for nearly two years. They'd both of them learnt a good deal about life here. There'd been giggles and tears, tiffs and companionship, and now the partnership was about to break up. They'd given in their notice for the end of August.

'I'd rather stay on here,' she said. 'I could keep it by the week.'

'When does Jenny arrive?'

'The day before the wedding. She lands at Southampton and comes direct to the inn at Raven Park. We're all staying there that night. Hans too.'

'Lucky Hans, lucky Jenny. What's she doing about her bridesmaid dress?'

'She'll bring it with her.'

Liz began to roam round the room, messing about with this and that, plumping up a cushion, pulling dead-heads off the gladioli, altering the position of a cigarette box. It was a restless claustrophobic mood, symptomatic of her condition.

'There should have been two of us – Jenny and me. Instead I'll be going round the bend with Mrs Standish breathing down my neck every hour of the day.'

'I wish you could be more philosophical,' Rachel said.

'She knocks the philosophy out of me. How would you like to be constantly in the company of someone who treats you like a . . . like a parcel? She can't wait to tear off the wrapping, open the box and get at the contents! I've no identity as far as she's concerned. None whatsoever! Except as a productive organism. The moment she's got her hands on the child I'm to be thrown into the trash-can, never to be seen again. It's an attitude I can't take.'

'It's part of the contract. You've got to accept it and be sensible about it.'

'Oh yes, she's got me where she wants me. But nearly

three months of isolation with her in Gstaad – that idea shakes me!'

'Use the time intelligently. Learn languages and make her respect you. After all, it's not a prison sentence. Don't turn into a bleating bore, Liz.'

Liz stopped in her tracks, stunned at such a base attack.

'I've got something to bleat about. You're all right. It's roses all the way for you.'

Rachel was seized with remorse. 'I'm sorry, Liz. I suppose my being so happy – so lucky – makes it all the harder for you – rubs it in. But, honestly, the way you think and act during this time is going to affect your baby. You've renounced your claim on him for his sake. Then think constructively for his sake too.'

'Do you really believe in that pre-natal influence stuff?'

'Of course I do. How can it be otherwise? A child is part of his parents. He's made up of their genes and hormones. No one can argue about heredity. It's irrefutable. Down at Ravenswood there are portraits of Jim's ancestors. There's one of a midshipman of Nelson's time, he might be Jim in fancy costume. Even the way he holds his head – back on his shoulders, his neck long. And he has the same strong narrow hands. All those things.'

'What's that got to do with my thinking? I can't think this baby into a different mould from the one he's in already.'

'You don't want to. But you can influence his temperament. He's absorbing everything from you – but *everything*. If you got drunk he'd get drunk! If you go berserk he'll surely be born with a crazy streak. Be positive, Liz. For his sake.'

'When did you put in all this research?' asked Liz with rare sarcasm. 'You seem to have wise motherhood at your finger ends.'

'Jim and I want children. As soon as we're settled in a home of our own we mean to start our family.'

'Some people never learn.' But Liz grinned as she said it, her natural good humour partially restored.

Roses all the way? To Rachel that was indeed how it seemed in the hot happy month of August when London was deserted. The roads to the coast were jammed with cars and caravans; beaches teemed with sunburnt bodies; the Lake District was a trippers' paradise, and Continental tours took the more enterprising and sophisticated British holiday-makers across the Channel. Cheap night flights were popular and the cry of the Caravel over the mews was heard with increasing frequency in the small hours between midnight and dawn.

'Everybody everywhere goes somewhere else at this season,' said Rachel drowsily. 'But nobody comes to London. London belongs to us.'

It was Sunday afternoon and she lay on the grass in St James's Park, her head pillowed on Jim's diaphragm. She had taken off her bolero and kicked off her shoes. Her suntop left her shoulders bare. His open-necked sports shirt revealed his brown throat, and his long fingers curled the bright strands of her hair. He said:

'It's going to be an early autumn, the leaves are falling already.' But he was thinking that the texture of her hair was softer than silk, its gold so rich in rippling lights that gold itself would be dull and dead by comparison.

Other couples lazed in the grass or sauntered under the trees and children played at the water's edge, or watched the antics of ducks and water fowl. Rachel and Jim scarcely noticed them. The park was theirs, London was theirs, the world was theirs. She stared up through the tracery of branches, seeing, as in a dream, the grey domes of White-hall, the spires of Westminster, and the top of Big Ben look-ing like the highest tier of an eastern pagoda.

'It's Arabian Nights,' she said. 'Domes and minarets seen through a skein of cobwebs, so ethereal and magical you half expect them to dissolve.'

'The mystic face of London.'

'Everything is more beautiful than it's ever been be-fore,' she said. 'Sometimes it all seems too wonderful to last.'

'Darling,' he said. 'Don't invite disaster. Big Ben and the spires of Westminster won't dissolve; nor will our . . . happiness.' He wanted to say 'love', but, after all, happiness and love were one and the same in this case, and love was a word he seldom used. You had your own creed about love, your private 'I believe . . . and for ever more' but you didn't have to talk about it.

She sat up and stared down at him with wide eyes as clear as the glistening water under the willows, shot with green and the gold of approaching autumn.

'It's you who tempt providence! Whatever happens, my darling, whatever happens, go on loving me!'

Thus she divorced them – those partners, happiness and love, and with the tone of her voice and the look in her eyes she made one of them indestructible.

Up to the present Mr Ferrit's curious hobby had been pure, in the sense that he had never before been tempted to exploit it for gain. Now, for the first time, he felt the corrup-ting influence of power.

There was money in this and it was only natural that Mr Ferrit's latent avarice should be stimulated by dreams of what riches could buy. A holiday in Majorca or the Isles of

Greece. A cruise to the Caribbean. A car of his own – a new one with a herd of horses under the bonnet. Italy.

Sleep was elusive, and there were nights when Mr Ferrit felt impelled to get up and make a tour of the Trident. Several of the mews dwellers were away on holiday and Mr Ferrit kept an eye on the premises for them. But whenever he reached Number Eleven he found it difficult to pass on. He would stand by the young Dixons' dwarf tree and gaze up at Mrs Olivier's open window, wondering how best to tackle his enticing but delicate problem. Mrs Olivier was probably quite a wealthy woman, but blackmail was a dangerous game and he didn't fancy it. Dirty, too.

Sometimes Mrs Olivier lay awake listening to his tuneless whistling – very light and soft – the insidious disturber of her rest. His step was silent because he walked at night on rubber soles. His nocturnal habits troubled her. In some obscure fashion she associated them with herself. Drawn by that thin piping, she would leave her bed in the dark and go to the window. Ten to one, he would be standing there just as he had done on her first night in London, only now the cat slept in her window-box and not in the tub under the orange leaves. Mrs Olivier could feel the vibrations of Mr Ferrit's concentration crossing the sleeping mews and exerting some macabre and irresistible compulsion. Like a ray, she thought, some deadly ray. When at last he released her by moving on she would lean back against the wall, shaking with an icy ague. He went slowly these nights, hands dug deep into the pockets of his stove-pipe trousers, the billowing jerkin and peaked cap making a sinister top-heavy shadow over the spidery legs.

In the day-time she avoided him, and, when she met him unexpectedly, she could scarcely bring herself to greet him. She felt sometimes as if they shared some shameful unacknowledged intimacy.

One airless Saturday night towards the end of August Rachel brought Liz to supper with Mrs Olivier. Jim was at Ravenswood but Rachel had stayed to see Liz off for Switzerland early on Sunday morning.

'Goodbye, Mrs Olivier,' said Liz soon after ten o'clock. 'I hate to miss this wedding. I'm terribly disappointed. You can't imagine.'

Her eyes filled and suddenly she began to weep with childish abandon. Mrs Olivier signed to her daughter to leave them alone, and Rachel went into the kitchen and began to do the washing up.

Mrs Olivier put her arms round the sobbing Liz.

'My dear, believe me, I understand.'

'Did Ray tell you?'

'Rachel has told me nothing. But I have eyes. You were a skinny bit of spaghetti when I arrived, now you're macaroni. Do you want to talk about it or not?'

Liz poured out her tale. 'I don't know if I'm doing right – I just don't know.'

Mrs Olivier was practical and direct. Her manner, while not unsympathetic, held neither censure nor pity.

'I can't tell if you're doing right or not. I don't know the people who are going to take your child. But this I know, you've come to a definite decision after much heart-searching, and you must stand by it. You've set your course and you must steer by it. And there's one warning you must bear in mind. Don't get sorry for yourself, don't look for sympathy, resist the temptation to confide. For everybody's sake – yours, the child's, your parents', and one day your husband's. You won't be the first person with something to hide. You'll be one of the vast majority of human beings. Marriage and your husband's children will overlay this experience. In the meantime do the best you can to launch this baby well. Then begin to live your own life again.'

Having examined the case and summed it up according to her experience Mrs Olivier called her daughter from the kitchen. When Rachel came in Liz was smiling through her tears.

'Your mother knows, Ray. Somehow I can face it better now.'

'I'll come and see you in Switzerland before I go home,' Mrs Olivier promised. 'If there's anything I can do at any time you can call on me.'

When they had gone Mrs Olivier went to bed. Human nature didn't change. You made your mistakes and did your best to make amends. That was life. But your past could catch up with you. The past was never dead, it had more lives than Lucifer.

The heat of the day had abated very little. The cobbles were silver under a waning moon. Mrs Olivier heard the sigh of the Dixons' bedroom curtains opening on their metal runners. The night was so still that she almost believed she could hear the young wife stir in her husband's arms.

She felt in the drawer of her bedside table and pulled out the bottle of pink capsules. Should she take one and make sure of a good night, or would it be wiser to give nature a chance? She decided against the sleeping-pill.

That night she had the dream again – the dreadful familiar Freudian dream of desire and frustration. Fundamentally it was the same, but there were variations on the basic theme. Sometimes she pursued the blond man down shadowy corridors; then, just as she was about to touch his arm, the dark passage would melt into a crowded room, and there he'd be, laughing and talking with somebody else. Always with his back to her. But she knew him – the light hair and bull-neck, the tapering virile body and massive shoulders. She must get to him and make him turn and look at her. He must see her and possess her. As the spider, knocking on the web, courts death as well as a mate, so the dreamer, compelled by some inexorable atavistic drive, pursued the dreadful culmination of her quest. Yet she was always denied the ultimate fatal orgasm, saved from herself and her doom by some trivial inadvertent interruption. To-night, however, he was very near. She had chased him bare-foot over the dark uneven cobbles between the sleeping mews houses. He had paused under a lantern to bend his gleaming head and stroke the black cat that wound to and fro about his long powerful legs. She tried to run towards him but her limbs were heavy, and she tried to call him but she had no voice. Slowly he straightened his broad shoulders and turned to look at her. She was paralysed now – shaking with dread, making a mighty effort to shout for help.

A tremendous knocking woke her. The hammering of her heart? Or someone pounding on the door? Her mouth was dry, her bones were water. She was too weak to move. The banging in her chest and in her ears was part of the nightmare.

'No, no, no . . . ' she kept repeating. 'Not that . . . not that . . . '

She switched on her reading lamp and dragged herself from the bed to the window and leaned out. A man was beating on the door.

'Who is it?' Her voice was faint and husky. She knew very well who it was.

He stepped back and looked up at the dark silhouette of her head against the subdued light. Her body was hidden from him by the curtain.

'I heard you call for help, Mrs Olivier. I was passing and I heard you cry out.'

She brushed her hand over her eyes.

'I'm sorry,' she said. 'It's nothing, Mr Ferrit. It was a bad dream. I get them sometimes . . . and cry out.'

'Is there something you're afraid of, Mrs Olivier?'

The question – so natural in the circumstances – came up to her with an inexpressibly sinister overtone.

'Nothing,' she whispered, huskily. 'Nothing real.'

'Sure you're all right?'

'Quite sure,' she said, her voice stronger.

He called goodnight and went away, whistling. He walked jauntily, she thought, with new self-confidence.

Tonight Mr Ferrit was no longer in doubt. He was a man sure of himself, sure, at last, of what he meant to do.

It took Mr Ferrit several days to run Onlooker to earth, and, when he had finally done so and persuaded the column-ist to visit him in his humble abode, Mr Ferrit was not at his ease.

Onlooker was a very different proposition from the hard-bitten photographer with whom Mr Ferrit had hobnobbed in the bar of the Queen's Head. Onlooker was supercilious and elegantly attired with a weary fine-drawn middle-aged face and hair greying at the temples. Everything about him spelled 'class', but Mr Ferrit felt that he was no less tough than the man with the ill-fitting suit and the flashlight gun. Both were accustomed to bringing down their quarry. If a one-day news scoop ruined or maimed a whole human life, what of it? A newspaper man had his duty to his readers. No one knew that better than Onlooker. He was well aware that half the world thrills to the way the other half lives – from up to down and down to up. Why, this fantastically morbid tome proved it! What would Mr Ferrit have done without the more lurid embellishments of the crime reporter's art?

Onlooker gazed at the contents of the huge scrap-album through tinted bifocals. His eyes were unastonished and disillusioned. Nothing could amaze him any more. His job had long since eliminated the faculty for surprise. But he felt a jaded curiosity about the mentality of this indefatigable 'collector'. You could be a *voyeur* of most eccentricities, Onlooker had found, but not of this! Mr Ferrit was a *voyeur manqué* – and *manqué* he would remain – of a very particular and perilous form of entertainment. Now where does this lead? Onlooker wondered. With a cynical twist of his lip he realised that, in this instance, it would probably lead on to the front page. It was really too good a story to break in a gossip column. It was stuff for the news editor. Yet, for the first time in years, he was not sorry to pass up a scoop. He didn't much care about this lot.

'A very interesting collection, Mr Ferrit. You're a specialist, I see – quite an expert in this rather strange line. You can't have missed much in the past quarter of a century.'

'During the war they fell off a bit,' confessed Mr Ferrit.

'Quite so. The individual killer is overshadowed by the mass in time of war.'

Onlooker wrinkled up his nose as if some odour offended him, and Mr Ferrit opened a window. Come to think about it, the little house did have an unaired smell, he must tell Emmie to give it a blow through once in a while. The old girl fluttered in and out of her fusty atmosphere as naturally as a bird comes and goes from its nest. Not much of a nest. Mr Ferrit had had a job getting rid of his sister this morning. He couldn't have Emmie around with Onlooker here. This was private business between himself and the press. Very private indeed. He'd given Emmie money to go to the cinema. That'd keep her out of the way. And the film she'd picked? The Gerald Bourne, of course. She'd see it through three times. He could bank on that. Gerald Bourne, Secret Agent, was Emily's number one hero. Which only went to show that, by and large, even the daft were normal or maybe the normal were daft. But more than that, it proved the news value of his story. Good old Emily!

'We have to be sure of our facts.' Onlooker was saying. 'Two hundred per cent sure.'

He set the originals of the shots of Mrs Olivier against the yellowed news flashes of two decades ago. 'Looks all right, but it'll need checking and re-checking.'

'That's your pigeon,' said Mr Ferrit. 'I'm sure of *my* facts. Now let's get down to business. What's this worth to me?'

Onlooker's cold eye gleamed fishily through the tinted bifocals. He mentioned a figure. Mr Ferrit snorted.

'I could do better with a Daily.' He named one. Onlooker did not call his bluff. He had started this ball rolling in his column and though he preferred not to be in at the death – personally, so to speak – he knew that this particular hunted fox belonged to his pack and no other. He doubled the number he'd mentioned. Mr Ferrit concealed his agreeable surprise and topped it.

'Take it or leave it,' he said.

'Done,' said Onlooker.

'One thing,' said Mr Ferrit, suddenly nervous. 'My name doesn't come into this? Not anywhere.'

'Not anywhere,' agreed Onlooker. 'Except, of course, on the cheque.'

13

ULTIMATUM

WHEN HER DOORBELL RANG ON THAT SATURDAY evening in September the last person Mrs Olivier expected to see was General Sir Jasper Fleet.

She knew that his weekends were dedicated to Ravenswood and that only the most urgent business could lure him to London during the summer.

'How unexpected, but how nice!' she exclaimed. 'I thought that on a Saturday you'd certainly be in the country. What can I get you? Tea? A drink?'

He had followed Mrs Olivier into the sitting room, but she might have been talking to a statue. He gave no sign of having heard her. He stood at the window, staring down at the mews, immaculate civilised hands linked behind his back. Her eyes were fixed on those hands. They were as tense and rigid as his back.

'Jasper,' she said quietly. 'What's wrong?'

Seconds can be an eternity and in that eternity before he turned round and answered her she knew what had happened. This is it, she thought. Somewhere in her breast an elevator crashed downwards. She moved instinctively to sit on the arm of a chair. The room whirled round her and settled down. Looking full into the light, she met his accusing gaze. Stern antagonistic face, neatly trimmed beard jutting fiercely forward, patches of florid colour in cheekbones as high and pronounced as those of his son.

'I have come to see you on a very serious matter,

Mrs Olivier. You can probably guess what it's about.'

She was pale as death but she met his eyes without flinching.

'I don't like guessing games.'

'Very well, then. Let's get straight to the point. No one knows better than you do that this marriage between my son and your daughter cannot—*dare not*—be allowed to take place.'

She took a grip on herself. 'Shall we sit down while we discuss this?'

'I prefer to stand. Shall we put our cards on the table?' he asked. He had all the advantages.

She shrugged her shoulders.

'I still have certain sources of information, Mrs Olivier. Those camera-shy pictures decided me to use them. You're a good-looking woman, photogenic. Why should you have this phobia about normal social publicity? You're a good mixer, why should you arrive in your birth place friendless? The reasons you gave seemed inadequate. They were also false. Your parents were not victims of the blitz, and your daughter is not the child of Gerhard Olivier.'

'She bears his name and in law she is his.'

'In fact, and in blood, she is the child of Lucas Wargrave.'

He was watching her closely, professionally interested in spite of himself. He was deeply outraged that this woman should have deliberately set out to do his family a great and irretrievable injury, and furious that she had tricked him. Him, of all people! But for those tell-tale press photographs she might have got away with her fraud. Even now, he did not underestimate her cunning or her fighting spirit. Would she try to placate him, her enemy? Or would she fight?

She had taken up her position in a high-backed chair, facing the window. Regal and arrogant. Her hands lay loosely in her lap, forced into a semblance of relaxation by

her will. He could feel the power of her will as he had felt
it with certain other antagonists who had crossed his path
in his secret service days.

'You don't deny it?' he pressed.

She said, with dignity:

'Perhaps you had better tell me exactly what your investigations have brought to light.'

'If you wish.'

She inclined her head slowly. She was saving her resources
putting herself into a state of suspended animation while
she made him talk, giving herself time to plan a course of
action.

'Much against your parents' will you married Lucas
Wargrave towards the end of the war, when he was an air-
gunner in Bomber Command. After Rachel – your child
and his – was born he deserted you.'

'Shall I pad out your information? Luke . . . was in a
Military Hospital in France when Rachel was born. He had
been shot down. When he came back he had changed. He
wasn't interested in . . . his wife and child.'

Sir Jasper saw that it had cost her a considerable effort to
speak the name which had not crossed her lips for over
twenty years. He continued less harshly, sparing her with
reluctant chivalry.

'After he left you and your child you formed a close
friendship with a South African Army officer, Major Gerhard Olivier. When your husband, Lucas Wargrave, was
. . . killed . . . ' He saw her blanch and close her eyes. She
covered the anguish and horror in her chalky face with her
large hands. He went on. 'When you were widowed you
immediately re-married. Your South African husband was
repatriated to his own country and you went with him,
cutting yourself off as completely as you could from the
past. Or so you hoped.'

She looked up, ugly with misery, her eyes blood-shot.
'Till now I succeeded.'

'Yes,' he agreed. 'Too well.'

He drew a pipe from his pocket and plugged it with unhurried care, 'May I?'

'Of course.'

He lit it and sat down facing her.

'Your husband, of course, knew everything?'

'Naturally.'

'Anybody else?'

'Not from me.'

'You'd have made an excellent agent,' he said. 'Unlike most women, you can stand emotional isolation.'

'I was not emotionally isolated. I had Gerhard. He was with me all the way.'

'How about Rachel?'

'She knows nothing.'

'Who decided that?'

She flashed a sudden challenge at him. 'What would you have done?'

'We'll stick to facts and leave hypothetical cases out of it.'

'All her life – we've tried to protect Rachel. From herself and from the world. We took a stand – that she should never know – and we stuck to it. Everything I said and did played towards that single goal. To keep her ignorant – to spare her and give her a fair chance. You've seen her home. You've met her . . . half-brother, Hans, and my brother-in-law, Christiaan Olivier – a good man. You know our friends and our background. Can't you put that in the scales against . . . the rest?'

He said stiffly: 'I understand that you did your best for your daughter, and you must understand that I will do my best for my son.'

She drew a deep breath and he saw her face change. He

recognised the moment of transition. She was going over from defence to attack.

'I assume that you've told Jim all that you know,' she said.

'Your assumption is incorrect. I've told Jim nothing.'

'Why not?'

When he did not reply at once she rose and stood facing him, her eyes on a level with his own. She was a tall woman and she could appear formidable. He recalled the revealing news shot in which she had 'charged' the press photographer. Sir Jasper was not easily intimidated, but he realised that he was being pushed towards quicksands. She pressed him for an answer.

'If you were satisfied that you knew everything why didn't you tell your son at once? He is the person most concerned.'

'I came to you,' he said sharply. 'I confirm my information before I pass it on.'

'Well, now you have confirmed it.' She made a sweeping gesture towards the telephone. 'Use my telephone and find your son. If he's not in his own flat he'll probably be in my daughter's. Bring him here. It's his future that's at stake, not yours.'

His eyes and his voice were steely.

'It's the future of our family – of our descendants – that's at stake.'

'Your son is of age. It's for him to decide what he means to do about this matter. He's not a child any more, to be directed by a brilliant father. Jim has a mind of his own. Very much so.'

'So have I, Mrs Olivier! Jim's judgment, in this particular case, would – as you know very well – be worse than useless. So *my* mind and *my* judgment will direct this situation.' He took a step towards her, threatening and aggressive. 'You – by every means in your power – have attempted to perpetrate a wicked, sinister fraud upon my family. You've represented your daughter in a light remote from the sordid truth, and you're not going to get away with it!'

He had drawn blood with his accusations, but she stood her ground. She clung to her point.

'In the last resort it's up to Jim.'

Her lip was away from her teeth, but it was he who held the whip. He cracked it now.

'On the contrary. It's up to you.'

'What do you mean?'

'Spirit your daughter away. Take her back to South Africa. Hide her – as you hid yourself twenty years ago – and leave Jim to get over it.'

Her eyes flashed contempt. 'What cowardice! Do you think Jim and Rachel are puppets? How could I take my daughter from her lover against her will and his? Am I to kidnap my own child?'

'There'll be no need for that. She'll go willingly – if she loves Jim. She'll go secretly, without his knowing.'

'Like a thief in the night! What are you trying to say?'

'I'm delivering an ultimatum, Mrs Olivier. You will tell Rachel the truth, the whole truth and nothing but the truth. Then offer her the chance of disappearing out of Jim's life. She'd go. I'd stake my life on that.'

'And if I refuse to do what you ask?'

'Then I will have to tell her.'

She swung round and stood staring down at the mews. It had its deserted weekend look, but the young Dixons must be home, for Flicky was sniffing the heavy tyres of Sir Jasper's Bentley and lifting his leg against the off rear wheel. The Maltese maid from the house at the end of the row tapped over the cobbles on her high heels, the pigeons wheeled and gathered for their crumbs. Mrs Olivier saw none of these things. She saw Rachel in the hour of her doom

– Rachel with her happiness turned to ashes, her faith in herself shattered and her love for Jim a sword in her heart. Oh, he was wily, this old fox whose teeth were buried in the throat of his enemy. The quality of Rachel's love for Jim was his only hope. Mrs Olivier turned her ravaged face towards him.

'This girl – my daughter – you show great faith in her, General Fleet.'

'Human nature is my business, Mrs Olivier.'

'You believe Rachel capable of supreme self-sacrifice – yet you don't find her good enough for your son.'

He considered her coldly.

'I haven't come here to plead a case, or even to prosecute. I've come to tell you what must be done. I would have liked your co-operation.'

Her laugh was bitter. 'You admit you handed me an ultimatum. Ultimatums don't invite co-operation. Capitulation would be more like it.'

'Since you put it that way, shall we go over the terms?'

She made a weary gesture. 'Go on.'

'I intend to be present when you tell Rachel.'

'No!'

He studied her, assessing the relative value of this point. Wisest, perhaps, in the long run to waive it. He thought that he could read her mind. She would try to play on Jim. He had forestalled her there.

'Perhaps you didn't know,' he said, 'but I'm picking Jim up at your daughter's flat after dinner tonight. He goes to Ravenswood with me – in my car. We return together early on Monday. I drop him in the city. Then I come here. I will be with you at ten o'clock on Monday morning. That will give you ample time – all tomorrow – to talk to Rachel and to make a plan.'

'And Jim?'

'Jim will remain in ignorance.'

'How heartless you are – how clever! You know that if you told him everything, he'd come to her at once.'

He shrugged and left her standing in the little sitting-room. Defeated? Even now he wasn't sure.

Rachel stopped little Yellow Peril on the Embankment opposite Battersea Park. The potted music was fainter here, the many-coloured lights among the trees more fairy-like. They could not distinguish the Saturday night crowd, but it was there, milling about, having fun, couples clinging to each other on the switchback or the big wheel as she and Jim had done, excited by movement and speed and the warmth of each others' bodies. Laughter of lovers, shrieks of children, Cockney voices, all were music in Rachel's enchanted ears. For her the whole world was touched with the same radiance that had set its luminous mark upon her features.

The exhilarating nip of autumn was in the September night and the golden leaves of the planes spiralled and eddied along the sidewalks and gutters in their swirling dance of the fall; reflections of lights and trees wavered in the surface of the river and the long barge-trains floated under the graceful bridges with the silent leisure of another age.

Jim watched Rachel's rapt face. He was touched, as always, by her infinite capacity for delight. She absorbed the scene, he thought, as if she feared she would never see it again, as if tomorrow she would be gone. Or blind. His arm about her shoulders tightened suddenly.

'It gives me goose-flesh when you look like that.'

She turned to him, wide-eyed. 'Like what?'

'As if you were seeing all this for the last time – as if you were afraid to miss so much as one falling leaf.'

She laughed softly. 'It's a bit the way I feel. After next week nothing will be quite the same. We'll be married. Oh, it'll be wonderful. But different. There's this moment – this on-the-threshold moment that can never come again – goodbye to one life, and hullo to another.'

The dash-board clock pointed to nine-thirty. 'Oh dear,' she said, 'we must hurry or we'll be late for your father. Rather odd, surely, his being in Town on a Saturday night.'

'It's not usual. But he does that sometimes – arranges all his London appointments and meetings in the course of one week, and stays at his club and gets it over. Anyway, he's having a new morning-coat made for the wedding. That means fittings. A pity he can't be in uniform with all his gongs, but that sort of glamour goes with the wind of retirement.'

'Not fair. Laura should have come to London with him. I'm sure he can't buy a morning-coat without her.'

Jim chuckled. 'Indeed he can! In any case, Laura has a lot to arrange at Ravenswood. Only a few days to zero hour.'

Rachel took a hand off the wheel to touch Jim's. 'Yes, she has, bless her. She's organised so much for us – all the things Ma can't do because she's a stranger. We're both frightfully grateful to Laura.'

'Listen,' he said. 'You'll have the little Yellow Peril all to yourself tomorrow, and the tank's full. Take your mother into the country for the whole day. To the river maybe. She'll like having you to herself.'

'I've arranged to go around to the cottage about eleven. We mean to go out somewhere. It's funny, we used to be so scratchy with each other. But lately it's been quite different. It's good between us now.'

When she turned into the crescent they saw that the Bentley was there before them, parked under the big tree.

'We're late,' she said.

He grinned. 'Dad's early. He's heading for home. That means I can step on it.'

'I thought he liked driving the Bentley.'

'So he does, but his night vision is atrocious. That's why I have to take him back.'

Sir Jasper refused to go in with them. He was impatient to get away.

'We've a long way to go,' he said. 'There's no time to waste.' His manner was curt.

'I'll see Rachel in,' Jim said. 'Then we'll be off.'

She fitted the key in the lock and he lifted her over the threshold. As the door closed behind them he set his back against it, still holding her in his arms. She slid down through his embrace till her feet touched the floor, but he did not let her go. In the darkness of the little hall they could not see each other.

'If I were to lose you,' he said, 'there would be nothing left.'

He felt the shiver pass through her nerves and over his own skin, bringing up the goose-pimples, shocking the breath out of his body, because for the first time in his loving of her he had admitted that one day – sometime, somehow, an end must come. He put out his hand for the light and switched it on. He cupped her face in his hands and looked down into it.

'You're lovely,' he said. 'So nearly mine! Less than a week.'

'I'm yours,' she said. 'All yours – now and always.'

14

GRIM FACE OF TRUTH

RACHEL WOKE ON SUNDAY MORNING TO THE RATTLE of the milk trolley in the crescent. It was eight o'clock and the area was a pool of primrose sunshine. She had slept soundly and she was filled with a vibrant sense of well-being.

Although a day with no chance of seeing Jim seemed a day wasted she did not resent Sir Jasper's action in taking his son down to the country. She knew that the General hated driving at night and that his Sundays at Ravenswood meant a great deal to him, and quite possibly he welcomed the opportunity of having Jim to himself just as her mother was looking forward to this day in Rachel's company. The Fleet family would go to church this morning – the dear little church where they would hear Jim's and Rachel's banns read for the third time. Next time they went to a service there it would be on the occasion of her wedding. She hugged herself, running her hands voluptuously over her own warm young body, giving it in spirit to her lover.

The little room was bare now, like the rest of the flat. Most of her baggage was already packed and out of the way, stored in the mews garage waiting to be moved in when Mrs Olivier moved out, while the things Rachel would need for her honeymoon in Jersey were nearly folded, ready to go into her air-mail suitcase at the last moment. A straw-filled packing case stood in the room Liz had occupied and Rachel's few kitchen utensils and bits of crockery and cutlery would be put into that on Friday morning. In the afternoon it would be transferred to Number Eleven the Trident, and that same day Jim would borrow Sir Jasper's Bentley to take Rachel and Mrs Olivier to the Inn at Raven Park where they were to spend the night before the wedding.

Everything was organised and in order. Rachel closed her eyes and allowed her imagination to take charge and look ahead. How lovely it was – the shimmering slipper-satin wedding gown with its tight bodice and long sleeves and full skirt! So simple and so absolutely *right*. She was in it now, with the orange-blossom holding the veil in place on her fair hair. Jenny, in an ice-blue dress, was holding up her train as she walked slowly up the aisle on the arm of her tall young brother, Hans, who would be at London Airport on Wednesday morning. And there, waiting for her in the church, was Jim, very straight and formal, beside his best man, the Naval Lieutenant whose cruiser was due back from the Mediterranean the day after tomorrow. The strains of the Wedding March were in her ears. Her great day was drawing very near.

Suddenly Rachel decided that she was famished. Her hollow tummy clamoured for a proper breakfast and she would not deny it.

She flung back the covers and sprang out of bed. The air was mild. No need to pull on a dressing-gown. She went into the kitchen in her short nightie, filled the kettle, and put a pan to warm on the gas-ring. Presently the tempting fragrance of coffee and fried bacon permeated the flat.

She sang as she opened the front door and brought in the paper and the milk. She glanced at the headlines. Earthquake in Asia Minor. Avalanche in Alps, six killed. UNO condemns *apartheid* – well, that was hardly news! Actress found dead after quarrel with fiancé, an empty bottle of sleeping tablets beside her. They were always doing that, poor things. Why couldn't they wait till the morning and make up the quarrel? She flung the paper on her unmade bed; she'd read it later between breakfast and her bath. That was one of Sunday's pleasures, not having to get up in a hurry. She took her little transistor into the kitchen. Egg and bacon always tasted the better for music. The weather promised well. Where would she take her mother? Jim had suggested the river. Bray perhaps. Or might it be nicer to picnic in some quiet place? She could fix up a picnic lunch in no time. When she'd cleared away the breakfast things she filled a thermos with steaming hot coffee and cut some sandwiches. There was ham and chicken in the fridge and a lettuce over from yesterday's lunch. She filled the tin containers and packed them with the thermos in the narrow wicker basket she and Jim always used and placed it ready in the little hall.

Rachel saw that it was nearly half past nine by the kitchen clock. Later than she'd thought. After all there wouldn't be time to go back to bed and read the paper from beginning to end. She sang in her bath for the sheer joy of living, and slipped into navy blue slacks and the sky-blue pullover that was Jim's favourite. Need she make the bed? No. Why not 'air' it for the day? She was humming the lastest dance tune as she picked up the paper and opened it. Might as well skim through it. See what gives.

So it was that very suddenly, and utterly without warning, Rachel's world came to an end.

Page three carried the paragraph that stopped her heart.

SOCIETY WEDDING FOR WARGRAVE'S DAUGHTER

'James Fleet, son of General Sir Jasper Fleet, K.C.B., etc., creator of Gerald Bourne, Secret Agent, will wed

Rachel Olivier next Friday in the tenth century church
of Raven Park near the Fleet family estate of Ravenswood. James Fleet's bride to be – adopted in infancy by
her South African farmer step-father, Gerhard Olivier
– was born in London, the daughter of Group Captain
Lucas Wargrave and his wife, Ann. Wargrave was
executed eighteen months later for the murder of
Amy Caxton, then serving in the A.T.S. Two other
victims met a similar fate at Wargrave's hands.'

Rachel slumped on to the bed. Her hands and face were
drenched in icy sweat and her teeth chattered. She felt
deathly ill. Just before she blacked out she managed to pull
the blankets over her.

When she came to the telephone was ringing. Let it ring.
She was still cold to the marrow of her bones but the sweat
was drying on her forehead and palms. Gradually the many
implications of what she had read began to filter painfully
into her consciousness like creeping poison. The telephone
had stopped ringing and the little flat was silent as the slow
stream of agony filled every particle of Rachel's being.

Confusion fogged her brain, but beneath it lay a thread of
hope. This horror wasn't true. It couldn't be! Her father –
Gerhard Olivier – surely she had belonged to him? And to
Môreson. Hans. He *must* be her full brother. They had been
so close – all three of them. This story was a monstrous lie.
But, dear God, if it were true, if the blood of a murderer –
such a murderer – ran in her veins, it was the end for Jim and
for her. She could never have children, nor even trust herself.
A dreadful mania might lie dormant in her blood, her blood
that was cold and cringing now as if the taint of evil chilled it.

Lucas Wargrave. Everybody knew that name, that handsome face. He stood in his Air Force uniform in that sinister
hall of fame – the Waxworks Chamber of Horrors – a wax

figure of great and terrible attraction, the brave air-gunner who had other ways of killing too.

Rachel began to shiver again in the grip of a loathing worse than fear. When next she looked at herself in the glass would she see Rachel Olivier, the girl she had always believed herself to be? Or would she see the daughter of a man whose unspeakable crimes had earned him a lurid claim to fame?

The sun had passed from the area and the hands of the clock showed ten minutes past eleven. The telephone was ringing again, insistent, drilling into her nerves. Who was it? Jim? Her mother? She didn't care.

Jim. If this were true – if she really was the child of Lucas Wargrave – she must never see Jim again. Only one person could tell her the facts. She must go to her mother at once. She must find out the truth. She dragged herself up, still shivering in the grip of this arctic inner cold, and slipped on a loose woollen jacket. She folded the paper tidily, and the foolish chocolate-box face of the dead actress looked at her from the front page. Rachel stared back at it with new understanding. 'There are things one can't take,' she said to the face. 'I know that now.'

Automatically she closed and bolted the windows and picked up the picnic basket in the hall. She climbed the area steps with leaden limbs and got into little Yellow Peril. She put the picnic basket in its accustomed place and started up the engine. In a very short time now – in a matter of minutes – she would know the truth. The thin ray of hope still shone through the clouds.

Mrs Olivier had not seen the newspaper story, but she was worried. Rachel was late and although she had telephoned the flat twice she had received no reply. She knew that this morning it was her duty to tell her daughter the whole tragic truth, and, though she dreaded the task, it was a relief to hear little Yellow Peril turn into the mews. The sooner she got it over the better.

She was on the landing to meet Rachel, but the moment she saw her daughter's anguished face she knew that the worst had happened. Somehow Mrs Olivier had been forestalled, and Rachel knew.

Mrs Olivier took the paper the girl held out to her mutely. She scanned the cruel paragraph with growing anger and dismay.

'How shocking! How could they do this – and you quite innocent!'

'Tell me it isn't true! Say it's all a dreadful lie!'

Mrs Olivier put her arm about the tembling girl and led her into the bedroom.

'Sit down,' she said.

Rachel sat on the bed, her head in her hands.

'You don't answer me, Ma.'

'What can I say? The facts in the paper are true. But can't you see that's only a fraction of the truth? One tiny fraction. His life interlocked with mine for a few weeks. That was all.'

'You were married.'

'Yes. I loved him then.'

Rachel was shuddering violently. 'It might have been you . . .'

'No! It was later that he – changed.'

'They hanged him'

'It wasn't right.'

'You say so. Only you. I know the case. Who doesn't? It's one of the famous trials. Lucas Wargrave, the pitchfork killer! They called him that because he slashed his victims with a devilish sign – and that man was my father! It can't be true . . .' she began to cry hysterically.

Mrs Olivier spoke sharply.

'Rachel! Be quiet! Your true father was Gerhard. He loved you as deeply as if you had been his own. He brought you up as his, and he would have given anything in life to save you this.'

'You should have told me. Long ago. I would have made my life . . . some other way . . . not hoped for marriage and children, like a normal girl.'

'Such morbid knowledge – such a cross to bear! We only wanted to save you, to let you grow up your sane, healthy, happy self.'

Rachel looked up suddenly, her eyes wild and wounded.

'You were afraid for me. Suspicious of my blood. I see it all now. Now I know why you hated me, why you scolded me, watched me and never trusted me! You used to make me feel guilty, different from other girls. I *was* different. I *am* different.'

'Hated you? I! If anything, I loved you too much. Don't dramatise this tragedy, my darling. It happened a long time ago –'

'But it happened to *me*! You were his wife, and you are still *you*. Unchanged. I am his child. Hans's children will be clean. Mine – if I had any – would be tainted. Possibly criminal, lunatic, dangerous to humanity – lepers!'

She was racked by dry sobs, a storm without rain, electric and destructive, blessed by neither comfort nor benefit.

'Oh, God . . . they'll have seen it at Ravenswood now . . . Jim will know!'

Mrs Olivier tried to hold her daughter in her arms, but Rachel shook her off.

'Why did you come to England? Why did you have to let me learn the truth in this dreadful shameful way? You brought it on me – from start to finish. *You*!'

She buried her face in the pillow and lay gasping.

The telephone was ringing. Mrs Olivier rose.

'I'm going to answer that in the sitting-room. It may be Jim.'

Rachel's sobs subsided. The storm was passing, leaving in its wake the arid desolation of unrelieved drought. She heard her mother's voice.

'A trunk call? Yes.'

Rachel put out her hand and lifted the receiver from the telephone extension next to the bed. She heard Jim's voice.

'Mrs Olivier, have you seen – '

'Yes, I don't understand how it came to be written. I know nothing about it.'

'My father tells me it's true.'

'Yes.'

'Does Rachel know?'

'She's only just found out. She's terribly upset. Quite desperate.'

'I'm coming to her. Tell her I'll be with her just as soon as it's possible. We only saw it when we got back from church. I'm taking Laura's car and I'm leaving home now.'

'I'll tell her. You'll find her here.'

When Mrs Olivier returned to the bedroom her daughter was still holding the receiver in her hand. She seemed dazed but quiet.

'Then you heard that, Rachel?'

She took the receiver from the girl and put it back on the hook. Rachel said:

'Yes. He's on his way.'

'He loves you.'

At long last Rachel's eyes brimmed and overflowed. She wept. After a time she lay with her eyes closed, as if asleep. A surge of hope and relief swept over Mrs Olivier. She brought a jug of water and a glass, Rachel opened her eyes and her mother saw that they were no longer wild.

'A drink of water?'

Rachel gulped it down gratefully.

'Can you rest a while? Jim will be here in just over an hour. Sunday morning into London is easy.'

'Yes. Leave me, Ma. I want to be alone – to rest.'

Not to rest, but to think.

Jim was on his way. Jim intended to stand by her. Out of loyalty. But Jim had another love. He had Ravenswood. He wanted a son for Ravenswood. How could he go on loving Rachel, knowing that now they dared never have that son? Love would turn into reproach. It could not be otherwise. She would be worse than a barren woman; she would be a woman suspect, one whose every mood would be under observation. That was how it had been in her childhood. She knew – how well she knew – what it was like to be watched! The tempers and tantrums of childhood, the infatuations of adolescence had never been taken for granted in her case. They had been laced with peculiar problems and dangers. She had been studied lest she display abnormalities. She shuddered. No wonder her relationship with her mother had been warped and prickly, apprehensive on one side, resentful on the other.

What would happen to her relationship with Jim after this? They'd had their tiffs, their sky-high flare-ups, and laughed about them afterwards. Her nature was hot and quick – 'gloriously inflammable' he'd called her – and he'd loved her for it. Would he find it less lovable now? A little menacing, perhaps. As lovers they'd known ecstasy, an intensity of joy in each other which neither had ever questioned. Yet now she was afraid of her own passions. She was afraid of the future, of the inevitable distortion of their love that had hitherto been uncomplicated, as much a part of their own private atmosphere as the weather and the seasons. The climate of their love was warm, and spring-like, its character fertile and bountiful. It was unthinkable that she should deny Jim children and herself a family because she was tainted by the laws of heredity. I should ring a little bell, she thought. Unclean! Unclean! She lay very still while the sad dangerous reflections soaked into the depths of her consciousness.

Mrs Olivier heard her daughter moan and went to her in quick anxiety.

'What is it?'

Rachel sat, propped up on her elbow. She looked as if she had wakened from sleep.

'Ma, I crave some tea – tea and dry toast.'

'I'll make it now.'

Mrs Olivier didn't trust her daughter's calm appearance. She knew that it was a coating of thin ice over deep disturbed waters where thoughts met and dispersed in darkness and gathered again to formulate a plan. But at least the suggestion of hysteria had evaporated and in its place there was an exhausted composure. As she was about to leave the room Rachel called to her.

'Please turn on the kitchen radio! Loud, so that I can hear. It should be time for the news any moment.'

'Darling, you don't have to worry. All that . . . newspaper stuff . . . it won't be on the radio.'

'I expect not, Ma. But put it on just the same while you make the tea and toast. And, please, will you butter the toast?'

'Of course.'

Mrs Olivier went to the kitchen and turned up the radio so that it could be heard in the bedroom. She longed for Jim to arrive. It was very important for Jim to convince Rachel that her life was not over. But would he be robust enough to stand against scandal, notoriety, and bitter parental disapproval? By now everybody would have passed the story around, one way or another. Mrs Shane, the Ravenswood help, had pointed it out to Laura. The Raffertys next door would know, even Colin, the little boy – 'Gee! Was Mrs Olivier really married to a *murderer*?' – and Mrs Meadows, of course, whose old man would say, 'Your Mrs Olivier kept some queer company in her day! And what about the girl?' The young Dixons would have seen it through sleepy after-party eyes that would suddenly jerk wide open. Mr Ferrit and his mad sister would gloat over it. Mrs Olivier put her hand to her head, hearing once again the cracked voice 'You're one of Ernie's people – he collects people like you . . . ' A thought drifted by and she almost caught it. Later she'd chase up that thought. And Cheryl, yes, of course Cheryl would read it too. Oh, God, it was a news story, it would flash across the ether to South Africa. The Johannesburg Sunday papers would carry it. Hans. Christiaan. It might get radio coverage there. And Hans due to fly from Johannesburg to London in two days' time! The Carstairs family would read it on board the mail boat in the Radio News Sheet. She felt the scandal snowballing by the minute. The kettle was whistling above the voice of the radio announcer. She warmed the tea-pot, put in the tea – rather strong – filled it and allowed it to stand. She cut the bread and slid it into the toaster. As she did so something touched her legs and she jumped.

'Lucifer, you!' The cat smiled up at her and trilled.

'Now, how did you get in?' she asked. 'I could swear Rachel closed the door after her this morning. She slammed it, in fact! And no one else has come in.'

She was just about to butter the toast when a cold draught blew up Jacob's ladder and straight into Mrs Olivier's heart. She was never certain, afterwards, if that icy blast really came from outside or whether it was the breath of fear and premonition of tragedy.

She ran down the stairs to the wide-open door and out into the mews.

She was just in time to see little Yellow Peril turn the corner of the Trident and disappear from sight.

15

THE MOON IS RED

WHEN RACHEL TURNED OUT OF THE TRIDENT TO-
wards the Cromwell Road she had no idea where she was
heading. Only one thing was clear in her mind. She must
get away – far from London, further still from Ravenswood
– and then, out into the country among meadows and trees.
There she must stop and think.

Soon she found herself speeding along the Western
Avenue, following the signposts for Oxford and the North.
She was an experienced driver, and, even now, in the
deadening aftermath of shock, she was in control of
Yellow Peril. Towns, factories, aerodromes and villages
flashed by and were left behind in their half-rural half-
urban pattern of fields and gardens, fly-overs and filling-
stations. Suddenly Rachel felt she was travelling like a hen
on a white line, mesmerically unable to assert her will and
change her course. She must get away from the great arteries,
from traffic and people, into a place of peace.

She turned right-handed off A.40, neither observing nor
caring where the leafy lane might lead. It was winding and
shadowy between high hedgerows and meadows where
cows ruminated tranquilly and horses grazed. A stream
snaked through a valley, and Rachel thought, *Water*. She'd
need water. She'd forgotten that. Green pastures and a
stream, scent of leaf-mould and bonfires. What more could
she want?

She was going slowly in low gear when the incident

occurred. A spaniel puppy, followed by a boy and a girl of about eight and ten, ran out of a concealed drive. Rachel braked and swerved to avoid the dog, but she felt the impact of the body against the back wheel, and the next moment the animal, more frightened than hurt, was tearing down the road ahead, yapping hysterically, lead flying, ears flapping. Rachel stopped the car and the children clambered into it.

'Please go after Honey quickly!' begged the boy. His older sister added: 'Mummy said we mustn't take her out, except on a lead. But she jerked it out of my hand.'

'We'll get her back,' said Rachel.

Fortunately the spaniel stuck to the lane and they found her, eventually, crouching under a hedge, panting and terrified, tongue lolling. The children fondled and soothed her. Rachel said:

'Well, anyway, she isn't hurt. Do you want me to take you home?'

'Oh no,' said the girl. 'We were only going for a walk. We'll take her home across the fields.'

The boy, who was kneeling beside the dog, looked up with a quick, toothless grin.

'It was jolly decent of you to help us catch her. It wasn't your fault she bumped into you, and it was fun for us to drive in your car.'

The girl glanced enviously at Yellow Peril. 'We've never been in a sports car before. Did you come from London?'

'Yes,' said Rachel.

'Where are you going?' asked the boy.

'I don't know,' said Rachel.

The children stared. Then they laughed. 'Is it a secret?' they chorused.

'More or less.'

'Shall we guess? Is it far?'

'It's far,' said Rachel. 'About as far as you can go.'

'I know, Land's End,' hazarded the boy.

'That's about it.'

'We were in Cornwall once for a holiday,' said the girl. 'And we went to Land's End. It's an awfully lonely place.'

Suddenly Rachel felt tears smarting in her eyes. She swallowed hard.

'I guess it is. Well, goodbye, you two. I'm glad Honey's all right.'

'Goodbye,' they called.

In her driving mirror she saw them looking after her, the boy with the puppy in his arms and the girl waving.

'It'll be dark when she gets there,' said the girl.

Her brother knew better. 'There's a full moon tonight. A harvest moon. Tonight the moon is red.'

A lost bemused smile touched Rachel's lips. Where would they look for her when she failed to return? Land's End? How could they find her when she herself knew neither her destination nor her destiny. Both were in the hands of fate. Jim would be anxious. So would her mother. Jim. His love for Rachel had brought only shame and scandal into his home. To her mother she had always been a problem. She saw that now. She followed the up-hill down-dale country road and branched off along narrow tracks leading she knew not where, and presently she was tempted by a gap in the hedge. Yellow Peril seemed to Rachel to find the way into that gap of her own accord. So it's here, she thought. This is the lonely place. But the time is not quite yet. The little car had come to a standstill in the lee of a high hedge on the fringe of a freshly reaped hayfield which rose steeply to a wood, thin and sparse in its tags of ruby and gold. An orchard, stripped of its fruit, separated the field from the stream further down the valley. The air was loaded with the pungent scent of leaves and stubble, unpolluted and whole-some. Suddenly Rachel thought of the picnic basket she had prepared so cheerfully this morning for her mother and herself. This morning? A thousand years ago. She reached for it and poured some hot coffee from the thermos. As she nibbled at a sandwich she discovered that she was hungry and glad of the chicken meat too.

The afternoon sun was warm but the grassy verge was still damp from a recent shower. Rachel took the ground-sheet which Jim always carried in Yellow Peril and spread it beside the car. She lay down on it, flat on her face, her head buried in her arms, the sun on her back. When she woke from the deep dreamless sleep of emotional exhaus-tion she saw that the shadows were already long on the grass. She felt wonderfully rested and calm, as if in her sleep all her problems had been resolved.

She left the car and climbed the hill towards the wood. She no longer wondered about her journey's end. She was steeped in profound fatalism. There were a few details still to be worked out, of course, but she would do that up there in the wood with this soft green world at her feet. Her brain was lucid, strangely apart from herself, directing her behaviour with unnatural detachment. She stood at the edge of the wood and looked out over the green fields con-tained by their flowering hedgerows and watered by the river and its tributaries. The scene, so typically English, was softened by the blur of woods and dells. Rachel absorbed it with nostalgic satisfaction as the memory of another wood on another hillside stole over her. A spring storm, fires of passion blazing high, gulls over the Channel. Ravenswood. The peacock and his mate in the walled garden, the pea-cock's frantic courting cries in the dawn, 'Healp . . . oo-ow-oo-ow . . . ' and the glittering spread of his tail. Well, the peafowl had babies now – leggy blond chickens. Only last weekend Rachel and Jim had laughed together, watching the mother putting her children to bed. She had flown to her roost on a leafy bough, calling the babies to follow her. When they refused she came back to fetch them, and they had jumped on to her back and taken a piggy-back upstairs to bed in the tree. Jim had said, 'I hope they survive the winter.'

Alone on the hillside, Rachel shrugged her shoulders, remote now from questions and answers, unmoved by problems great or small. The silver glimmer of the stream in the valley caught her attention. It wasn't far from where she had left the car, only a few minutes' walk. Sleek cattle grazed in the lush water-meadows down there and a fisherman sat on the bank. How peaceful he looked! Somewhere in a fold of the hills distant church-bells chimed the hour of Evensong. Rachel wandered down the hill in her unhurried far-away mood. She had lost all sense of personal identity. She was no one in particular any more, neither Ann Olivier's daughter nor Jim Fleet's bride to be. She belonged to no one and no place. The empty Transvaal veld, the swelling Sussex Downs, the London crescent and the Trident were all one to her. She was anonymous, part of this quiet countryside, though she did not even know what county it might be. Bucks? Oxfordshire? What matter? It was the heart of the whirlwind, the place of peace the place she had sought for her purpose.

The sun had gone off the Trident and still Rachel had not returned. Nor had the little yellow car been seen outside the crescent since she had driven it away that morning. It had not appeared outside Jim's flat, or at Ravenswood. Where could she have gone? Mrs Olivier had asked the question of Jim and of herself countless times in countless forms.

'She knew you were on your way. We were expecting you. It makes no sense.'

'That's what frightens me.' Jim lit a cigarette from the stub of the one he had been smoking and began to pace again. 'From what you told me she . . . did a sort of bolt. Got you to put on the radio in the kitchen so that you wouldn't hear her slip out. She meant to avoid me. It was quite deliberate.'

'She was very shocked and desperate at one time this morning. But when I left her to make the tea she seemed quite calm. Rational and sensible.'

'It's no wonder she was shocked, poor girl! It wasn't much fun for us at Ravenswood either. Why, in God's name, didn't you tell me everything long ago? I was the one with the right to know.'

His eyes blazed in their deep bruised sockets. His face was gaunt, the skin stretched taut over the prominent bones.

'Recriminations won't help, Jim.'

'I know. The point at issue is whether we should inform the police.'

'And add to the publicity we've already received. Rachel's picture in the paper as a missing person. Her name. The circumstances of her flight.'

'I think we should consult my father. He has friends in the Special Branch – '

'Your father will be delighted that Rachel is out of the way!' she said bitterly. 'He wanted her to disappear. He went so far as to urge me to make arrangements for her to disappear. We'll get no help from him.' She put a hand to her aching forehead and pushed back the heavy dark hair. 'It's nearly seven o'clock. Pour me a Scotch and soda, Jim. I'm going to get an aspirin, my head is bursting.'

She went into her bedroom and opened the drawer of the bedside table. The aspirins were there in their tinfoil strips.

She crushed two into a medicine glass and put the rest back. She must get some water, yet she did not move. Something held her in the bedroom. Something was troubling her, but for the life of her she could not think what it was that struck a faint warning note in her consciousness. She sat on the edge of the bed, holding her throbbing head between her hands. Perhaps she'd better take three while she was at it. She opened the drawer once more, and it was then that the warning bell suddenly clanged through all her nerves like a fire alarm, hideous, discordant, dangerously significant. Aspirin and headache were swept out of her mind, she went through the drawer with trembling fingers. Dear God, let me find them! Let them be here!

'Jim!'

He met her on the landing. She stood swaying in the doorway, her eyes distraught.

'We must tell the police without delay! Immediately.'

He took a step towards her and put a supporting arm round her.

'What is it?'

'My barbiturates – my sleeping tablets – they're missing. The bottle was more than half full. *They're missing*, Jim!'

The fisherman on the river bank had put away his tackle and his catch, two fine perch. He moved stiffly, for he was old and full of rheumatism.

He saw the girl in slacks and a blue pullover kneeling on the bank, trying to fill a thermos flask with water.

'That's not the best drinking water,' he said gruffly.

She sat back on her heels and regarded him with a puzzled frown. In the fading light he thought she had a lovely face, but there was something written upon it that troubled him. He was a bit of a crank, a bit of a poet in an old-fashioned way. As he looked at Rachel he thought of the Lady of Shalott, and wondered why.

'It doesn't matter,' she said, gently.

'Oh yes, it does, young lady. Look, I'm on my way home, so you can have this.'

He offered her a bottle of clear water.

'Thank you,' she said. 'That's kind of you.'

'It's safe. I've got a phobia about water. A very dangerous drink – if it isn't filtered.'

She smiled as she took the bottle from him. 'You're very thoughtful.' She emptied the thermos on to the grass.

'Now are you satisfied?'

He nodded approval. 'You're camping near here?'

'Not far,' she said.

'My car's over there. Round the bend of the river. Want a lift anywhere?'

He pointed away from the hayfield where Yellow Peril was parked in the lee of the high hedge.

'No, thank you.' She seemed to hesitate for a moment. 'My friend is waiting for me over in the opposite direction.'

He bade her good-evening and she watched him wander on along the river bank, round the curve and out of sight. A lame old man, homeward bound.

'My friend?' she whispered to herself. 'My friend . . . is waiting.' Although she was not afraid she could not bring herself to say the name of the dark friend.

In the car? Or beside it? No, not in Jim's car. Not fair to Jim to spoil so many good memories. She knelt down and straightened the ground-sheet on which she had slept so soundly earlier in the afternoon. She would sleep there again. Tonight. She wondered how it would feel – the thing she meant to do. She mustn't make a mess of it. There were a great many capsules to get down. Perhaps she should have the water ready so as to get it over quickly before the first ones took effect. How fast would they work? You read about an overdose but the papers never told you much about the practical side of it. You had to guess at numbers. Twenty, thirty, forty? She had no idea how many the bottle contained. Enough, she reckoned, and that was all that mattered. She recalled the time she'd gone with Laura Fleet to the church bazaar at Raven Park. There'd been a bottle like this, only bigger. Transparent and half full of beans, and you had to guess the number of beans. Her guess had been nowhere near the mark. Laura's, on the other hand, had been pretty good.

There were two plastic mugs in her picnic-basket and there was also the lid of the thermos. She filled each with water and stood them carefully on the grass beside the ground-sheet, scooping hollows for them so that they would not upset.

She slipped on her woollen jacket, for it was growing cold. The sun had set and in the east, behind a scroll of branches, the full moon rose like a huge Japanese lantern. Enormous, glowing, raspberry-red.

Land's End the little boy had said. It was the farthest place he could think of, and his sister had added, 'It's an awfully lonely place.' Yes, it was awfully lonely – this world's end to which she had come – but no less lonely than life with no Jim, no children, no future. She said aloud to the harvest moon:

'God, if I'm breaking Your law, forgive me.'

She inhaled deep gulps of the cool night air, the pure country air she loved. Then she knelt on the ground-sheet and opened her bag. The night breeze rustled the leaves in the hedgerow, an owl hooted and a cloud crossed the face of the moon.

It was quite simple. She shovelled the little pink torpedoes into her mouth in twos and threes. They went down easily enough, and the water was adequate. She lay back. The cloud had passed upon its way. The huge face of the moon stared down at her. It was the last thing she saw – that great raspberry moon with the shadowed shapes upon it. Her heart was thumping now, faster, faster, louder, louder, hammering in her chest and in her ears, rocking her to pieces like a great locomotive. There was a tingling in her fingers and toes, and now, too late, she was afraid.

'Help me, God! Please help me!'

Her prayer was lost in the thundering night – the night that was red as blood.

16

REACTIONS

MR AND MRS HUGHES HAD BEEN PLAYING BRIDGE with friends in the next village and the last rubber had been the battle of the evening. So it was nearly midnight when they set out for home under the full moon which was now no longer red but a silver so luminous that the blanched countryside lay deeply tranced under its radiance.

Mrs Hughes turned on the wireless and was just in time to hear the last news and a police appeal. Would anyone able to give information about a yellow M.G. sports car number 621 DMX, driven by a fair-haired young woman of light build, probably wearing navy blue slacks and a blue pullover, please telephone 999 without delay. It was a matter of very great urgency.

'Well!' said Mrs Hughes. 'What's the blonde been up to? Robbing the Bank of England?'

'A yellow M.G. sports? That's funny, weren't the kids talking about a girl in a yellow sports car?'

Mrs Hughes sat up very straight.

'So they were! Honey was touched by the wheel of the car and ran away and the girl told the children to get in and they chased the dog. Joyce said the girl was on her way to Land's End.'

They were silent, turning the matter over in their minds. Mr Hughes drove a little faster. 'I think we should get back and report it.'

'We must wake the children. Micky may even remember

the number. Where cars are concerned he has a fantastic memory. Photographic. And Joyce will certainly be able to tell us what the girl was wearing and how she did her hair.'

The Sergeant of the Oxfordshire Constabulary who interviewed the Hughes family at one o'clock on Monday morning was soon convinced that the children had indeed driven with Rachel Olivier in the yellow sports car, but he could not shake their story that she was on her way to Cornwall.

'We talked about Land's End,' said Joyce, 'because we'd been there ourselves. That's where she was going. She said so.'

'This young lady was proceeding from London,' said the Sergeant. 'She must have travelled on the Oxford road. That's the opposite direction from Cornwall.'

'She might have changed her mind,' said Micky. 'She didn't seem to care much where she went.'

The Sergeant scratched his head. 'Did she seem upset?'

'She was sort of sad looking,' said Joyce.

'Yes,' agreed Micky, digging his fists deep into the pockets of his new camel-hair dressing-gown. 'When my sister said Land's End was a lonely place I thought this girl was going to cry.'

The Sergeant took his leave and the children were hustled back to bed by their parents.

Colonel Barker listened to the seven o'clock news while he drank his morning tea – the best cup of the day.

The police appeal was repeated, but this time listeners were informed that the yellow M.G. had been reported in Oxfordshire and might have been seen in Cornwall.

A blue pullover, fair hair, light build. Colonel Barker had seen no yellow M.G., but he had seen a girl answering to the description – a girl with sad haunting eyes. He had

given her his bottle of water down by the river and he had
felt a distinct qualm at leaving her. But she had said her
friend was waiting for her. Something about her had made
him think of the Lady of Shalott. Now what? Ah, yes
. . . 'And they cross'd themselves for fear, All the knights at
Camelot: But Lancelot mused a little space; He said, "She
has a lovely face, God in his mercy lend her grace, The
Lady of Shalott." '

Colonel Barker climbed painfully out of bed and hurried
to the telephone as fast as his rheumatism allowed. He told
the police what he knew. The officer to whom he spoke was
interested. The time and the place at which the Colonel had
encountered the girl suggested that she might certainly be
the driver of the yellow M.G. and, if so, it also established
the fact that she had been alive and well up to seven-thirty
on Sunday night.

So it was that a police van lurched through the gap in the
hedge soon after seven-thirty on that misty Monday morning, exactly twelve hours after Colonel Barker had given
Rachel the water bottle. Little Yellow Peril stood guard
over her like a faithful horse. The bonnet was damp and
slippery with mizzle and so was the grass. The girl lying
on the ground-sheet was cold and very still. The water
bottle lay overturned near her hand with two plastic mugs,
the thermos top and the small empty bottle that had once
contained pink capsules.

'Looks like we may be too late,' said the Sergeant, as he
went on one knee to take her wrist and seek the pulse of life.

Christiaan Olivier and his nephew had finished their
evening meal at Môreson and the Bantu maid had brought
coffee on to the stoep. Hans looked at his watch as he had
done every few minutes during the past hour.

'Seven-forty,' he said. 'Twenty more minutes to go.'

His uncle helped himself to coffee. 'The call might be late.'

'It'll be twenty to six in London now. We're two hours ahead here.'

'For God's sake, man, stop pacing about like a lion in the zoo. You give me the jumps.'

'I'm sorry,' said Hans. 'I've got the twitch myself. What am I to do about tomorrow's flight? There'll be no wedding, but I think I ought to go just the same.'

Christiaan refrained from saying that there might well be a funeral. Instead he put a horny hand heavily on his nephew's shoulder.

'Your Ma may need you. We must wait till the call comes through. Then you can decide. We'll know more when we've talked to her.'

All they knew at present was what they had heard over the wireless on the six o'clock news – that Rachel Olivier had been found early that morning in a hayfield in a deep coma, suffering from an overdose of sleeping tablets. She had been taken to a London hospital in a critical condition. A cable from Ann Olivier, sent earlier in the day, had confirmed the report. Now they awaited her telephone call.

Hans's mood was shocked and excitable. He was angry with his mother and his uncle and the world at large. Poor Ray!

'Oom Christiaan, you knew all along about my mother's past marriage. Why didn't you tell me? I'm the man of the family now. I should have been told.'

'It was your Ma's business. She told no one except your father.'

'She told you.'

'Nee, my boy. She told me nothing. It was your Pa who told me shortly before he died. He reckoned your Ma should have one friend to share that knowledge with her. When first she realised that I knew everything she was angry. Afterwards it was a relief.'

'The Fleets . . . when they were here . . . oughtn't you to have said something to the General?'

'If I'd given him so much as a hint he'd have done everything in his power to stop the marriage.'

'Well, then, Jim should have known. It was wrong to keep him in the dark.'

'Who are you to judge?'

'If I were Jim Fleet I'd feel cheated not to be told. Not to be trusted.'

'You've seen what the shock's done to your sister . . . '

'Ja, I can imagine what it meant to Ray to learn a thing like that! Dammit, we know in this country what black blood can do to a family. It's always there, ready to come out, it may skip generations and then suddenly there's a dark one – one you can't mistake. It must be the same with other inherited features. How can Rachel have children – knowing who her father was – *what he was*? How can she risk transmitting that sort of madness to her descendants?'

Christiaan plugged his pipe and stood for a while in silence looking away out to the far hills dark under the Milky Way and the Southern Cross. The first rains had broken and the veld was a lush carpet starred with flowers and fragrant with the scent of spring. A loom of moonlight silvered the eastern sky although the great disc had not yet risen above the horizon. At last he turned to his nephew.

'You young people see everything without shadows. Black and white. Sane and insane. Good and evil. It's never as simple as that.'

Both men started as the telephone shrilled in the *voorkamer*. Hans was at the instrument in a few leaping strides.

'Mr Hans Olivier? . . . stand by for London. Mrs Olivier on the line . . . '

Hans heard his mother's voice as clearly as if she were in the room with them. There was a faint buzzing accompaniment but not enough to disturb audibility.

'Hans, your sister's condition is unchanged. She's still in a coma. But there's hope.'

'What are they doing for her, Ma?'

'Everything possible is being done for her. Everything.'

'Ma, you sound done in. Are *you* all right?'

'I've had very little sleep in the past twenty-four hours. I've been at the hospital all day. But I'm home now and they'll call me if there's any change. Jim is here with me. He's staying here.'

'Jim? I'm glad. How have his folks taken it – General and Lady Fleet?'

'Not well. It's impossible to blame them.'

'Look, Ma, I know the wedding's off, whatever happens to Ray, but I'm going to take that plane tomorrow. I guess you need me.'

'Yes, come to me,' she said. 'Come, darling. And now is Christiaan there?'

Hans handed the receiver to his uncle. The older man's voice was gruff with emotion.

'Annetjie, keep up your heart. When do they think Rachel might come round?'

'There's no knowing. Perhaps tomorrow, perhaps the next day . . . if at all . . .'

He saw her through her voice – the matt drawn face, coarsened by strain and sleeplessness. He could hear the unshed tears in her throat and feel the weight of her heart transfer itself like a physical load to his own.

'Annetjie, I'm with you in thought. And if that's not enough Bronkhorst can manage here for a bit and I'll come to you.'

'Thank you, Chris. I know you mean it. I'm too tired to

think now. I only want Rachel to get better so that I can bring her home to Môreson. I must bring her home, Chris.'

'You will, my girl. Have faith. Here's Hans again.'

There were hasty farewells cut short by the relentless pips followed by the sick frustration of nearness achieved and severed. Hans put down the receiver slowly and went back on to the stoep and out into the starry night beyond. He felt helpless and far from those he loved most. Mountains and oceans separated the Transvaal and Trident Mews. Seven thousand miles of dark infinity stretched between him and Ray, between Môreson and the hospital ward where his sister lay in the profound oblivion that was the ante-room to death.

Christiaan, standing alone on the stoep, saw the tall figure of his nephew silhouetted against the light of the rising moon, but he made no move to join Hans in the garden. He knew that the young man would be thinking about Rachel, resenting his mother and blaming her for whatever might befall his sister. Hans could not be expected to understand the sacrifices Ann had made for her daughter's sake, or to realise that to enter and maintain her dedicated state of secrecy had required her to alter the course of her entire life. She had been forced to forego every close or intimate relationship she might be tempted to form, since an exchange of confidences is an essential – if dangerous – ingredient of friendship. She had, in her youth, been gay and gregarious. yet she had married a man much older than herself with whom she had gone to live in an out-of-the-way place far from the city lights – a place which she had grown to love. She had made an admirable fist of it and Rachel had turned out a fine girl. But now all her efforts had gone for nothing. Worse, they had led to a tragic act and possibly even to the death of the girl she had tried

M

to the best of her ability to save from the consequences of her father's sins.

Christiaan sighed heavily. His pipe was dead. He knocked it out and slipped it into his pocket. How well he recalled the day when Gerhard had brought them to Môreson, the dark young wife and the child with the silvery hair they had all believed to be Gerhard's own. Those few who might have known or guessed the truth had kept it to themselves and the secret had been buried and obliterated by the years. That first day at Môreson Ann had come towards Christiaan, hands outstretched, a strong supple girl with a gipsy face alight with glowing health. Her black hair had gleamed in the sun and the warmth of her smile had taken his breath away.

'You're Chris,' she had said. 'My new brother!'

Then she had laughed and her eyes had flashed before she'd looked away. She had known, even then, that he did not feel like her brother and never would. But that knowledge, like so much else, had remained forbidden territory between them.

He went down the steps into the spring night.

'Totsiens,' he called to Hans. 'Ring me from London when you have news. Reverse the charges.'

'I'll do that thing.'

Hans matched his step to his uncle's and strolled with him to the Chevrolet. A cat dozed on the bonnet.

'That's luck,' said Hans. 'A black cat.'

'You're as superstitious as your Ma.' Christiaan shooed the animal. 'Voetsak, ou' kaffer-kat! Bring us a bit of luck, if you know how. We can do with it.'

Stunned with weariness, Mrs Olivier fell asleep as soon as her head touched the pillow. It was raining hard and Lucifer slept on a kitchen chair undisturbed by the patter of rain on the skylight. In the studio Jim had placed a basin under the leak that was periodically patched up and was once more in need of attention. Mr Ferrit could probably fix it sometime tomorrow. The drip-drip splashing into the enamel bowl at irregular intervals seemed to Jim to fall on to his own raw nerves. He had telephoned Laura this evening and for once he had found her unsympathetic and out of tune with him.

'Your father has cancelled everything – all the wedding arrangements and reservations. You understand, Jim, nothing can take place from Ravenswood in the circumstances.'

He had replied with asperity.

'I don't think you understand the circumstances, Laura. Only a miracle can save Rachel. Tell my father that. It'll be good news to him.'

He had heard her gasp of dismay as he put down the receiver, a sour taste in his mouth as if he had eaten something bad. But his antagonism towards his own family was nothing to his bitter resentment against Mrs Olivier. She had practised an ugly deception on all of them. Most of all on him. She should have had the guts to tell him the truth and let him work out the answers for himself. Drip-drip-splash. Drip-drip-splash. Yes, he had told himself the same thing a hundred times, and there was nothing to be gained from it. Rachel's pale lifeless face floated before his eyes. Tubes dripped their vital liquids into her veins, those blue streams so delicately traced under her fair skin. A nurse with big brown eyes watched over the patient behind screens that told their own tale. Mrs Olivier had bent over her daughter, brushing her cold forehead with her lips. Kiss of Judas, Jim had thought, hating Rachel's mother. Drip-drip-splash.

In the shoddy slip of a house in the first prong of the

Trident Mr Ferrit lay awake, prey to new, curious and exciting sensations. Pity was not among them. Nor guilt. He was probing the subtler channels of power – narrow, dark and tortuous.

He had studied his big book before going to bed. Emily, always restless round the time of the full moon, had pored over it with him.

'Your people,' she'd said, with pride.

Over a period of twenty-five years he had collected and pasted in cuttings connected with the trials of sex maniacs and murderers who had gone their sinister way to Broadmoor or the gallows. As some people were addicted to crime fiction, so Mr Ferrit was obsessed by this particular field of criminal activity. It wasn't the crime alone that fascinated him, it was the whole set-up, the people, good and bad, involved in it. Ann Wargrave had intrigued him from the moment he had first set eyes on her pictures in the papers of the day. You couldn't forget that face, so full of fire. At the time he had speculated about her relationship with the murderer – the devilish pitchfork killer. She'd been Wargrave's wife. How had she escaped? Had she found no cause to fear her husband? Any man would want a woman like Ann Wargrave. She had that sort of magnetism. It was written all over her. And Lucas Wargrave, attracted to a woman, was a creature more dangerous and deadly than the most savage beast in all the jungle. How had it gone with him and her? Mr Ferrit had followed the evidence word by word. Ann had stood in the box and sworn that her husband during the period of their marriage had appeared to her to be normal. Yet only a few months after the birth of their child he'd killed three women under terrible circumstances in the space of a few weeks.

Mr Ferrit did not regard his existence with his daft sister as a 'life'. Nor did he amuse himself with lady friends on the

side. Or friends at all, come to that. His real life was vicarious, the projection of himself into the skins of others. The
Trident was an important part of that double existence. He
borrowed something from everybody. Sometimes he was
Ginger Rafferty, the dashing airman, or young Charlie
Dixon with his desirable wife and his less desirable dog.
He had for a while been the West African lover who had
visited the house at the end of the mews when Lucifer's
young ladies had lived there with boy-friends sniffing around
like dogs to the scent. Watching and observing the living,
keeping his big book of the slayers and the slain – his
people – Mr Ferrit lived dangerously, but only in a dream.
Now at last he felt that he had gone beyond the dream
– though still in the safety of a state remote from reality.

During the past twenty-four hours, since Rachel Olivier
had been in the news, her life hanging by a thread, it had
been borne in upon Mr Ferrit that if that thread snapped he,
like the principals in his notorious collection, would be
responsible for the death of a fellow human being. By allowing Onlooker to see his album and meet his people – among
them Lucas Wargrave – Mr Ferrit had tipped the scales of
destiny. If Mrs Olivier's daughter, with her tossing hair
and her friendly smile, failed to wake from her deep sleep
he, Ernest Ferrit, would at last be linked irrevocably with
those he studied so closely and knew so well – his chosen
brotherhood of doom. He would paste the final postscript
to the Lucas Wargrave story into his big book, and whenever he read it or looked at the face of the young woman
with the lovely hair he would say in his heart:

'*This one is mine.* This is the one *I* killed. I, Ernest Ferrit
of Trident Mews, killed Rachel Olivier, natural daughter of
Lucas Wargrave, the famous murderer.'

Yes, he too would have a place in his own diabolical hall
of fame. But no one would know of it. Not even Emily.

17

LUKE WARGRAVE

THE HOSPITAL TO WHICH RACHEL HAD BEEN TAKEN was an old one. It had once stood among the river meadows of the countryside but had long since been absorbed into the great sprawling heart of London. The various blocks were built round grassy courtyards and birds nested in fine old trees. It has a cloistered atmosphere and, for all its own internal hustle and bustle, it seemed peacefully islanded from the surge of city life.

To Jim Fleet the days and nights of suspense seemed interminable. He had been given permission to stay away from the office and most of his time was spent at the hospital. On Tuesday afternoon Rachel was still in the deep coma from which it seemed she would never be roused. That was the afternoon Mrs Olivier began to talk. The ward sister had advised them to go out and get some fresh air.

'Walk in the garden,' she had said. 'I'll see you're called if there's any change.'

Jim had lit Mrs Olivier's cigarette and his own, and they strolled up and down the gravel path between the green lawns, still spongy from the rain. The sun shone fitfully but it was pale and watery with little strength in it. Starlings swarmed in a great elm with their wild elemental shrillings high-pitched above the murmur of the city.

'Jim, we must talk about him,' she said.

He looked down at her, one eyebrow raised. 'Rachel's father?'

'Yes. I've been thinking that you may be right. Perhaps I should have told you everything from the beginning. There are no precise rules for such situations. How can there be? One uses one's judgment and mine could easily have been at fault.'

'That's finished. Where do we go from here?'

'I must tell you about him – what little there is to tell that you don't already know.'

He was silent and forbidding, a hard unapproachable young man who was not inclined to make it easier for her. She went on.

'I was younger than Rachel is now when I first met Luke Wargrave. I was in the WAAFs and he was in the R.A.F. It was a wartime love affair. How can I expect you to understand?'

He said coldly: 'I can try.'

'Their lives were short, those boys. They didn't have time to go steady.'

She threw the words at him contemptuously. She had lived with death and danger. The threats to her generation had been immediate and continuous. Bomber crews flying nightly over enemy territory accepted death as their shadow.

'Luke was an exciting personality – then. He had only to enter a room for the women to start getting out their lipsticks and compacts. But it wasn't just animal magnetism that attracted me. There was more to him than that. His father was a doctor, like mine, and Luke had been to Rugby. He was a good all-rounder, though his scholastic record was erratic. He was brilliant, but lazy. If there hadn't been a war he'd have gone to Cambridge. Instead it was the R.A.F. He wanted to be a pilot but he had defective colour vision. So he became a rear-gunner. He was very fearless, very deadly.'

'I believe you,' he commented grimly.

'My father didn't go much on Luke. He disliked seeing me swept off my feet, completely infatuated. He felt that these war-time romances had no roots – no permanency – and he opposed every step of ours.'

'Pity he failed. He was a good judge of men.'

'Of men, perhaps, not of his daughter. His opposition was all it needed. My mother, of course, backed him up. It just made Luke and me more determined to go our own way.'

'Why did you have to marry him? Was it necessary to go that far?'

She stopped in her tracks and glared at him. Then she burst out laughing. It was a harsh ugly sound.

'Believe it or not, we thought it necessary. We actually believed our baby should be born in wedlock. We wanted our child to have its father's name. *Wargrave*. There's a laugh for you, Jim Fleet! We thought if Luke was killed at least there'd be his child – his claim to immortality. Funny, isn't it? Very funny! We didn't realise then that he'd establish stronger claims to having his name remembered. It wasn't much of a marriage at that. We had a week's leave for our honeymoon and after that we both went back to our jobs. We couldn't even share our lodgings. I was in a hostel in London and Luke was stationed at Wallingford in Oxfordshire. Night after night our bombers went over Germany on those endless raids that were stepped up and stepped up, and I knew as well as he did that the chances were that he would never come back. I wish to God he never had!'

'I endorse that.'

'Jim,' she said earnestly. 'You must believe something. Luke was wild and selfish, but he was generous too and he wasn't really evil. Not when I first knew him. Not when Rachel was conceived. That . . . evil phase . . . came afterwards.'

'Try to tell me about it.'

He led her to a bench and they sat down. She spoke very quietly.

'Luke's aircraft was shot down over Germany. He was taken to a military hospital severely wounded. When he was discharged from hospital he was drafted to a prisoner of war camp. His leg had been shattered and he must have gone through a tough time. The Germans were short of anaesthetics and drugs then, but he was strong – very strong. When he was demobbed after the war he was fit enough physically with only a limp to tell of that crash, but he had changed in himself. Something had happened to him. His eyes, at times, became like a lion's, intent but mindless. You couldn't argue with them. Oh, how can I explain it?'

'You're not doing badly. Did he suffer any head injury?'

'Not that I know of. It was never even suggested, but I suppose there was some weakness, some tendency that was suddenly exaggerated by what he had gone through. The war *did* change certain people – you know it did! It woke the sleeping violence. Rachel was only a baby then. She and I were living with my parents. He came to see us . . .'

She pushed back her hair, and looked at Jim with dull heavy eyes. Her voice had thickened and some of the suffering and shock she had experienced at that time began to dawn on him. The fear too.

'I didn't want my parents to know what he was like – this stranger who could turn from a man into a wild beast in a moment. I didn't want to have my father say "I told you so" or have him pity me. I hoped my husband . . . would become himself again.'

'Mrs Olivier,' Jim said. 'Surely you must have guessed then what terrible potentialities were latent in your husband – perhaps not even latent, but active, even then?'

She raised her head and looked him straight in the eyes.

She's honest, he admitted to himself. At heart she prefers truth to lies. She said:

'It was then, when he came back, that I was first afraid of him. Any hint of resistance to his will brought out a cruel sadistic streak quite foreign to the Luke I'd known before. I couldn't believe it at first! I told myself I was imagining things, that I must try to understand how it was for a man who had been a prisoner, starved of sex and love for many months. But I knew, deep down, that it was much more than that. He had forgotten what it was to be . . . tender. That's what scared me – that and the other thing, the look in his eyes at certain times when it came over him – when he was possessed of the devil.'

She shivered and buried her face in her hands. Jim, too, was chilled, caught in the miasma of the young wife's terror of dangers too monstrous for contemplation. Mrs Olivier braced her shoulders and made herself continue.

'I believe now that Luke was frightened too. Frightened of himself, terrified that he might do me an injury. I believe that in those first days of his return from Germany he was fighting a dreadful inner battle with the devil that took charge of him. He was fighting alone and in the dark. No allies. Can you think how dreadful that must have been? He was a lost soul. Jekyll and Hyde, and Jekyll always in terror of the visitations of Hyde. I'm certain – I'd stake my life on it – that he left us, deserted me, for our own sakes. After his fashion he had loved me. I am not given to pity, but with all my heart I pity Luke. I was even sorry for him then – long before I began to appreciate what must have happened to him.'

They were silent in the gathering dusk. Nurses going off-duty and the night staff coming on passed by them, little cloaks swinging jauntily. Mrs Olivier hardly saw them. Jim's voice roused her.

'And you were Ray's age when all this happened to him – and to you?'

Her arm was along the back of the bench and her head rested on it in an attitude of dejection and defeat. The sun had set and a chilly ground-mist coiled round their ankles.

'Yes. I was Rachel's age – the mother of a baby girl I loved very dearly.' She rose. 'Let's go in, Jim. Let's go to Rachel now.'

Jim did not go with Mrs Olivier to the hospital on Wednesday morning because it had been agreed that he would meet Hans at the airport at noon. But when he telephoned the air terminal for confirmation he was informed that the South African flight had been delayed and was not due in till late afternoon.

As he hung up he heard the door-bell ring and Mrs Meadows answer it.

'Mrs Olivier is at the hospital, madam, but Mr Fleet is here. Would you like to see him?'

Jim cursed Mrs Meadows inwardly. She had no caution in her. She rushed at life and people and always wanted to please everybody. An absurd attitude, particularly trying at the present moment.

'Yes, indeed I would,' said a clear pleasant voice. 'I'm Mrs Braithwaite – an old friend of Mrs Olivier's.'

Jim groaned. Mrs Olivier's old friend certainly had him trapped. She was already on her way upstairs. There was nothing for it but to get rid of her as quickly as possible.

'It'll do Mr Jim good to have a little company,' Mrs Meadows was saying cheerfully. 'Take him out of himself. I'll make you both a nice pot of tea.'

Jim was on the landing to meet his uninvited visitor. He saw a short fresh-faced woman with an agreeable smile and a head of burnished auburn hair. She was hatless and, although her figure was matronly, there was something youthful about her appearance. She had candid blue eyes and the hand she offered him was small and dimpled.

'I'm Mrs Braithwaite,' she said. 'Cheryl Braithwaite. Ann Olivier and I were intimate friends in our youth. We were in the WAAFs together. I recognise you from your photographs, Mr Fleet.'

'There's been too much of that lately. Will you come in. I'm afraid I have to leave very shortly – for the hospital.'

Mrs Braithwaite sat down.

'I'm just staying for that cuppa I was promised and then I'll be off. What is the news of Rachel?'

'She hasn't regained consciousness,' he said.

'Oh, my dear, I am so sorry. Such a terribly anxious time for you and her mother.' Her voice was full of concern.

He offered her a cigarette but she refused it. He lit one for himself, observing as he did so that his fingers were nicotine stained. As a rule he smoked comparatively little.

'Mrs Braithwaite, I feel I ought to recall your name. But Mrs Olivier doesn't talk very much about her days in the WAAF. She's not one for reminiscing.'

'I know that. She has her reasons.'

'You said that significantly, Mrs Braithwaite. Did you know her before she was married?'

'I knew her before her first marriage, Jim. I knew Rachel's father.'

She was treading carefully, he realised, in case he was in ignorance. Suddenly he made up his mind to learn all he could from this little woman with the kind open face.

Mrs Meadows came in with the tea tray.

'Quick work, you'll grant me,' she said. 'But the kettle was on the boil.'

When they had helped themselves to tea Cheryl said:

'I met Ann in the Churchyard garden not long ago and we had a talk. I had the impression that she was very lonely – not in the companionship sense of the word, but in herself. You do realise, don't you, how very completely she isolated herself from her past life when she decided to marry Gerhard Olivier?'

'Intentionally, Mrs Braithwaite – and completely, I agree. Did you know Gerhard Olivier well?'

'Well enough to know that he was a fine man.'

'Then you must have known – '

'Luke Wargrave. Yes, I knew him too.'

'What was he like?'

'Wild as a hawk. Moody. Attractive in his own way. Excellent company. He had an amusing satirical way of expressing himself. He could make people laugh.' She broke off with a wry little smile as Jim's left eyebrow shot up. 'People aren't all in one piece, my dear. You could never have guessed Luke had that evil side to him. Not when Ann was in love with him, anyway. Her parents didn't like him, I admit. They thought he was irresponsible. In any case, her father mistrusted hasty war marriages. A lot crashed, you know. Her father thought that she was mistaking infatuation for love.'

Jim leaned forward.

'Was she?'

Cheryl's blue eyes, guileless but wise, met his frankly.

'No. She was desperately in love with Luke. More than that, she loved him. She's a tough woman, Mr Fleet – '

'Jim.'

'Jim, then. She had a hard core – still has, no doubt – and she could have made something of her marriage to Luke Wargrave if only that mad, sinister, murderous streak hadn't flared up. I suppose it was there, dormant, from the beginning, but the months of incarceration in a P.O.W. camp probably brought it out.'

'Did she never talk about it to you – guess at it – when first they were married?'

Cheryl reflected. Woman's confidences, thought Jim with a shudder of distaste. There's nothing they don't tell each other. But she's got to tell me as much as I can get her to. This little red-haired woman had become important to him and he was aware that she was willing to help him to the best of her ability, and to help Ann Olivier too. She was not intruding out of curiosity but out of goodness of heart in memory of a past friendship. She said thoughtfully:

'He had a touch of cruelty in his nature. Ann admitted that. It was always there but she could take it. It was never perverted – then. He was selfish and demanding but she was young and hot-blooded herself. She enjoyed being mastered. But after he came back it was another story. Rachel had been born then; the war was over and there was the future to think about. But Luke didn't seem to care. He was no longer the same person Ann had married. That was when she began to suffer and to be afraid.'

'You evidently knew her very well, Mrs Braithwaite.'

'I told you so. We were closer than sisters. She could tell me anything.' Her face crumpled childishly. 'That's why it hurt me so much when she cut me right out of her life – as if she couldn't trust me. She did the same thing to her parents. It wounded them bitterly. She was very tough about that.'

'She felt she had to be,' he said, surprised that he should be defending Mrs Olivier.

'That's what Gerhard Olivier tried to make us understand. It was after Luke deserted Ann that Gerhard really came into the picture seriously. He was always there when she needed him. Unobtrusive, safe. She needed safety very badly. He was much older than Ann and he adored her. She liked and respected him but she was never in love with him. She never pretended to be. She was absolutely honest with him.'

'That's what I'd expect.'

'He told me how it was. He said Ann and her child needed him and that was good enough for him; the rest would follow.'

'Somehow I believe it did. Rachel had a very happy home. She was devoted to her father – to Gerhard Olivier, I should say –'

She made a quick impatient gesture. 'Nonsense, my dear! Gerhard Olivier deserved to be called Rachel's father. Surely twenty years of affection and care amount to more than an interlude in the night!'

'In some ways, yes. Please go on.'

'Gerhard married Ann very quietly after – she was free. He adopted Rachel legally. Only a very few people knew anything about it and those of us who did willingly promised that the child should never find out her true parentage from us. Gerhard had been wonderful to Ann through the ordeal of the trial – all that dreadful publicity.'

'I wish I could get hold of a full report of the trial.'

Cheryl put down her tea cup and glanced up at him. 'Do you? Well, you can. I kept all the cuttings. Every one of them.'

'Will you let me have them?'

'Of course. I'll send them to you.'

'I'll come and get them.'

'If the little yellow car outside is yours – as I assume it is – you could take me home right now, and I'll give them to you. I can lay my hands on them because I've been re-reading them since all this happened.'

Jim rose.

'I'll take you up on that, Mrs Braithwaite. And then I

must get along to the hospital. Mrs Olivier is expecting her son from South African today and I was to have met him this morning, but his plane is late. That's how it happened that you found me here.'

'Perhaps it was all to the good. Providence must have intended us to meet.' She spoke with naïve sincerity. She had risen and, as Jim looked at her, it occurred to him that she was a contented person and that her simplicity accounted for the illusion of youth surrounding her like an aura.

'I'm sure it did. You've been so helpful already. You've put a great deal into perspective for me.'

'I'm glad,' she said. 'Don't judge her harshly, Jim. Ann has great faults and greater virtues. She was loyal to Luke Wargrave to the bitter end. She went through a big ordeal in the witness-box to try to save him from the gallows. If only the psychiatrists had been the kings of the court in those days, as they are today, Luke Wargrave would never have been conden.ned to death.'

'You believe that?'

'I do,' she said firmly. 'And I knew him.'

18

THRESHOLD OF HELL

MRS OLIVIER WATCHED JIM FOLD THE YELLOWED cuttings he had been reading and put them into an envelope. He tucked them into the pocket of his jacket and glanced up at the clock over the door of the visitors' room. Just across the corridor was the little ward in which Rachel lay unconscious.

'Time to think about going to the airport,' he said.

'I wish I could come with you, but I keep hoping for some change.'

'Why don't you go and meet Hans yourself? You've been here all day and you need an airing badly. I'll stay. A pity you haven't a licence or you could take Yellow Peril.'

Mrs Olivier's tired eyes brightened.

'I could get a taxi or go by bus from the West London Terminus.'

'Do that. Meet him and have your evening meal at the airport in comfort. Then come on here afterwards.'

'I think that's a good idea, Jim. This suspense is slow torture. Wondering if she'll ever wake – and if she does . . . '

'Don't!' he said.

'At least you have no sense of guilt. I have.'

He gave her one of his long searching stares and it seemed to her that he was no longer young. His eyes were ageless in those deep sockets that grew hollower and darker by the day.

'You've done your best for Rachel – according to your lights. No one could do more.'

'Those cuttings of Cheryl's. You've been studying them all afternoon. Not very cheerful reading.'

'At least his victims were women who take terrible risks – women who sell their bodies to strangers – the street walkers of the darker beats.'

'What drove him to that devilish compulsion beyond our understanding? What hideous discords were ringing in his brain?'

'He signed his crimes diabolically. The straight vertical slash and the short horizontal one crossing it to symbolise a pitchfork.'

She covered her eyes. Instantly he was contrite.

'I'm sorry. I'm immersed in all this – trying to find a way out of the wood.' He touched her arm. 'You should be getting along. I'll come down with you and find you a taxi.'

The day had been oppressive with a low ceiling of heavy cloud, but when Mrs Olivier arrived at the airport a cold wind with rain on its breath had begun to blow. She had half an hour to spare before the South African flight was due to arrive. She sat near one of the long windows commanding the landing strips and watched the great mechanical birds from all over the world fly in and come to rest. She was glad to relax and have something to look at other than the awful stillness of her daughter's form in the hospital cot, the design on the waiting-room carpet, or the autumn courtyards under the high hospital walls.

At last flight 107 from Johannesburg was announced and Mrs Olivier went close to the window, her heart beating faster. No sign yet, only a drumming somewhere above the storm clouds. Then the great wing-span broke through, wheels touched the runway, the ladder was run out to meet the aircraft and passengers were descending. Hans? Yes, that was Hans all right! No hat, no overcoat, assured easy stride. He looked so strong! She needed that strength to lean upon.

When he came up through the channel for 107, ahead of the straggle of other passengers, she was there to meet him. He put down the light grip he was carrying and held her tightly in his arms, too moved for speech. But the question was in his eyes. She shook her head.

'No change as yet.'

He thought: My mother is old and ravaged and ugly. He had never loved her more.

'What now?'

'We'll have a meal here and then get a taxi to the hospital. You'll stay with me in the mews cottage for the present, and Jim will go back to his own flat.'

'Has Jim been with you through all this?'

'Yes.'

'Good for Jim. His parents?'

'I haven't seen them since it happened.'

'Or heard from them?'

'Laura sent a message hoping Rachel would recover.'

They found a corner table and ordered grills and a bottle of claret.

She filled in the gaps for him, telling him all that it had been impossible to say on the telephone. The waiter brought black coffee and Hans asked for the bill.

'Ma,' he said. 'If Ray breaks through – will she be just the same? Will she be all right?'

It was the question she had dreaded.

'We don't know. There's a danger . . . that she may not be . . . all right. It was a long time before she was found. Probably all of twelve hours after taking the barbiturates. She'd been exposed to cold . . . '

He frowned. 'Exactly what do you mean about not being all right? What could be wrong if – when – she wakes up?'

'There could be brain damage.'

'In that case, Ma, it would be better if she didn't wake up?'

'I don't know,' she said. 'I simply don't know, Hans.'

The storm broke in earnest soon after nine o'clock that night. Thunder and lightning, lashing rain, a wild wind that rattled windows and banged doors. The Women's Medical Ward on the top floor of the old part of the hospital was vulnerable to the full force of the gale. The other patient in the small adjacent ward had left and her bed was empty. Gusts beat furiously against the tall narrow panes, causing the curtains to breathe and sigh although the windows were closed.

'Ray! Ray! Wake up, Ray!'

Jim's voice called her back from somewhere far away – from Land's End. The children, the dog, the fisherman, the field, the wood and the harvest moon stirred dimly in Rachel's returning consciousness. She forced her eyes open. The red moon in the black sky multiplied. The hedge was very high and forbidding. It swayed as if to crush her. The moons began to converge upon her. Now they were no longer moons but grotesque masks, inky faces splotched and streaked with sulphurous yellow. She closed her eyes. The intolerable pain in her head threatened to burst it apart, every bone in her body ached.

'Ray, my darling!'

'Jim, I hear you.'

Her tongue was made of flannel, padded with dust.

'Water,' she begged.

A thin tube found its way into the corner of her mouth between her dry lips. She sucked at it feebly.

'Head very bad?' asked a male voice, strange to her – a quick bossy voice.

'Ghastly – can't see.' The words were difficult to bring out; they made queer noises.

'It's the all-time high in hangovers,' said the new voice, with a smile in it. 'That'll teach you to swallow barbiturates by the score, young lady.'

'Where am I?'

'In hospital. You were found in a field and brought here.'

She raised her lids again, afraid of what she might see. Oh, God! Oh, God! Was she raving mad? Evil is in the eye of the beholder. Behold, my mother! She sits beside my bed and tries to take my hand. But she has no hands. I have no hands. Her face is broader than it is long, grape-dark, smeared with old mustard; her lips snarl. But her voice is infinitely tender.

'Rachel, my child, do you know us? Jim is here. And Hans.'

Two more gargoyles swung towards her. She closed her eyes and sank into the dark abyss.

When next she woke she was alone, except for the guardian, who leaned forward.

'Awake?' The guardian was dressed as a nurse.

It was dark and the noise of the storm was deafening. Her head was a little easier, but her mouth was parched. A night-light burned dimly. Weird discoloured fingerless hands busied themselves about her. The face stooping over her was wide and jaundiced, the hair under the white frilly cap was bouffante indigo. Some new rinse, of course, but so hideous and frightening!

The night sister swept in with a torch. All Rachel saw of her was the torch and her glasses – a bobbing light and two headlamps. The headlamps were salvation. These people –

their masks were evil but their hearts were good. They were trying to make her more comfortable. How did good people get into hell?

'You've been out for three days and a night,' said Headlamps. 'We must change these dressings and rub your back and your heels.'

'Why dressings?'

She discovered bandages and tubes about her painful body.

'That's how you've been nourished – through your veins. And your blood has all been purified on the artificial kidney. Maybe you've seen that on T.V. It's one of the modern miracles of medical science.'

Purified? Now it began to come back – the deed, and the reason for it. But there was no miracle that could purify blood with the taint of murder and madness in it.

'The ship,' she said. 'It rocks.'

'This ward is high. We feel the wind.'

Sounds echoed through the aching vaults of her head. Noise within noise. The storm outside, jets tearing the angry sky, and, in the adjoining ward, the moans and mutterings of the sick and the steady snake-hiss of an oxygen cylinder.

'This'll do your head good.'

With great difficulty Rachel swallowed the liquid the nurse offered her. Headlamps nodded approval and continued on her rounds.

Next morning the faces around her had lengthened agreeably, but they were still a macabre colour. She did not dare to ask for a mirror. She examined her own hands anxiously. What, no nails? The things on the ends of her arms were like stuffed rubber gloves, featureless. She explored her face with them. Her skin was kelp washed ashore by a storm, not supple and glossy from the water, nor sun-baked, but somewhere between the two. Dead and soggy, immovable over its framework. Her hair was knotted fur, drenched by noxious sweats, dried stiff and hard.

Two doctors came to see her. The senior physician was small and aggressive with grey hair and a clever fox-face. She recognised his curt voice from the night before. The young doctor with him had a kind tired face. When they had completed their examination the physician questioned her.

'Where are you?'

'In hospital.'

'What day is it?'

'Monday . . . the church-bells were ringing last night . . . no, last night was the storm . . . '

She gave up. It was difficult to speak with her flannel tongue.

'It's Thursday,' he corrected her brusquely. 'Can you remember people? Who was here when you woke up yesterday?'

'My mother . . . my brother . . . '

'Well done. We didn't think you knew them. Who else?'

She turned her head away.

'Jim . . . don't let him come here!'

'Don't you want him?'

Sounds of distress broke from her. He said more gently.

'Never mind. He'll be here when you do. Would you like to see your mother?'

'Nobody,' she said. 'Nobody.'

'Perhaps later today,' suggested the young doctor.

'Not while I'm like this.'

'Like what?'

She tried to focus their faces and failed. Everything danced; the red-brown eyes of Fox-face mocked her. Her tongue stuck to the roof of the mouth.

'Not seeing properly,' she muttered.

'What happens when you close your eyes?' asked the young doctor.

'I see hell.'

She caught the glance that passed between them.

'I think she should have a chat to Brace,' said Fox-face.

'Who's Brace?' she asked.

'A psychiatrist.'

'Or Keanes.' The young doctor's smile was reassuring.

'Who's he?'

'Our padre. He was in the Navy for a time, he's a very human human being.'

'Or both,' barked Fox-face. He turned to the ward sister and gave her various instructions. Chest X-ray. Electro-cardiogram. Visitors? Yes, if she asked for them. No, if the idea upset her.

The gleam of their white coats vanished as they disappeared through the open door into the Womens' Ward.

Presently she heard a rumble in the corridor and over the top of her screen appeared the curved head of a prehistoric monster. It came to rest, staring down at her over the white screen. Small and snake-like on its long neck. A dinosaur, she thought. Why a dinosaur in my room?

'I've come to X-Ray your chest,' said a young woman in a white coat. 'Nothing to worry about.'

She folded back a portion of the screen and revealed the stumpy mechanical body of the 'dinosaur'. She made the creature do her bidding, smiled at Rachel and trundled it off again. Two internes came to electrocute her. Of course, that was how it was done in America. Not the rope but the electric current. She waited for pain and death. But they left her alive and unharmed. The nurse came in, brimming over with vitality and good nature.

'Your mother's here. She brought you your own nightie

and cream and powder and things. I'm sure you're dying
for them, aren't you?'

Rachel, who had felt only the ache in her body and the
wall of wood in her chest that made it impossible to touch
the food they brought her, was suddenly aware of the
coarse hospital garment against her skin. Mrs Olivier had
followed the nurse before her daughter could ojebct.

'Darling,' she said. 'You look quite different!'

Rachel managed a smile.

'So do you. You're not mustard yellow and purple any
more.'

'Was I?'

'No,' croaked Rachel. 'I guess I was the purple one.'
She held out thin unrecognisable hands and arms.

'Bruises, darling. They'll soon be gone.'

Rachel fingered her bandaged wrist.

'Does it hurt?' asked her mother.

'Yes.'

'There're stitches there,' said the cheerful nurse. 'Now
let's get you changed.'

Rachel felt better when she was wearing her own loose
flimsy nightgown. The nurse had left them and Mrs
Olivier said:

'What about a mirror?'

Rachel shook her head.

'My hands are seaweed, my hair's fur and my skin sticks
to my bones.'

'Nonsense, child!' But Mrs Olivier did not press the
matter. 'Jim – '

'No,' said Rachel.

'Hans?'

'Not yet.'

'Liz cabled from Switzerland. She sends her love.'

'Liz . . . ?'

'Don't try to think, darling. Just rest. I'll leave you now and come back this afternoon. If there's anything you want nurse will phone me. I'll be at home.'

When Mrs Olivier had gone Rachel closed her eyes. She longed above all things to doze. She was desperately tired. 'Please don't let it happen,' she prayed. 'Please let me sleep before it begins.'

But there was the shimmer – the T.V. screen before it is properly focused, with endless flickering jigging silvery motes raining, running, chasing each other until the picture assumes its pattern. Ah, this was the one that came most often. It began in beauty. The shimmering was not always frightening. It had, at times, the summer feel of Africa, of the heat-haze dancing over the veld, the lakes and rivers of mirage all vibrant in the living light of a vast empty land. Clear in the shimmering light were the blue stars she welcomed. Hyacinth blue, twinkling in transluscent brilliance, falling like 'the quality of mercy . . . the gentle rain from heaven upon the place beneath', unbelievably comforting. Stay with me, blue stars! Now the picture was forming. Yes, it was the wood. This too was beautiful, with glades of sunshine among the trees, and she knew that in the wood, if she could enter it, was a shining sanctuary of love and joy. Hold it, she begged. Hold it! But the blue stars – the bluebells of the spring-sweet wood – were falling out of sight and the horror was beginning. The trees swayed and heeled over like the masts of sinking ships subsiding in a vast cataclysmic upheaval. Oceans rose and fell, craters and chasms opened in the swirling nebulous floor of the universe, cliffs swayed and crumbled in a purgatory of disintegration where all was lost and corrupt and the blue stars obscured. But the last point of anguish was what she dreaded most. Don't let it happen! Don't let him sign it! The blue stars faded in the universal grey and in their place came Satan's signature. The phosphorescent pitchfork. When she saw that she knew that she was damned – possessed of the devil – a lost soul orbiting alone in the wastes of infinity, capsuled in a sense of desolation beyond grief or pain.

And this, she knew, was hell.

19

INQUISITION

WHEN MRS OLIVIER LEFT HER DAUGHTER'S BEDSIDE and returned to the mews cottage she found Laura Fleet waiting for her.

'Mrs Meadows has just gone. She gave me tea and it's still hot. I'm going to pour you a cup. You needn't tell me how you like it, Ann. I'll give it to you the way it's good for you.'

'Thanks.'

Mrs Olivier left her wet raincoat on the landing and sank into an armchair. Laura went into the kitchen and came back with a steaming cup.

'Strong and sweet. Mrs Meadows tells me Rachel regained consciousness last night. How did you find her this morning?'

'I suppose you could say she's better. She can move and hear and speak in a fashion. But she isn't seeing – very well.'

'She's been through a great deal, Ann. A terrible traumatic emotional and physical experience. The poison had time to get right into her system and her bloodstream. It's a mystery she's alive at all.'

Mrs Olivier looked at Laura with puzzled weary eyes.

'How do you know all this? Why are you here? I thought you were finished with us. What do you care about Rachel – you and Jasper?'

'Jim keeps us informed. We do care about Rachel, and we also care about Jim. What's happened is over and done with. In your place I dare say I should have done the same – if I'd had the courage and the follow-through.'

'I'm afraid for Rachel, Laura.'

Mrs Olivier's hand shook as she lifted her cup to her lips. The tea slopped into the saucer.

'Damn. I'm clumsy and cold. I'll light the fire.'

But Laura was before her. The electric radiator soon banished the damp chill of the stormy day and Mrs Olivier leaned forward and warmed her hands at it. Laura said quietly:

'In what way are you afraid for Rachel?'

'Her eyes. She doesn't see us properly, but there are things she does see. God knows what! Her eyes are haunted. I've seen that look before in somebody else. It's a dreadful thing to see in a person you love. She has the look of a lost soul.'

'She's been where you and I can't follow, Ann. It could take quite a time for her to come back.'

'She's knocked on the gates of hell,' said Ann Olivier grimly. 'I know.'

Laura's attentive silence and the sympathetic enquiry in her gentle moon-face invited confidence. Suddenly Mrs Olivier wanted to let it all spill over.

'A psychiatrist called Brace saw her this morning.'

'Creswell Brace? He's famous.'

'That's the one. He saw me after he'd seen Rachel. I suppose in a way I could dot the i's and cross the t's for him. She has hallucinations – nightmare visions of everything good and beautiful sinking into a sort of atomic end of the world. She longs to sleep but daren't close her eyes for fear of these hellish pictures signed by the devil – '

'Signed? Ann, what can she mean by that?'

'That signature? It's a vertical stroke with a short curved one across the top to make a pitchfork. When she sees

that . . . signature . . . she suffers extreme despair. To her
it appears to be the sign of diabolic possession. You see its
significance, don't you?'

Laura was deeply shocked. She had read accounts of
Lucas Wargrave's crimes and trial and she recalled only too
clearly the way in which he had signed his dreadful work.
The razor slash on his victim's bodies – the pitchfork.

'What does Brace think?'

'He says she has identified herself with her father. That the
poor child is convinced that she is possessed of the devil –
as Luke was. She believes that she has tried to commit
murder – '

'Murder! Rachel? But this is too horrible!'

'Self-murder, she calls it. She's lost, Laura. She's in some
sort of pit of despair where we can't reach her. She didn't
want to see me, but I insisted. She refused to see Hans or
Jim. Hans is very upset. I've sent him to meet the boat train.
Jenny Carstairs arrives this morning and I've told him to
spend the day with her.'

'Jenny – the bridesmaid? Of course. Oh dear, how
different it all is from what it should have been! Jenny and
Hans are rather fond of each other, aren't they? I remember
from seeing them together at Môreson.'

Laura sighed. Môreson – that seemed a long time ago!
She'd thought of it recently as a clever act in a long story
of deception. Now she saw it differently – as the wide clear
space in the life of a woman who had known war and an
aftermath more terrible than battle. To Ann Wargrave –
Ann Olivier – Môreson must have been a haven of refuge.

'Has Hans not seen his sister then?' she asked.

'He was with her last night when she recovered consciousness. He and I and Jim. It was Jim who called her back from
wherever her spirit was wandering. It was his voice she
answered. We – Hans and I – we couldn't get through to her.

She came back for Jim. Yet now that she's fully conscious she won't see him. She doesn't want any of us.'

'My dear,' said Laura. 'She wants and needs you all – her mother, her brother, and – most of all – her lover; but she isn't ready for you yet.'

'Will she ever be?'

'What does Brace say?'

'He says this temporary mental breakdown is due to shock combined with the barbiturate poisoning. She's had a very severe emotional shock. He's not committing himself further. He'll see her again tomorrow. If only I could make her listen to me – but I can't get to her. She's locked herself away.'

'Ann, there must be a key – if it can be found. We drove to town last night in answer to a telephone call from Jim. He rang Ravenswood at about six o'clock. That was before Rachel woke up. Jim wanted to see his father urgently.'

'If it was about Rachel I'm surprised Jasper took any notice.'

'Jim is our only son.'

Ann Olivier glanced up sharply, and Laura smiled.

'Yes, I did say *our* son. He's been mine as well as Jasper's since he was a little fellow. What does Jim know of his own mother except that she walked out on him? I'm the one he turns to. That's what counts.'

'Like Rachel and Gerhard. Gerhard was her real father.'

'I was thinking that.'

'Jasper doesn't see it that way.'

'No. I'm afraid not.'

'The circumstances are very different, aren't they? And the circumstances are unalterable.' Ann Olivier's face was a woodcut, deeply shadowed.

Down in the mews they heard the sonorous chant of the

Rag-and-Bone man, the rumble of his cart and the clop-clop of hooves. It was background music in the Trident and they took no notice. Presently Laura said:

'Jasper's coming here to see you, Ann. He'll be here any time now.'

'Oh no, I can't bear it!'

Mrs Olivier jumped to her feet and went to the window. Laura saw her rigid back and beyond it the fringe of leggy petunias and geraniums tossing in the wind that had blown the rain clouds away.

'Jasper started all this – here in this room. I can never forget it. That day I knew he hated all of us. Nothing has changed, except that it's worse now – far worse!'

'Jasper didn't start it, Ann. Fate did. Those pictures when you had the fracas with the press photographer. Somebody spotted who you were and tipped Onlooker off.'

'Inny o' lumber – 'nyo' lumber.'

Alf and Michael, his mule, were plodding back along the mews and Emily Ferrit was with them. The old hag looked up at the window as they went by and it seemed to Mrs Olivier that she leered.

An echo sounded in Mrs Olivier's ears. 'You're one of Ernie's people, he collects people like you.' Other echoes too – the thin whistling of Mr Ferrit strolling down between the sleeping houses of the Trident. The first night she'd seen him, a shadow falling across the cobbles pointing at her doorstep. The first morning she'd come upon him, washing a vintage Bentley, his peaked cap over one eye, his cheroot dangling from the corner of his mouth. 'Could of sworn I'd seen you somewhere before. I know your face.' *I know your face* . . . I know your face . . . Mr Ferrit had allowed himself to get into conversation with the press photographer who had taken those disastrous pictures. Mr Ernest Ferrit had been quoted as saying of the cottage

'They goes in single and comes out wed.' Mr Ferrit – apart
from Mrs Meadows – was the only person who now sought
out Mrs Olivier to ask after Rachel. Jane Rafferty and Mary
Dixon made embarrassed inquiries if they ran across her,
hating to cause her distress or appear to pry, painfully
conscious of the sordid circumstances surrounding Rachel's
grave condition and of the stigma that attached to both
mother and daughter. But Mr Ferrit displayed no such in-
hibitions. He haunted Mrs Olivier's corner of the Trident
and waylaid her whenever she returned exhausted from the
hospital. He asked about Rachel avidly as if her recovery
were a matter of morbid personal importance to him.
There had been something almost menacing in his anxiety,
something pressing that gave her a *frisson*. He'd stand with
his spidery jockey's legs apart, his skinny body tipped forward on the balls of his feet and his thin lips drawn back
from sharp discoloured teeth. 'Do you think she'll get better,
Mrs Olivier?' And what could she answer? Only 'We
hope so, Mr Ferrit.'

Mrs Olivier swung round to face Laura.

'You're right. Somebody else might have started it.
Jasper was doing no more than his duty – to Jim, to his
family, even to Ravenswood, Rachel understands all that.
Better than I did, maybe. If she hadn't understood so well
she would never have done what she did. A lovely healthy
girl with all her life before her.' But in her heart Rachel's
mother was forced to add, all her life, yes, but a life without
Jim, without children, with the sword of a terrible inheritance for ever over her head.

They heard a car draw up and the slam of its door. Mrs
Olivier gathered herself together.

'Tell him to come up, Laura. The door isn't locked.'

His step on Jacob's ladder was deliberate and elderly. None
of its usual spring in it. Yet when he came into the room

General Fleet appeared as forceful as ever. Well groomed, alert, in command of the situation. Mrs Olivier made no move to cross the room and greet him. She stood where she was, facing him, her back to the window, her attitude defensive, her strained face dark with suspicion.

Laura watched them in silence as if they were two dangerous animals best left to fight it out undisturbed. Laura, like many people close to nature, could at times assume the patient immobility of a hunter, wearing her stillness like a cloak of invisibility.

Sir Jasper looked at Ann Olivier for a long moment, his gaze holding hers, shining a relentless torch into the hidden places of her soul. The window was open, the heater had been turned down to half its full strength and the room was only just warm, yet he observed the beads of perspiration start out on her forehead. She put up a shaking hand to push back her hair in the gesture he knew well. She cleared her throat with a little sound that made Laura flinch. This is how he breaks them, Laura thought. This hypnotic use of silence, this pitiless protracted assessment before going into action. She was aware – just as he was – that the breaking point for Ann Olivier was very near. Laura was not enjoying herself. But Jasper had insisted upon her presence. 'One way or the other I'm going to get at the truth – the final absolute truth,' he had said, 'and you must witness it.'

Laura had always been struck by the animal quality in Ann Olivier. It was in her swinging stride and the careless grace and muscular strength that belied her years. It had been very evident in the news picture of her attack on the photographer, and Laura was sure that Ann's instincts – whether sexual or maternal – were strong, protective and primitive, constantly straining against conventional disciplines. She had the look of an animal now, cornered, wounded, but still prepared to attack.

'Why have you come? Her voice was husky. 'Why are you here, Jasper?'

'I have come to ask you some questions, Ann. A great deal depends on your answers.'

She sat down and looked up at him. There was no room for pity in Jasper Fleet, no temptation to reflect upon the lifetime that had brought Ann Olivier to the pitch where truth could no longer be twisted, clouded, or withheld. He had a duty to perform and he must keep his purpose clear and to the point. Let the complications crowd in later, if they must.

He sat opposite her, leaning forward, his fine hands on his knees, his beard bristling and aggressive, his eyes intent but not unkind.

'Don't be afraid. Just answer my questions. I'm not against you, Ann. I want to help and I must have your co-operation. All right?'

She nodded, licking dry lips.

Am I seeing her beaten into the dust? Laura wondered. Or could this hour of defeat bring forth some strange sort of victory? She heard her husband's rasping voice and the clinical precision of his first question. She thought: This is the inquisition – this is the 'soul saving' torture! Tremors ran down Laura's spine and she felt as she had done when the vet had asked her to hold a savagely mauled dog while he attempted to cleanse the animal's wounds. She knew what was coming. She knew that all Ann Olivier's short passionate life with Luke Wargrave – the love of her youth and the father of her child – was about to be stripped naked, dissected, minutely examined, and finally cast aside. She turned her head away as she had turned it away from the suffering dog.

After a time Laura Fleet went to the kitchen and fetched a glass of water for Ann Olivier. She lit a cigarette for her.

The practised scalpel of Jasper's interrogation had worked fast and with uncanny skill. Ann had finally succumbed to the hypnosis of his eyes and voice as if to an anaesthetic. Her resistance had ebbed and walls of secrecy, fortified and preserved over more than twenty years, had crumbled and fallen, letting in the strong harsh light of total honesty.

'So it boils down to this,' Sir Jasper said at last. 'Wargrave came back to you at the end of the war? Home to you?'

'Yes.'

'And almost immediately he deserted you?' As she inclined her head, he continued. 'You then had strong reason to believe that your husband had undergone some terrible change of personality – that he was aware of this and was anxious to save you from the demon he was liable to become at certain times.'

'Yes,' she said in a low voice.

He stood up and looked at his watch.

'Laura,' he said. 'It's twelve-forty-five. I'm going to have a bite at my club. There's a lot to be done this afternoon. Do you want a lift anywhere?'

'No,' she said. 'I'm staying here.'

They heard him go down Jacob's ladder, and it seemed to Laura that his step was lighter than when he'd come.

Mrs Olivier sat stiffly on the chair where he had left her. Her large hands covered her face and tears rained through the chinks between her taut fingers. She *is* like an animal, thought Laura. She doesn't know how to cry, poor thing. But Laura Fleet was very good with animals. Within the hour Ann Olivier had been fed and watered, put to bed with a hot bottle and covered with a soft eiderdown.

'Sleep,' said Laura, stroking the dark head on the pillow. 'Sleep all afternoon, if you can. When you wake we'll go to Rachel.'

'Where's Jim?' asked Mrs Olivier. 'Why hasn't Jim been in touch with me today?'

Laura drew a very deep breath.

'Jim has gone to the prison where Luke Wargrave spent his last days on earth. Jim will be in touch with you, my dear. Later.'

20

THE SIGNATURE

THE PRETTY NURSE BROUGHT A BOWL OF ROSES INTO Rachel's room.

'Where are we going to put them? Spoilt, aren't you?'

'Who are they from?'

The nurse gave Rachel the card, but she shook her head.

'I can't read yet. Everything dances and shimmers.'

'Do I dance and shimmer too?'

'Yes.'

'Makes me sound like a film star.' She took the card from the florist's little envelope. 'It says "Get well quick. And come to Switzerland, Ray darling. Liz." '

'Liz! How would she know?'

'Does she live in Switzerland?'

'For the present.'

'Maybe she gets the English papers. Maybe she telephoned your mother to find out what hospital you were in.'

'Was . . . all this . . . in the papers?'

'About you being found in the field and brought to hospital? Yes, it was. Want these near you?'

'On the window-sill, please. Red ones – I love red roses.'

'You wouldn't have got the colour right this morning. You must be seeing better.'

'I believe I am.'

'What colour is my hair?'

'Fair.'

'This morning you said I had indigo hair and a yellow face.'

'I'm sorry.'

The nurse laughed. 'That's all right. I checked with an independent witness. There are more flowers for you outside. I'll get them.'

She fetched a vase of tall carnations and read out the card. 'With love from Laura Fleet.'

'Pink and white,' said Rachel.

'You're doing fine,' said the nurse, and left her to go to the Womens' Ward.

Laura Fleet! Did the carnations mean that Laura forgave her for the pain she was causing the Fleet family? Instinctively Rachel's eyes sought a single spray of delicate pink orchids in a small slender glass vase at her bedside. They were more like exotic butterflies than flowers, their wings hovering and quivering like everything else. Jim's flowers. If only they would stay still! Her mother had read her the message 'With all my love'. And Mrs Olivier had added, 'He means it.'

'Am I intruding?'

The man in the black cassock had entered the small ward. He stood by the cot, looking down at Rachel. His cassock made him appear taller than he really was. His domed forehead was fringed with a fluff of light hair and his eyes were bright and friendly.

'My name is Keanes,' he said. 'I got a message from Doctor Armitage – the house physician – that you might want to see me.'

'Have you come to ask me questions?' Rachel asked wearily. 'There was a psychiatrist here this morning. Everybody keeps asking questions.'

He pulled out the wooden stool and sat on it. He had a wide attractive grin that made him look rather mischievous.

'I know. Brace told me you were in trouble. But in this case the boot's on the other foot. You're the one who's entitled to ask the questions. I could try to answer a few, if you like.'

'I'm a coward,' she said bleakly. 'I tried to kill myself.'

'Lucky you failed. You have a second chance.'

'So I'm back to where I started from. Nothing is different.'

'Oh, I shouldn't say that. *You* must be different – after what you've been through – what you are still going through. For one thing you know now that sliding out of a tough situation isn't the answer.'

'Suicide is a crime, isn't it? Self-murder. And the penalty for murder is death. Hanging. That's funny, when you come to think of it. Justice ought to do my job for me – as it did for my father. You know about him?'

'Yes, I know about him. Luke Wargrave was very greatly to be pitied.'

He saw surprise spark in her sad expressive eyes.

'He was possessed of the devil,' she said. 'Nothing could be more terrible. But Justice doesn't pity. It condemns – with horror and disgust.'

'Possessed of the devil. You're right of course. But we all are – in varying degrees – from time to time. The devil is part of our make-up, but sometimes he gets the upper hand, even complete control. He becomes the soul's dictator. That happens to people like your father.'

She said, hopelessly. 'It has happened to me.'

Desmond Keanes was not easily shocked, but the despair in the soft husky voice of the girl and the look in her strange light-green eyes jerked at his heart.

'Try to tell me,' he said.

'I broke the law – not man's law but a much bigger law than that – when I tried to take the easy way out. I knew it was wicked, deep down inside me, but I did it just the same.'

'What makes you know it was wicked?'

She passed her hand across her eyes and shook her head.

He leaned forward. 'Perhaps I can help you. Our lives are not our own to dispose of as and when we think fit. Whether we know it or not, we are part of a divine and purposeful plan with a place to fill and a task to perform.'

She said weakly: 'And the punishment for . . . sliding out . . . is hell. Since I woke up I've been punished. What do you think hell is? Where do you think it is?'

'Who can say? Hell has many names and aspects. Who can describe it? Perhaps you can. The ancient Jews called it Gehenna after a valley outside Jerusalem – a valley desolate and lost, the dumping ground of refuse consumed by perpetual fires – the ultimate end, a place without hope.'

'A place without hope. That's right. But it isn't Gehenna or the furnaces in the depths. It's the break-up where nothing stays good. It's your soul alone in space – trying to get up among the blue stars and being sucked down into the awful heaving sea where everything swirls away and falls apart. Death isn't sleep and darkness. It's this vibrating infinity that could be bright and beautiful if it didn't heel over into hell – the place without hope.'

She was flushed and excited and for a moment he wondered if he might be doing more harm than good. Her eyes beseeched his help.

'Get me out of it!' she begged. 'Get me out of hell!'

Desmond Keanes drew upon those inner reserves of power that seldom failed him.

'Christ the Redeemer gave his life for you – for all of us. He paid on the Cross in love and blood and anguish. We belong to Him – among what you describe as the blue stars – His love, His compassion and His forgiveness are infinite. Ask Him to help you. Have faith.'

He rose and gave her a blessing, his hands lightly touching her hair.

'Now you will sleep,' he said. 'You will sleep in God's love.'

She smiled at the man of faith and watched him flap away in his long cassock, his heavy shoes firm and masculine on the polished boards, the fluff of hair bright and silvery in the pale afternoon sun.

She closed her eyes and saw the wood with the glade of summer gold among the trees. Bluebells danced in patches of incandescent light. If only it would stay this way! But soon now the trees would begin to tilt and topple and then there would be the knife-keen moment of excruciating agony – the slashing symbol – the pitchfork in the corner, Satan's signature. But the trees stood firm in their strength and beauty, growing towards the light.

A maid brought Rachel food and she refused it. The night nurse came to wash her hands and rub her back and heels and then at last she was alone.

Dare she close her eyes?

The heavy lids fell. The scene was the one she feared the most. The little car and the high hedge looming over it, the red harvest moon that would presently swim towards her with a fleet of menacing satellites, the field with furrows that would open into canyons to engulf her. And then, when the blue stars were drowned and lost and all hope abandoned, Satan would sign the scene of destruction.

The red disc paled, the face within it was kind. Clouds flurried across this moon-face that was Laura's and the blue stars twinkled. Satan was impatient. He did not wait for the moon to set and the world to fall apart. Already the dread vertical slash sliced the sky and hung like a fiery sword in the scintillating firmament. But where was the horn-shaped head of the pitchfork – the diabolical emblem? Strange, but the short sharp stroke had failed to curve. It was a straight cross-bar – the hilt of a sword, or the arms of a cross, pulsing in the vibrant night – the night of no horizons.

Rachel woke to see the night sister coming through the Women's Ward. The welcome beam of the torch bobbed ahead of her, the comforting headlamps gleamed.

'What time is it?' Rachel asked her.

'Nearly midnight. Have you been awake, dear?'

'I've had a wonderful sleep.'

'No bad dreams?'

Headlamps set her torch on the bedside table where it illumined Jim's spray of orchids. The winged petals were dusted with a silvery bloom Rachel had not noticed before. She looked at them in wonder while the sister's cool fingers took her pulse.

'No bad dreams,' said Rachel. 'And I can see you now. I couldn't before. You have a face – a very nice one.'

'I've had it an awfully long time,' said Headlamps dryly. Indeed it was a seamed and homely countenance, determined but compassionate, and suddenly the padre's words echoed in Rachel's ears. 'Look for Him – He is all around you.' The night nurse had come round the screen and stood waiting beside her senior.

'Anything you want, dear?' Headlamps asked Rachel.

'Yes. But it's too late.'

'Let me be the judge of that.'

'Even you can't give me what I want,' said Rachel. 'I want Jim. He was here earlier. Now he will be gone.'

Headlamps made a sign to the nurse, who disappeared into the corridor where Rachel's bowls and vases of flowers lined the wall.

'If you want a sedative later ring and ask nurse,' said Headlamps. 'She'll bring you a hot drink and a tablet. Good-night, dear.'

'Goodnight, and thank you.'

Rachel watched the sturdy departing form of Headlamps; the dark cape swung over her shoulders for the night was cold. The light from the Women's Ward threw its soft glow against the pleated cream panel of the screen. Only one panel now, so that she could see the ward night-nurse seated at the long table in the pool of light writing up her notes. Rachel found that she could close her eyes without fear of the flickering nightmare visions that had haunted her since her first return to life. Headlamps' firm footfall faded down the corridor and only the uneasy mutterings from the long ward and the hiss of the life-saving oxygen cylinder broke the silence of the night.

The step of a man outside Rachel's room was strong and purposeful above the confused restless sounds of sickness. One of the housemen? Some emergency? Her eyes snapped open as he came quietly into the room, a tall familiar figure silhouetted against those faint shaded lights so softly reflected here. She sat up and put out her bruised bandaged arms.

'Ray, I've been waiting for this – waiting for you to want me.'

'I want you, Jim.'

He sat on her bed and she felt the strength and tenderness of his embrace. His arms enfolded her and crossed over her back as they had so often done, but now the lightness of her body pierced his heart. Never before had he known so thin a layer of satin flesh between his palms and her fragile bones.

'Darling . . . there's nothing of you. Why did you do it, Ray? Why, why, why?'

Her small dry face was against the warm powerful column of his throat and he felt, rather than heard, the little sound she made, half laugh, half sob.

'I couldn't face life without you.'

'You didn't even give me the chance to tell you that you didn't have to.'

'I know that now – nearly too late.'

'Know it now – and always!'

In her eager return to life he was most acutely aware of her recent nearness to death. He buried his doubts and resentments and held her close, afraid to hurt her, afraid to let her go – this infinitely beloved girl restored to him from the shades.

She reached up to touch his shock of dark springing hair, and with the action her alien hands lived again. They were no longer kelp washed up upon a desert shore. They were her own hands equipped with a woman's sensitive fingers interlaced in her lover's crisp warm hair. The tips of those resurrected fingers traced the line of his eyebrows and the hollow plane of his cheek. She said:

'I can feel again. I love you. I am alive.'

21

'GOODNIGHT, MR FERRIT'

MR FERRIT BOUGHT HIS EVENING PAPER AND strolled into the Trident without haste. Emily would be out. Saturday was her afternoon for the pictures and she often sat the programme through twice. When he entered the house he found a message in his sister's illegible scrawl telling him to ring Mrs Rafferty. As Mr Ferrit had nothing better to do he decided not to telephone but to go and see Mrs Rafferty at once.

He left his paper unopened in the living-room, lit one of his cheroots and sauntered out into the September dusk. He distended his nostrils, sniffing the damp autumn air and the pleasant fragrance of a bonfire in the churchyard garden. So they were burning leaves already? A sign of the end of summer. There was a misty bloom in the air, the sunset was red and murky, the flowers in the window-boxes had withered, the creepers were shedding their leaves and the young Dixons' vine was almost bare. Only the dwarf oranges remained jaunty and unconcerned by the change of season.

A bicycle ridden with great dash, bell tringing, swooped round the corner of the third prong with Flicky barking furiously at the wheels. Colin dismounted with his usual flourish.

'Hullo, Mr Ferrit! Come to fix the window I broke?'

'What brings you here this weekend? It's not half-term or holidays, is it?'

'Nope. Had to go to the dentist this morning to get my

brace changed.' Colin produced a fearsome grimace to illustrate his point. 'So I'm staying over till tomorrow night.'

'Lucky you! How did you break a window?'

'Swinging Uncle Ginger's new golf club. I got a smashing drive.'

'So it seems!'

Colin grinned. 'I made that pun on purpose.'

'Smart.'

'It's this pane here, behind the grille. The shot was a bit low as you can see – a hockey shot. Uncle Ginger said he couldn't really congratulate me.'

'I don't suppose your aunt congratulated you either.'

'No,' agreed Colin. 'Have you heard the latest news from the mews?'

'Can't say I have.'

'About Rachel Olivier.'

Mr Ferrit stood rooted. His heart had given a most extraordinary lurch.

'What about her?'

'She's married Jim Fleet.'

'*Married*?'

'Yes. In hospital. The hospital padre married them early this afternoon. And Jim's gone back there now to fetch her away in his father's Bentley.'

Mr Ferrit's mouth fell open. He rescued his cheroot with a shaking hand. Colin stared at him curiously.

'I say, aren't you pleased?'

'I'm stunned,' said Mr Ferrit. 'I thought Miss Rachel was a very sick girl.'

'She was, but Aunt Jane says she had a fine constitution and Jim's her best tonic.'

'When did you hear all this?'

'Three o'clock this afternoon. Mrs Olivier and her son, Hans, came home from the hospital at the very same moment Aunt Jane brought me back from the dentist. Mrs Olivier told us herself. It's in the paper too. Come and measure up that window, Mr Ferrit. The door isn't locked, but don't let Flicky in. He always tags after me.'

Colin parked his bicycle in the garage and frisked into the house. Mr Ferrit threw away the stump of his cheroot and followed the boy slowly into the shadowy twilight of Jane Rafferty's exotic lounge.

'This is the pane. You see there isn't a hole. It's just this star, more like a comet, really – with this long crack for a tail. Uncle Ginger says it speaks well for the glass that it didn't shatter.'

Mr Ferrit examined the pane. 'And what did your aunt say?'

'She was livid with both of us. Said she found us both childish.'

'This glass is expensive, Colin. Are you going to pay for it out of your pocket money?'

'If you even suggest such a thing to Aunt Jane I'll never speak to you again.'

'I couldn't bear that,' said Mr Ferrit.

'Aunt Jane told me to get the tape-measure out of her work-basket if you came while she was out. I'll fetch it.'

Mr Ferrit stood gazing out at the darkening mews, his hands thrust deep into the pockets of his stove-pipe trousers. Married? They wouldn't have let her marry if she hadn't been well on the way to complete recovery. The little yellow car was parked outside Number Eleven. Thanks to him, Ernest Ferrit, she'd gone off in that only last Sunday, humiliated and desperate, knowing herself to be a murderer's daughter – intending to call it a day. Touch and go she hadn't made a killer out of *him*. Yes, and once he'd got thinking about it that was what he'd wanted! He'd felt enormous – god-like – when he'd believed she was going to

die. If she'd died it would have put him into the murderer
class without so much as lifting a finger! The notion had
gone to his head. He'd been drunk with it for days. He'd
ached for it – physically ached – for that consummation,
the final proof that just for once he, Ernest Ferrit of Trident
Mews, had exercised the power of life and death over a
fellow human being. Not in the positive blood-thirsty
see-red way of his own picked band of thugs who used a
woman brutally and destroyed her, but subtly – the brains
behind the deed. Onlooker and the girl herself had done it
for him. But the doctors had brought her back to life. They'd
cheated him of his triumph.

He stared down at the little yellow car and suddenly the
ghost of a girl was at the wheel, her lover beside her. The
young man always let her drive and Mr Ferrit guessed he
liked it that way so he could put his arm around her and
fondle the back of her neck, or maybe just sit there drinking
in that fresh young face. For the first time in the past five
days he pictured Rachel as she was – a girl in love going
forward to meet the great adventure of marriage, not just
the fictional victim of a crime he'd never have had the wit
to conceive or the guts to commit. Me, I'm chicken, he
confessed in a blaze of self-knowledge. To kill without the
intention to kill – no credit in that. He'd been taking false
credit all this past week, kidding himself along, pinning
medals on himself, putting himself among the strong ones
who possessed women and made an end of them like certain kings and queens of ancient times. He, Ernie Ferrit, did
that too but he did it the shadow way, the watcher's way.
There'd been occasions, though, when he'd felt impelled to
wring his sister's neck. When Em interfered with his people
and thumbed through his album he saw red, but never red
enough. He just didn't know how to get the brake right
off. So what? So Em was still round his neck like a bloody

great millstone and there'd she stay till kingdom come. When it came to action the best Mr Ferrit could do was to sell a friend down the river for thirty pieces of silver. Thirty pieces of silver? He'd done a helluva lot better than that. Enough for that holiday in Italy. What price Capri? The black-eyed signorinas and the hot golden sun, the songs and the vino! Anything could happen in Italy. Mr Ferrit began to whistle softly to himself.

'Sorry I've been so long,' said Colin. 'I had to turn that workbasket upside down and inside out to find the tape-measure.'

'Your aunt will be pleased,' said Mr Ferrit, taking the measure from him. He fished a note-book and a stub of pencil out of his pocket. 'You write down the measurements I give you.'

Colin licked the tip of the pencil. 'Go ahead,' he said.

When Mr Ferrit and Colin went out into the mews they found Hans Olivier and Jenny Carstairs just getting into little Yellow Peril.

'Going off somewhere?' Colin asked wistfully.

Hans had already met the boy and Mr Ferrit and now he introduced them to Jenny who was quick to sympathise with Colin's envious gaze.

'Want to come for the ride?' she asked him. The boy's eyes sparkled.

'Gee, yes! But where to? I ought to be here for supper.'

'We'll give you supper,' said Hans. 'Though it'll be a late one. We're going down to a place by the river. We dump Yellow Peril there and pick up General Fleet's Bentley and come back to London.'

'Whoopee! But I must leave a message for my aunt.'

'I can do that,' said Mr Ferrit. 'Trust me.'

'Gee, thanks.'

'Do you know the way to the Great West Road?'

Hans asked. 'I've had instructions but a guide would be better.'

'It's the airport road,' said Colin. 'I know it. I'll be guide.'

Within seconds they were roaring down the Cromwell Road.

'Boy, you do step on it! Don't you?'

Jenny laughed, loving this keen little chap with the hair that grew like Hans's with a totally unmanageable crest on the crown.

'General Fleet's Bentley,' said Colin after a while. 'Jim went off in the Bentley to fetch Rachel from the hospital and take her on their honeymoon.'

'That's right. We're going to recover it for the boss.'

'Will we have supper with Jim and Rachel?'

'No. When we've swopped cars we'll go to a Road House we've been told about. We won't even see Jim and Rachel.'

But there Hans was wrong. The inn was on the bend of the river hidden by trees. Grass terraces led down to the water's edge where great willows trailed their tresses. There were fairy lights in the garden and Colin thought it was the most magical place he had ever seen. Hans went to the hall-porter to exchange the key of the M.G. for that of the Bentley.

'Here it is, sir, but Mr Fleet said to let him know when you showed up.'

The porter dialled a room telephone and Jim answered. They could hear his voice.

'Bring them up to the sitting-room, please.'

Jim met them on the landing.

'Come along in – but only for five minutes. My wife isn't quite herself yet.'

'My wife! Listen to him!' Jenny laughed and rushed in ahead of him to hug Rachel.

Hans and Colin followed them into the pleasant room

with French windows leading on to a little balcony over-looking a shining loop of the river.

Rachel lay on a long wicker garden chair in a filmy pink gown and Colin thought that she wasn't much like the sweater-girl he knew who was always in slacks or shorts. She was pale and she looked like someone in a dream. His dream or hers? Colin wasn't sure. But when she smiled at him it took his breath away. In all his eight years he had never felt quite like this. His eyes prickled, his cheeks burned and he was struck dumb. Jim laughed and rumpled his hair.

'I know how you feel, my lad. A glass of champagne?'

Colin saw the bottle with the gold neck in the gleaming ice-bucket. He heard the pop of the cork and the soft fizz as Jim filled the wide shallow glasses where the tiny bubbles chased each other to the top. They all clinked glasses and drank to Jim and Rachel, and Colin said:

'Oh, boy, this is the best day in all my life!'

'That goes for me too,' said Rachel.

'Oh, by the way,' grinned Hans. 'I nearly forgot this. It could be important. General Fleet gave it to me for you.'

He fumbled in his pocket for an envelope addressed to Jim and handed it over. Jim took it with a puzzled glance.

'Dad must be losing his grip. He's given us a cheque already.'

'He said it was the best wedding present he could find for you – so don't despise it! So long for now.'

When Hans and Jenny deposited Colin at the Rafferty's later that night he was in a happy haze of sleep and cham-pagne.

'Well,' said his uncle. 'What a rip you are! Your aunt's in bed and asleep. Next thing I know you'll be wanting your own latch-key.'

'Gee, that's a good idea! I think I'm squiffed.'

'Don't go to bed with your shoes on, that's all I ask.'

To his wife Ginger Rafferty said:

'Colin's drunk and in love. At eight years old! What do you know?'

She laughed and put her arms out to her husband.

Sir Jasper and Laura Fleet had enjoyed the play at the Savoy Theatre and they lingered over their late supper in the Grill. They had asked Mrs Olivier to join them but she had steadfastly refused, insisting that she must be alone this evening, and that in any case she was expecting a telephone call from South Africa.

'It was no good persuading Ann against her will,' said Laura, sipping Turkish coffee and admiring the emerald lights in her crème de menthe frappé.

Sir Jasper grinned. 'You couldn't. She has a will of iron.'

'So have you. And you're a secretive beast into the bargain. Where have you been all day? Is there another woman in your life – after all these years?'

'I've been checking on Ann Olivier's story.'

Laura raised her eyebrows. 'Does Jim know?'

'Not yet. His efforts yesterday were unproductive and I've not had time to give him the benefit of mine. Jim got very little from the prison authorities – except that Luke Wargrave had apparently been liked.'

'How astonishing!'

'Warders come into contact with many strange characters. They have different standards of judgment from ours. Remember, they saw the man, not the maniac.'

'Tell me about your own activities. What have you been up to?'

'This morning I went to see the solicitor who handled the defence of Lucas Wargrave. A very interesting morning. Old Carbutt-Smith, the senior member of the firm, was quite a youngster then, but he recalled Ann Wargrave very well indeed.'

'Who doesn't?'

'Just as she told us, she had begged the lawyers to obtain some material evidence to prove that her husband might be prone to temporary fits of insanity, She was convinced that something had happened to him – as she put it. But he strenuously denied any head injury and there was no scar to suggest anything of the sort. He knew the nature of his acts and that they were wrong. That was obvious because he was cunning about trying to cover up his tracks afterwards.'

'What was new then, Jasper?'

'This. The Government pathologist at that time was a very remarkable man of science with all a scientist's curiosity. He was famous for his attention to detail, his remarkable powers of observation and his interest in criminology. He was as deeply concerned with the minds of murderers as he was with the remains of their victims. You could almost say that the first was a hobby and the second was hard work. He also happened to be a personal friend of Carbutt-Smith.'

Sir Jasper cupped the fine globe of his brandy glass between his palms and inhaled the bouquet of old brandy.

'Allen Lorrimore was, of course, called by the prosecution to give evidence with regard to Wargrave's victims. It was one of his last cases, and one that fascinated him. Wargrave's previous record was erratic, but it certainly wasn't criminal, and on the bodies of all three of his victims he had made this diabolical sign – the pitchfork, or perhaps it was more like a fish-spear. It was, if you like, a cross gone wrong.'

Laura shivered and drew her fur more closely round her shoulders.

'There was a touch of Jack the Ripper about the whole

thing. These women were creatures of the dark alleys. Vice and menace were their familiars. Men like Wargrave are an occupational hazard to such women, and well they know it.'

'Poor things . . .'

'Quite so.' Sir Jasper waved them away crisply. His investigations were concerned with the mentality of Lucas Wargrave and the fate of his victims was incidental. 'Carbutt-Smith knew that Lorrimore was keenly interested in cerebral abnormalities and in accidents or blows that might cause a growth. Lorrimore made a special study of such matters, and had his own theories on the subject. In the course of his duties he was frequently called upon to make post-mortem studies of executed criminals and it so happened that it was he who performed the autopsy on Lucas Wargrave. His interest in the man had been further stimulated by discussions with Carbutt-Smith, so he took portions of Wargrave's brain for microscopic examination. He found that there had indeed been definite damage at some time, resulting in pressures that must have caused severe inflammation of certain important nerve centres. In his opinion the damage was quite enough to cause insanity. Lorrimore wrote a report on his findings and sent a copy to Carbutt-Smith who included it among his notes. I have had photostat copies made of that report for Jim and Ann Olivier. I have also arranged that those copies will be with the recipients tonight.'

'Jasper, what a wonderful wedding present for Jim!'

He raised his glass.

'To Jim and Rachel – and the future.'

Jim and Rachel sat in the deep window seat overlooking the bend of the river. It was stippled by starlight and the shadow of willows, pitted here and there by the rise of a fish and the widening silver circles that betrayed the secret flowing life beneath the surface. Pale mists crept across the dark quiet lawns and clusters of fairy lights in the boughs of a tall tree cast their wavering reflections into the onyx water like bouquets of exotic flowers.

Behind them a fire crackled in the hearth lending the room its own dancing fantasies. Shadows leapt and capered on the white walls, flirting with the warm glow of the flames flickering over the massive oak beams. Rachel's cheek rested in the hollow of her husband's shoulder.

'I like your new dressing-gown. The wool is so soft and light.' She rubbed her face against it, relaxed and content.

'You're purring,' he said. 'And I like the silk of your hair. That's light and soft too – and the scent is new. Disinfectant. Rather nursery and innocent. Not at all bridal, I should say.'

She laughed. 'That young nurse with the big brown eyes washed it for me this morning. I was complaining that it felt like seaweed.'

'Not to me. To me it feels like very fine satin, a little warm still from the sun.'

'I can't believe I was in hospital this morning. All this last week has been one long nightmare – waking and sleeping.'

He drew her closer to him, feeling her pliant body mould itself responsively to his. He was painfully conscious of the new spiritual quality in her and of the long dark journey she had made alone – a journey from which she had so nearly failed to return. She seemed more perceptive and delicate, yet stronger too.

'That was long ago – in the world we're going to forget. But before we put it away from us forever I want a promise from you.'

'Whatever you like.'

'From now on we share – the good and the bad. No more desperate decisions taken alone. What matters to one matters to both.'

'Double the good and halve the bad – the arithmetic of love.'

She leaned suddenly across him to take the photostat document from his pocket.

'This is good. Finding this was the best thing your father could have done for us. How did it happen? How did he do it?'

'That morning when I talked to Cheryl Braithwaite, your mother's friend who'd known her through all those bad times, a lot of things seemed to fall into place. Mrs Braithwaite had known Wargrave too and I began to get a picture of him as he was before the crash – it was not an evil picture, Ray – and I felt I must follow it up and learn more about him. I rang Dad at Ravenswood to ask for his help. He's always fair and just, and I knew he wouldn't let me down. We made up our minds to delve into every possibility – go over the case again to the best of our ability. Dad knows a great many people and it wasn't too difficult.'

'New evidence – that came too late,' she said sadly. 'I wonder why that solicitor didn't show this to my mother. He must have guessed what it would mean to her – for my sake as well as her own.'

'By the time he received it Ann Wargrave was Ann Olivier. She'd wasted no time. She was on the way to a new life in a new country – and she covered her tracks well.'

She held up the stiff shiny paper, slightly smudged. It was dark by the window and lurid reflections touched it briefly – her passport to posterity. She said, with a faint puzzled frown, 'This doesn't really register with me. Oh, I know it's wonderful – that it means we needn't be afraid of having children – but this man, this Lucas Wargrave, I can't focus him as my mother's husband – my father.'

'Don't try.' He smiled and touched her hair with his lips. 'He was before your time.'

'I've hated her,' she went on, 'hated my own mother, yet all the time I was resenting her she was thinking of me – putting what she believed to be my interests first. She could have been wrong the way she went about it, but she was sincere.'

'She was dedicated. This last sad, difficult week I learnt that. I learnt a lot about your mother, Ray. She's a great woman.'

'That new life she made in South Africa after my father was – '

'Hush! Forget that?'

'That life – Môreson, Pa, Hans – in a way, my home, my father, and my brother were her gifts to me. It was *my* life she made there, not her own.'

'She'll be free to make her own now,' he said gently. 'Your life is with me.'

He took the photostat gently from her.

'My father is a very methodical man. You may be sure he'll keep a copy of this. It's of no further interest to you and me. It's played its part.'

He rose and crossed the room to the fireplace.

Rachel saw him drop the paper into the leaping flames. She watched the document blacken and curl and fly up the chimney in a spray of sparks and powdery flakes of paper. It seemed to her then that all her mother's agony and her own shock and grief and fear of the past week went with it as the last puff of silvery ash fluttered into oblivion.

Ann Olivier did not burn her copy of Lorrimore's

report. She put it carefully away with her most important papers. She had telephoned Christiaan earlier that evening when the precious document was safely in her possession. Since then she had felt calm and strangely free – free of deception, free to think about her own future. Her robust frame was here in the mews cottage but her spirit – the essence of herself – was far away in the Transvaal. The Southern Cross would be bright among the glittering constellations of that distant sky and spring flowers would star the grasslands. Christiaan had said, 'The rains have fallen and the dams are full.'

How strange! It was there that she really belonged while all this time she had believed herself to be a Cockney at heart – a city dweller. She had told Christiaan that she would be back soon after Rachel's honeymoon.

'They're flying to the Channel Isles as soon as Rachel's fit. And next week Hans goes abroad with the Carstairs family.'

'What about you?'

'I'm going to Switzerland to see Liz. Then, when Rachel and Jim are settled in here, I'll be on my way to South Africa and Môreson. Home.'

'Home to me, Annetjie.'

That was when Ann Olivier realised that her whole life with its ups and downs, and the tragic events of her youth and the long years of trying and failing to forget, had led her inevitably to this second homecoming. With Chris she would find happiness based on truth.

A late car purred into the mews. Hans perhaps? No, the young Dixons were returning from a party. She knew the way Charlie revved his engine before switching off. She went to the window and drew aside the curtains. Flicky was greeting his master and mistress as if they'd been absent for weeks and then he was streaking off down the mews in pursuit of Lucifer.

'Flee-kee! Flee-kee!' Up-down, up-down. Two notes of music. The girl's voice was clear and flute-like in the quiet night. I'll remember it always, thought Ann Olivier. Flicky was bustled indoors and the lights went up, an orange glow against the curtains.

Soon there'd be another young couple in the mews. Rachel and Jim, right here. And Lucifer. Too bad that such a companionable cat had been saddled with such a haughty name. Lucky would have been more like it. But there it was - same old story, good and evil all mixed up in accordance with the scheme of things, even unto a cat and his name. She must let Lucifer in. It might rain tonight. The air had a cold softness, a damp feel of laden clouds.

She went downstairs and opened the narrow red door. The cat was waiting. He squeezed past her shapely legs with his back arched and his tail erect. He uttered his trill of appreciation. And then another small sound held Mrs Olivier spellbound. A thin tuneless whistle. Mr Ferrit on the prowl. Self-appointed night-watchman and Onlooker's informant. It was curious, she felt neither anger nor apprehension now, perhaps because she had nothing to hide any more, nothing to fear. Maybe that was the cause of her new sense of lightness and freedom.

Mr Ferrit paused when he saw Mrs Olivier on her doorstep. His face was heavily shadowed with the light obliquely behind him.

'You're late out, Mrs Olivier. It's past midnight.'

'So are you, Mr Ferrit.'

'I couldn't sleep. I thought I'd see that all was well down here. Number Nineteen's empty - the folk on holiday.'

'I see.'

He rocked a little from his heels to the balls of his feet, a mean, spidery figure too contemptible to merit hate.

'How is your sister?' she asked.

'She cut the paragraph out of the paper tonight - the bit about Miss Rachel getting married. She's pasted it in a big album we keep. We want you to know that we're pleased, Mrs Olivier. Very pleased. In a way, Miss Rachel getting better is a sort of reprieve.'

She only saw his face dimly, but his voice was sincere. A reprieve. For Rachel? Or for Mr Ferrit? Or for her, Rachel's mother, who had been the cause of it all?

'Yes,' she said. 'That's the way I feel about it too. Goodnight, Mr Ferrit.'

Mrs Olivier went into the little house and up Jacob's ladder where the lucky black cat awaited her.

The familiar whistle floated up to the open window and faded as the man in the mews turned the corner of the Trident and disappeared into the autumn night.

THE MAN IN THE MEWS

After the death of her South African husband, London-born Mrs Olivier leaves her Transvaal farm to spend the summer in her native city which she has not seen for over twenty years.

Her daughter, Rachel, who works in London, has found Mrs Olivier a mews cottage in the Trident, one of those tucked-away cul-de-sacs that still breathe the atmosphere of the days when horses stamped in the stables and carriages rumbled over the cobbles where now cars like Jim Fleet's Yellow Peril squat outside the pretty converted coachmen's quarters.

Rachel is in love with Jim Fleet and fiercely resents her mother's intrusion upon her new-found freedom. She realises that only maternal solicitude could have brought Mrs Olivier back to the city she had sworn never to revisit.

The antagonism between Rachel and her mother is further heightened by the intervention of Jim's influential father, General Sir Jasper Fleet, once an important figure in the Security Service, who becomes suspicious of Mrs Olivier's past and the curious self-imposed isolation of her London existence. Other people too are interested in Rachel's enigmatic mother, chief among them being Mr Ferrit, the 'man in the mews', who lives a sinister vicarious life which finally enables him to unearth Mrs Olivier's fearful secret.

The story, played out against the background of Trident Mews, the South Africa highveld and the Sussex estate of the Fleet family, is concerned with the stormy love of Rachel and Jim and the dark forces remorselessly building up against these young lovers. Suspense and tension gain momentum until the whole grim truth is laid bare and the characters concerned are forced to face its full implications and find their own solutions.

The Man in the Mews

a novel by Joy Packer

METHUEN

First published 1964 by Eyre & Spottiswoode (Publishers) Ltd
© Joy Packer 1964
Reprinted 1977 by Eyre Methuen Ltd
and 1983 by Methuen London Ltd
11 New Fetter Lane, London EC4P 4EE
Printed in Great Britain by
Redwood Burn Limited
Trowbridge, Wiltshire

ISBN 0 413 43740 x